More Praise for Sally Gunning's Peter Bartholomew Mysteries

Books by Sally Gunning

Hot Water
Under Water
Ice Water
Troubled Water
Rough Water
Still Water

Published by POCKET BOOKS

STILL WATER

A PETER BARTHOLOMEW MYSTERY

SALLY GUNNING

POCKET BOOKS
New York London Toronto Sydney Tokyo Singapore

An *Original* Publication of POCKET BOOKS

 POCKET BOOKS, a division of Simon & Schuster Inc.
1230 Avenue of the Americas, New York, NY 10020

Copyright © 1995 by Sally Gunning

ISBN: 0-671-87138-2

First Pocket Books printing December 1995

10 9 8 7 6 5 4 3 2 1

POCKET and colophon are registered trademarks of Simon & Schuster Inc.

Cover art by Tristan Elwell

Printed in the U.S.A.

For my brother, David, my sister, Jan, and my husband, Tom, the stars of my three favorite horse stories.

Acknowledgments

Many thanks to Carol and Bill Appleton for coming up with the snazzy cars, to Irving Demoranville of the University of Massachusetts Cranberry Experiment Station for guidance on the care and feeding of cranberry bogs, to Marilyn Whitelaw and the senior Tom Gunning for the consultations on classic films, and to Elizabeth Keiser for contributing the appropriate magazine. Again, my thanks to Brigid Mellon for the fine editing and, as always, to my husband, Tom, my love and thanks for the sound critical advice, the laughs in all the right places, and those three little words, "Dinner is ready."

CHAPTER
1

Peter Bartholomew peered over the newspaper at the tiny old woman in the huge mahogany chair and said, "Who?"

"Simmons," said Sarah. "Anthony Simmons. The fellow who bought Heath Farm. Lordy, Pete, don't you know anything anymore?"

Sure, Pete knew something. At least he vaguely remembered hearing something. The Heaths had sold the farm and moved back to the mainland. Apparently, they'd sold it to someone named Anthony Simmons.

"He's from Connecticut. Briar Hills. Been here since August. Folks thought he'd leave after a month or two, but here it is October and he hasn't gone yet. Set himself up on the farm with all his horses. He's got money someplace, I'd say—fixed the house up like Buckingham Palace and the barn like the royal stables. So are you through reading the news?"

Pete looked down at the *Islander* newspaper. Since Sarah had been dishing out most of the news, there was still a lot of newspaper as yet untapped, but Pete was in no hurry. Back in high school, when Pete first hung up his sign—*Factotum—Person Employed to Do All Kinds of Work*—the half-blind Sarah Abrew had been one of his first customers, hiring him to read her the daily paper. Twenty years later it was still Pete's favorite job, but he didn't want to give Sarah the upper hand by telling her that too often. "Where'd you hear all this about the Simmons place anyway?"

"Same place you'd hear it if you'd let go of your wife long enough to poke your nose out the door."

Pete felt his neck grow hot. He'd been forty-five minutes late this morning because he *hadn't* been able to let go of his wife.

"Ex-wife," Pete corrected her.

"They don't ex each other the same way they did in my day, I'll tell you that. Honeymooning after the divorce. Mind you, I've known a honeymoon to come before a wedding a time or two." Sarah tipped back her head and cackled.

"Jeez, Sarah."

Sarah rapped the braided rug with her cane. "Don't you Jeez' me. You think you invented it? Now where was I?"

"Simmons," said Pete quickly. "Where'd you hear all this anyway?"

"Fergy Potts. She stopped in with the wedding pictures. Her granddaughter got married. You didn't know that either, did you?"

Pete didn't. He'd been shockingly uninterested in the world outside his own four walls of late.

"Skinniest bride I ever saw! Anyhow, Fergy heard most of it from May. May heard it when she delivered her jelly to Beston's Store. He's a widower, you know. Or he was till he married this wife. Claire, her name is. Newlyweds. Mother-in-law's staying there, too. And he's got a daughter from the first marriage that's visiting. So you haven't come across this Simmons? Stuck to himself when he first came here, but all of a sudden he's out and around, asking a lot of questions. May says he's a nice enough young fellow despite all the questions."

Pete had learned to be wary of these island adjectives. He knew, for one thing, that to call Simmons a "young fellow" only meant he was under sixty-five. And "nice enough"? He must have bought some of May's jelly.

Pete opened the paper and finished off what news there was—a one-car–one-tree accident on Shore Road, a warning not to feed the migrating geese, a notice about the upcoming town meeting. He folded the paper, crossed to Sarah's chair, and kissed her cheek.

Sarah gripped his hand. "Bring Connie next time you come," she said. "Maybe that way you'll get here on time. And by the way, I haven't been talking about this Simmons fellow just to pass the time. Fergy says most of his questions were about you."

Pete straightened up. "Me? Why me?"

"Now how the devil should I know?" snapped Sarah. Then she added something she'd been adding a lot these days. "You take care, you hear?"

Pete was on Shore Road, almost to the causeway that connected the island of Nashtoba to the mainland, when he heard tooting behind him. He looked in his rearview mirror and saw his partner, Rita Peck, in her silver Dodge Omni. He pulled over. Rita pulled in beside him. Her seventeen-year-old daughter, Maxine, was in the passenger seat. Two heads of gleaming black hair, Rita's a conservative bob, Maxine's a spiky stubble, leaned toward him and started talking.

"I've been at the dentist," said Maxine. "What a creep. He didn't give me any Novocaine."

"Someone came looking for you," said Rita at almost the same time. Then to Maxine, "You do *not* call that nice Dr. Smith a *creep.*"

But Pete was used to juggling these two by now. "Tough break," he said to Maxine, then to Rita, "Who was he?"

"Some man." Rita sketched an arch in the air with nails that were perfect blood red ovals. "Tall. Thin."

"Well he dug halfway to *China,*" said Maxine, pointing downward with one fingernail. Her nails were bright green and cut square at the ends.

"It was only a *cleaning,*" said Rita. Maxine's teeth again. "He wouldn't tell me who he was, Pete." Back to the stranger now. "But I *think* he was one of those new people. From Heath Farm."

"What did he want?"

"*First* it was the cleaning," said Maxine. "And then he came along and did all this *jabbing.* And now I have to have a filling."

"Which you would not have to have if you'd been doing what he told you to do in the first place—*flossing,*" said Rita. "I *asked* him what it was about and he wouldn't tell me. He said he needed to speak to you *personally.* All very hush-hush. So I told him to come back at two. I knew you'd be there at two because I won't be. You did remember, didn't you?"

"Two?"

"*Pete.* I've got to meet Sylvia about the curtains for the office. I told you."

"Oh. Right. Two."

"He had a great car for an old guy," said Maxine.

4

"He's not *old,*" said Rita. Behind her daughter's back, Rita rolled her eyes at the roof.

Her back to her mother, Maxine rolled her eyes, too.

So Anthony Simmons was asking questions about Pete. Looking for Pete. Pete decided it might not be a bad idea to ask some questions of his own before this two o'clock meeting. On the island of Nashtoba there was one place that always seemed to have the answers to all the questions.

Beston's Store.

Beston's had started out as a plain old hardware store. It would have stayed a plain old hardware store, too, if it didn't have a porch attached to it. It might even have stayed a hardware store despite the porch if Ed Healey and Bert Barker had jobs or if the telephone repairman, Evan Spender, spent more time repairing telephones. But no. There they sat, day after day, hour after hour, and after a few months of it George Beston decided to put in a Coke machine to accommodate them. Come winter it got cold on the porch so he installed an old railroad stove and moved the benches inside. He threw in a coffee machine and some donuts, too. At first people who had stopped just to pick up some nails ended up sticking around for coffee. After a while people started stopping by just for coffee, but like as not they found something else at Beston's to buy. The next thing the islanders knew, George Beston was selling Cyrus Pease's cider, May's jelly, and Alice Wimer's homemade bread. Come Christmas he mulled the cider and added Christmas wreaths and wrapping paper. Next a few gift items appeared. Pretty soon there wasn't much you couldn't buy at Beston's Store.

And there wasn't much the old men on the porch

couldn't tell you. If you could stand it long enough till they got around to it, that is.

"Well, well, well, look who's crawled out from under his rock," Ed Healey sang out as Pete hit the steps.

"Some rock," said Bert. "I wouldn't mind being trapped under her."

"Here, Bert, have a Coke," said Evan. He handed Bert a tall green bottle and slid more coins into the machine. "Coke, Pete?"

Pete accepted a Coke, more to acknowledge the rite than to quench the thirst.

"So," said Ed, "what brings you around?"

"I hear you've seen something of this newcomer, Simmons."

"Too much, if you ask me," said Bert. "Nosy fellow. Don't see hide nor hair of him till he wants something, then all of a sudden he's waltzing around here like he owns the place. Who's he think he is, anyway?"

"He's the new director of the Wequassett Trust," said Evan.

Pete raised his eyebrows. Sarah hadn't mentioned that. The Wequassett Trust was a conservation organization over on the mainland with a big budget, important friends, and lots of clout.

"He was here yesterday," said Evan. "And again this morning." He looked sideways at Pete. "He's been asking about *you,* as a matter of fact."

"What kinds of questions?"

"Mr. Fancy-Dancy," said Bert. "Mr. La-dee-da."

"And he was asking about me?"

"About Factotum, actually," said Evan.

"And about you," said Ed. "About what kinds of work you do."

"About what kind of lamebrain this so-called

person-employed-to-do-all-kinds-of-work really is," said Bert.

"Don't worry, Pete," said Ed. "We filled him in on everything."

And so much for Anthony Simmons, thought Pete.

But Pete was wrong—Simmons walked into Factotum on the dot of two o'clock. At least Pete was pretty sure it was Simmons—he was tall and thin and looked to be in his late forties, just the right age to seem young to Sarah and old to Maxine. And Pete knew right off he wasn't from Nashtoba—first of all, he was looking around like he was in the wrong place, and second, he was wearing a camel hair coat.

The coat was certainly in the wrong place. Pete watched Simmons glance at the lumpy rattan furniture and the cockeyed floor lamps in a room that had once been Pete's living room, before Factotum took hold. At the moment the room also held the most recently acquired jobs for Factotum—a pile of flyers for Martelli's two-for-one night, a bicycle with a flat tire, four window boxes in need of paint, and a cardboard carton whose lid had been punctured with holes. The stranger eyed the carton dubiously.

"Josh Dilts's lizard," said Pete. "It's not eating. Josh hired us to take him to the vet. His mother wanted to flush it down the toilet."

The stranger eyed Pete as dubiously as he'd eyed the carton. "Peter Bartholomew?" He asked it as if he hoped he wasn't.

"That's me."

"I've been hearing quite a bit about you, about the kinds of work you do." The stranger's eyes flicked again to the lizard. "At least I was led to assume—"

"And assuming your name is Simmons, I've been hearing about you, too."

7

The stranger blinked. "I . . . hearing? I don't . . . Yes. Anthony Simmons." He thrust his hand belatedly toward Pete.

"How do you do?" said Pete.

"Ah. Yes. How—" Simmons stopped there. He seemed unable to make up his mind whether to bolt or hang in. "So what is the going rate on taking lizards to the vet?"

"Sharpening six pencils," said Pete. "So you've heard about Factotum."

"Yes," said Simmons. "They say you do everything. Even—" He hesitated, the shadows of the men on the porch lurking nearby.

Pete finished for him.

"Find bodies? Solve murders? Track down crooks? I hate to disillusion you, but what you see here is a lot closer to the truth." Pete waved a hand at the assortment before them. "But it's true we do pretty much anything. Is there something we can do for you?"

"I . . . I'm not sure. At first I thought . . . I don't know—" Simmons cast a furtive glance at the door. "Is there somewhere private—?"

Pete was afraid he was going to say that. He led Simmons into what had once been a bedroom but was now Pete's office. Sort of. The assortment in the outer room was nothing compared to what had collected in Pete's office. He pushed a bag of lawn fertilizer off an old trunk and motioned for Simmons to sit. Pete leaned against his desk. It was the best he could do— the desk and the chair behind it were covered with cans of old paint.

"You knew me," said Simmons finally.

Pete shrugged. "Not really. The island talks."

"And you? Do you talk? There are certain confidential aspects to this matter."

"I talk if I have to."

Simmons assessed Pete silently. "All right," he said. "Fair enough. But would you have to involve others, other Factotum personnel?"

Pete didn't feel like telling him that other than Rita, Factotum's personnel consisted of his ex-wife and a muscle-bound twenty-two-year-old kid. "That depends."

"I'd prefer that you tackle this alone."

"Tackle *what* alone?"

Simmons didn't answer.

"Look," said Pete. "Alone is okay if I'm putting up a couple of storm windows. But if you're looking to build the pyramids—"

Simmons smiled. Strangely, it was the smile that showed Pete how tense he was. "I assure you I don't want to build the pyramids."

"And you don't have a lizard in need of a vet?"

"No."

Pete pushed a hand through his hair. "Okay," he said. "That's two questions. How many do I have left?"

Something almost like pain shot through Simmons's face. "I apologize. I assume you're a busy man, and I'll get straight to the point. I have a . . . There seems to be a . . . It's the barn," he finished lamely.

"Barns I can handle," said Pete. "What does it need? A roof? A floor? Paint?"

"Stairs," said Simmons. *"And* paint."

"Okay," said Pete. "I'll look it over and give you a quote. Next week, say?"

"Next week. Certainly." But Simmons said "certainly" the way Rita might have, which usually meant "certainly not." Still, he stood up.

Pete joined him. Pete was tall and lean, but Simmons was taller and leaner. He looked brittle, and he swayed as he stood, like a dead branch in the wind. He stepped to the door and grasped the knob, but he didn't turn it. "There *is* one more thing," he said.

Somehow Pete wasn't surprised. "What's that?"

"I believe someone is trying to kill my wife."

CHAPTER
2

"Are you sure?" It seemed like the kind of question Pete should ask.

They had rearranged themselves for a longer term now—Pete had cleared off the chair and pulled it around in front of the desk for Simmons, and Pete sat on the top of the desk, leaning on his hands, his muddy workboots dangling a safe distance from the camel hair coat.

"That's the thing of it," said Simmons. "I can't, of course, be sure. I just can't completely convince myself this is a matter for the police. And considering other constraints, other—" He stopped, looked away, unbuttoned his coat. Under the top coat there was a jacket and tie. Then Pete noticed the pants matched. He couldn't remember when he'd last had a man in a real suit in his office.

"This is why I've come to you," continued Simmons. "You're absolutely right, Mr. Bartholomew, I'd heard about you, about the—"

11

"Pete. And you mean you heard about the murders. But as I said before—"

Simmons held up a hand, half hesitant, half obstinate. Yes, Pete could see him as director of the Wequassett Trust. "Let me finish, please. Contrary to my first few impressions, I've come to believe that I'm in the right place. I'd like you to at least hear me out."

Pete couldn't remember getting into too much trouble just listening. "Okay," he said. "Shoot."

"Thank you. To begin. Since my wife and I moved here, there have been a series of . . . accidents. I believe the beach plums were the first. My daughter, Rawling, picked some beach plums and left them in a bowl on the kitchen counter. My wife ate some and became ill. A severe headache, blurred vision, vomiting. The symptoms indicated poisoning of some sort to me. Through my connections at the trust—" He hesitated to see if Pete knew what trust. Pete nodded. "Through the trust I was able to have the remaining fruit tested. They found evidence of a strong pesticide. They were picked not far from one of the cranberry bogs, and I at first assumed the fruit was treated either accidentally, or on purpose along with the rest of the bog. I thought nothing further of the matter. What made me change my mind was the stairs." He stopped and peered at Pete, suddenly looking doubtful, but whether his doubts were over Pete or over his own tale, Pete couldn't tell.

"The stairs?"

"The stairs. My wife sculpts. Did I tell you that?" Pete shook his head.

"She has a studio in the loft in the smaller barn. I'd been using the Shearson Brothers for the construction work, and before they renovated, they supposedly did a thorough safety check. You've heard of Shearson Brothers?"

Pete nodded. Shearsons was a large, well-established construction firm of excellent repute that operated out of Bradford, the "capital" of Cape Hook. It always amazed Pete how the Anthony Simmonses of the world could come into an area cold and smell out the class act.

"The Shearsons indicated to me that the structure of the small barn was sound. They first remodeled the loft with proper windows, worktables, shelves, that sort of thing. They cleaned up and painted the lower interior and had begun the exterior when—" Simmons looked away. "I didn't involve myself in the details of the work. I didn't actually examine the stairs. We're considering a major purchase at the trust and I've had many long meetings, late hours. Neither did I grill the Shearsons about the stairs. I assumed . . . They certainly knew Claire was . . ."

It was the first time he had used her first name, and it seemed to make the incident personal again. Real. He twisted his hands, one inside the other, and suddenly Pete felt sorry for him. Clearly he was a man who was used to delegating jobs while retaining the ultimate responsibility for them. Pete helped him along. "Something happened to the stairs?"

"Something certainly *did* happen to the stairs." The shock and outrage in Simmons's voice seemed fresh. "They collapsed. *Collapsed.* But that's not the worst of it. Claire had decorated the walls with some old farm equipment. When she fell through the stairs there was an old hayrake underneath them that had been hanging on the wall. Those tines—"

This time Pete decided not to help Simmons along, at least not about what might have happened on those tines. "But your wife was all right?"

"She had the presence of mind to catch herself on the rafter as she fell and swing herself out of the way.

13

She was . . ." Simmons stood up and probably would have paced, but he was hemmed in by paint cans, grass seed, fertilizer. He sat back down. "She was unnerved. Completely unnerved. I, of course, fired the Shearsons at once."

So much for the well-reputed contractors. Still, blaming the Shearsons for the misdiagnosis on the stairs was one thing; accusing someone of attempted murder was another.

"I know that barn," said Pete. "It's an old one. It wouldn't surprise me if some stairs collapsed."

Simmons shook his head. "They'd been rebuilt not long ago. That was what the Shearsons told me. Come out to the farm. See for yourself. The Shearsons said those stairs were sound."

"What else would you expect them to say? That they saw some flaw that nearly killed your wife but decided not to fix it?"

"That's why I fired them," said Simmons. "Either they were incompetent or they were lying, it had to be one of the two. But when you come out to the farm, you can see for yourself."

Pete squirmed uncomfortably on the desktop. Now they were getting down to it. But down to what? It wasn't much either way.

"And the beach plums?"

"In the light of the episode with the stairs, I took a closer look at the beach plums. I can show you where they came from."

"You can also show the police."

"I can't call the police. I told you."

But he hadn't really. "The police don't arrest you if it turns out your fears are unfounded, you know."

"I can't call the police. At least not yet. Even you, you who has seen murder firsthand, you don't really believe my wife is in danger, do you? I might be wrong. And there are other reasons besides. My wife—"

Anthony Simmons sat down. His face changed. It looked like the face of a man who was deciding whether or not to cut his own throat. Pete could tell exactly when he made up his mind to do it, too.

"When Claire was nineteen, she was raped by a police officer. It happened in her own home town, a small town in New Hampshire called Millburton. At that place, at that time, it was not accepted that there could be such a thing as a bad policeman, just as there are bad people, and there was a considerable amount of feeling against her in the community. But Claire took it the whole nine yards, all the way through an ugly, terrifying, demeaning trial, and she did it nobly. The ultimate result was that the officer was convicted and incarcerated. The ultimate price for Claire was much worse. She . . . she . . . What concerns the discussion here is that she became pathologically afraid of the police."

Simmons stopped talking.

Pete didn't exactly chip right in with something else. After that, what was there to say that wouldn't sound inadequate or, worse, offensive? "I see," he said finally.

Simmons looked up. "I wonder if you do. We're not talking about a momentary panic when she sees a uniform. This is something more than that. She'll be in line in the supermarket behind a man in a sweatsuit, and she'll decide, somehow she'll become convinced, that the man is a policeman. She'll . . . she'll crumple. She'll disintegrate. She'll become unable to function, to move. I can't explain it to you. I can't force her to face them. Not yet."

"And you think that has something to do with this?"

15

Simmons looked blank.

"The . . . the police incident," said Pete. "If you think someone's trying to kill her, you must have given some thought as to who and why."

"I have. Yes, I certainly have. But somehow I never considered that."

"Is he out of jail?"

"I . . . For heaven's sake! I can't imagine he would be. I, of course, never considered—"

"When did this happen?"

"It happened when Claire was nineteen. She's now thirty-two. That's thirteen years ago. I suppose he could be. I suppose he very well could be. Lord, do you suppose? No, I'm sure that's not it. She's moved several times since Millburton. Her name has changed with marriage. I doubt if he could find her, even assuming he wanted to. No, I'm sure that has nothing to do with it. However, I truthfully can't give you the name of anyone else, anyone in my wildest dreams who would wish to hurt Claire. When you meet her, you'll understand. Actually, it's partly because this sounds so foolish that I want your help."

"I don't see what you expect me to do."

"The stairs need to be repaired. Claire is extremely anxious to get back into the studio, and I, of course, won't allow her to use those stairs until they're completely rebuilt. She has pressed me to reengage the Shearsons, but that I will not do. I have, however, promised to engage an alternate contractor immediately. Let me hire you to fix the stairs. Come out to the farm. Meet Claire. Look at the stairs. I'll show you where the beach plums came from. If you feel there's nothing to my fears, so be it. Fix the stairs and go. If you happen to agree with me that there might be something amiss, well, I'll have to take further action."

So that was it. The listening part of the program was now over, and they were up to the part that had proved to be trouble for Pete in the past—the part where he had to say yes or no. But it seemed pretty clear to Pete what was going on here. According to Sarah Abrew, this Anthony Simmons and his wife Claire were newly married. If Claire was thirty-two, she was probably ten or fifteen years younger than her husband, and with a nightmare such as Simmons had just described in her past, it was no wonder he'd tend to feel protective, even paternalistic. Pete figured all he had here was the Case of the Overly Anxious Bridegroom. All Simmons needed was a dispassionate third party to check things out and ease his mind. And the man had spent a considerable amount of time researching just the right dispassionate third party to ask. It was flattering, really, that he'd chosen Pete for the job.

"Okay," said Pete. He waited for the crash of thunder or the eerie music from the wings, but there wasn't any.

Simmons sat back, pleased, then almost at once he hunched forward again. "You said something about coming out next week. Now that you more fully understand the nature of the problem, I'm sure you will also understand that I'm most anxious to have this resolved."

He was the kind of man who applied pressure so graciously it was hard to resist. And besides, on the island of Nashtoba there were few things so pressing that they couldn't be put off a day or two. Pete stood up. "How about if we run out there now?"

The relief on Simmons's face was gratifying.

Rita's face was another matter.

They ran into her coming in as they were going out.

Pete introduced Simmons, and she greeted him pleasantly, but as Pete went to follow Simmons out the door, Rita grabbed him by the elbow and yanked. "Where do you think you're going?"

Pete explained.

Rita's eyebrows knotted. "And what about the Hermitage? You were going to the Hermitage this afternoon. We have no idea what we're getting into out there, and you said you'd check it out this afternoon."

The Hermitage was the unoffical name given to the home of the island's only recluse—he had bolted himself in his house, only coming out as far as the porch to collect deliveries and only then after the delivery truck had left. No one had laid eyes on him in twenty years. Until last month. When the groceries sat on the porch uncollected for a week, the delivery boy had notified the police. The police chief, Will McOwat, had gone in and found what everyone expected him to find—the hermit had died. And two nights ago, over a beer at Lupo's, Will told Pete that he'd never seen a house in such a mess. Pete had been only mildly interested until the hermit's cousin from Pennsylvania had called Factotum the next day and hired them to clean out the house before he arrived in two weeks.

"The Hermitage won't take long," said Pete.

But Rita's eyebrows stayed knotted. She'd heard what the chief had said.

Pete lowered his voice, in case Simmons was in earshot. "And neither will this farm thing. Really, Rita. I'll be at the Hermitage by tomorrow morning."

Rita's eyebrows regrouped but not necessarily for the better. It did occur to Pete that he'd seen this particular eyebrow formation before and ignored it at his own peril. He supposed he should call Simmons back inside and explain that he had some urgent housework to do or that the lizard had just taken a turn for the worse . . . He followed Simmons out the door instead.

CHAPTER
3

Anthony Simmons's "great car" was a Range Rover. It looked like a plain old sport sedan, but Pete had recently read about a few of its extra features— leather seats, six-disc compact disc player, eleven speakers, a chassis that elevated automatically in case of bumps, and, if Pete remembered correctly, a price tag of fifty-five thousand dollars.

Simmons insisted on leading Pete to the farm, as if Pete didn't know where it was. On a small island like Nashtoba, it would have been pretty hard for a forty-acre farm to hide, but Heath Farm tried. They swished through dry sand over tar until they had almost reached the tip of the island, then Simmons swung left onto a dirt road that had been full of muddy potholes the last time Pete had been by. Not so now. Still, despite a fortune in grading, the road remained narrow and steeply pitched, banked with uncomfortable drops. At the bottom of one of the drops, Simmons stopped, got out of the Rover, and walked back to Pete.

"Those are the beach plum bushes, there. And see the bog?"

Pete saw the bog. It was still the deep, rich maroon of ripe berries not yet picked. In the distance he saw the bog's owner, Jasper, mucking around in the drainage ditch, and, along the right side of the bog, the spiky beach plum bushes.

Simmons got back in his car and drove on. He took the final turn and stopped in the drive behind a classic light yellow Mercedes convertible. Actually, he stopped in front of it. The Mercedes was facing out. Beside the Mercedes, looking like a mule at the Kentucky Derby, was a muddy blue Toyota Corolla. Pete pulled in behind that.

Pete got out, looked around, and whistled. The Heath Farm Pete knew had never looked like this. The last time he had seen the farm, it had consisted of a house with sagging trim, a long, low outbuilding with many missing shingles, a salt-box-style barn that was two decades away from its last paint job, and a shed that had been left to rot. All had been surrounded by scrub pines and bull briars.

The Simmonses had fixed all that. Or at least they had fixed most of it. The small barn was still unfinished, but they had replaced the house trim, turned the long building into a stable, and converted the shed into a two-car garage. All three finished buildings gleamed with fresh white paint and smart yellow trim. The corral was surrounded by immaculate white plank fences, and a still-green pasture rippled over the gentle hills past a quiet pond, stopping at the white pine forest.

Pete got out of the truck and Simmons joined him. "I'll be interested to see what you think of the workmanship," said Simmons. "Whatever my current concerns about the Shearsons, they were capable of following instructions and working fast and well, not something I was expecting to find out here."

And exactly where did he think he was, thought Pete, 1810 Bolivia?

But still, Pete was impressed and he said so.

"We cleaned it up a bit, cleared out some scrub," said Simmons modestly. "But the one who had the eye for it all was Claire. It's amazing what an artist can see. The barn, or the eyesore, as Claire calls it, somewhat ruins the effect, as you can see."

The salt-box barn was between the stable and the house, half hidden by the projecting corner of the porch. Apparently the Shearsons had left midjob, with the exterior only half scraped.

But Simmons was now gazing at the Toyota, smiling. "Good, they're home." He turned to Pete. "My daughter, Rawling, is visiting."

"The one who picked the beach plums?"

"Yes. My wife Nancy's child. Claire is her stepmother. Rawling's here to meet Claire, to get acquainted, I suppose you'd say. My wife, that is to say, Rawling's mother, Nancy, has been dead a little over ten years. We . . . I mean Claire and I . . ." He gave up. After a minute he added, "I think my marriage came as something of a surprise to Rawling."

Pete could see why. There had been one too many wives in the previous sentence. He started toward the barn, but Simmons stopped him with a word.

"Wait. Please. One important item. I do not want my wife to suspect the nature of this visit. Is that understood? You're here strictly to fix the stairs."

"She's not worried about all these accidents?"

Simmons shook his head. He'd gone all brittle again. "She sees them as just that. Accidents. She blames herself for the fruit. It was there, on the counter, in a bowl. She didn't bother to wash it. She believes the stairs were another accident, and she's to be left to believe that. And I'd like to take this a step further. I prefer that my daughter not know anything about this either. I prefer, as a matter of fact, that you speak to no one here about what we've discussed. No one at all. Have I made myself clear?"

"Sure," said Pete. "Most of us speak pretty good English out here."

Anthony Simmons grew stiffer. Then the stiffness broke, and he grinned. "I'm sorry. I . . . Oh, God, look, I don't know what I'm saying anymore. Just forget it, will you? Things have . . . things have been rather tense. Will you bear with me? Come in, I'll introduce you to Claire, and then we'll look at those stairs."

As they approached the house, the door opened, and a tall young woman with flyaway auburn hair strode toward them across the lawn. Fast.

Simmons's face lit up. "Rawling! Here, I'd like you to meet Peter Bartholomew. Pete, this is my—"

"Hello," said Rawling. She met his eye straight on, thrust her hand into his, and jerked it down and away, barely breaking stride. "Good-bye."

"Where are you going?"

"To the store. We're all out of fruit. I don't know why you take her car out of the garage every morning"—Rawling jerked her head at the Mercedes—"since apparently she doesn't plan to drive."

"Take the Mercedes," said Simmons.

"No thanks," said Rawling. "I'll take Greg's, if somebody will move that truck." She said the word *truck* the way she might have said the word *muck*.

Pete moved his truck.

Rawling knifed herself into the Toyota and roared away.

Anthony Simmons looked pained. "She's twenty-five," he said as if it might explain something. "She's just completed her master's at Smith."

Lucky for Smith.

"Now let's find Claire." Simmons picked up the pace, like a horse who smelled the barn. He crossed the glossy porch in two strides, pulled back the heavy door, and ushered Pete inside.

What happened to the Heath house? Pete wondered. Then he realized it was the walls. There weren't any. The whole length of the house was one long room, the far end an authentic farmhouse kitchen with brick fireplace, hanging copper pots, cast-iron stove, bench-style table; the middle, a sunken sitting area tastefully interspersed with antique furniture, ending on the other side with a formal dining table flanked by eight tall chairs. In front of Pete a wide staircase rose gracefully toward the far wall, turned left, and disappeared. The sunken part of the room was carpeted. The rest of the floor was covered in wide pine planking, gleaming and bare.

Pete checked out his boots for mud. Then he checked out the man and woman sitting in the antique chairs.

"Ah! Lillian," said Simmons. "And Greg, too." He strode down the steps and up to a woman who possessed all the coloring and liveliness of a block of marble. He laid a hand on her shoulder and bent down. "Lillian, this is Peter Bartholomew. He's come to give us a quote on the stairs. Pete, this is my mother-in-law, Lillian Bowles."

"How do you do?" She took Pete's outstretched hand and smiled, but both movements were minimal, wary, in keeping with the stone motif. Still Pete noticed she was striking. Stunning. And, he decided after a minute's thought, nowhere near as old as she first appeared.

24

"And Greg, Greg Hempstead, Rawling's . . . ah . . . friend."

Ah, one of those. Hempstead rose and grasped Pete's hand, but said nothing. His hair was almost the color of Rawling's but without the life. He had the kind of jaw that was used to being clenched. And a taste for older men seemed to run in the family—Hempstead was a good ten years older than Rawling.

"Where's Claire?" asked Anthony.

Hempstead shrugged. "She left just before Rawling. Through the back door."

Simmons's eyes flicked to Pete's. Pete had already gotten a bead on the layout and had noticed that the shortest route to the stable was out the front door. As a direct route, the back door could only lead to the old barn, and Anthony didn't want Claire in the old barn. "Excuse us, please, Lillian."

Lillian Bowles accepted this old-world courtesy with a nod.

They went out to the barn. It was built salt-box style, high at one end and low at the other. It was the front side that needed the paint. They pushed open the heavy doors and went through.

The Shearsons may have been terminated mid-exterior paint job, but they had done up the interior like no barn Pete had ever seen. Most barns Pete had come across were dank and full of hay dust, with old, unused farm paraphernalia rusting and rotting in the corners. In this barn the floors had been scrubbed and oiled, the walls covered with new weatherboard, and the farm paraphernalia hung and displayed in the manner of true antiques. There was a tin watering can, a hurricane lantern, a fruit basket, sleigh bells on a thick leather harness, an old plow, the hayrake. It was dark, but overhead, two small windows collected light from outside and beamed it down. As Pete looked up, he saw a collection of fishing rods, old and new, suspended in the rafters. Of course, thought Pete, the pond would be stocked.

"Claire?" Simmons called.

When no one answered, Anthony's voice went up a notch. "Claire?"

The barn was partitioned into what must once have been large stalls. Simmons disappeared into one. Pete peered into another. Empty. He moved under the stairs and looked up. The Shearsons were right—these weren't old stairs. Pete looked at the hole where the two missing treads had been and then at the ground below. Although the hayrake had been returned to the wall, the two fractured treads had been left where they'd fallen. Pete picked them up. Dry rot. He could see where the wood had pulled free from the nails. Pete frowned. He didn't like it. And when he came right down to it, neither did he like secretive husbands or spoiled stepdaughters, and although he'd never admitted this to anyone but Connie, the last time he'd enjoyed being near a horse was when he was six and the horse was attached to a metal post and went up and down. He decided to refuse the job. He returned to the door.

In the corral a young girl sat perched on a palomino. The first thing Pete noticed was that the girl's hair and the horse's mane were the same yellow blond. She rocked in her saddle in perfect rhythm to the lope of the horse, and it looked like one of those paintings they put on calendars. If the girl were older it would have looked like a perfume commercial or an ad for jeans. Suddenly the girl turned the horse, angling across the corral toward the gate. She looked up, saw Pete in the doorway of the barn, and something about her body or something about the way she came alert to a stranger standing in the door of her barn told Pete who she was even before Anthony came up behind him and breathed it.

"Claire." There was a world of relief in his voice.

She raised a slender hand and waved. Pete was put in mind of a feather in a breeze.

Simmons cleared his throat. "That's Claire. Come on."

He moved across the ground between the barn and the corral in an awkward, lunging trot. As Pete followed him, two separate thoughts struck him. The first was that he'd already started to think in horse metaphors. The second was that Claire Simmons was the reverse of her mother—as he got closer, she looked older. She tossed a slender leg over the back of the horse, kicked her other boot out of the stirrup, and slid to the ground. It was a long way down.

"Claire, this is Peter Bartholomew. Pete, my wife Claire. He's come about the barn."

Claire Simmons tossed the reins over her horse's neck and patted him before turning to her husband first and then to Pete. Her eyes were brown, like the eyes of the horse. "Hello," she said.

"Hello," said Pete.

"Give Dapper to John, will you?" said Simmons. "And come in so we can talk."

"All right."

She was hardly five feet tall and slender. The horse loomed over her. Pete lingered, watching, half afraid to take his eyes off something so small at the mercy of something so big, but for some strange reason the horse decided to do what she told him to. They walked, Claire Simmons in front, horse behind, toward the stable. Before they got there, John Forbes stepped through the stable door.

Forbes was a fellow islander. Pete wasn't surprised to see him there—Forbes changed jobs a lot more

often than he changed shirts. He looked much the
same as he had the last time Pete saw him, only
dirtier. He acknowledged Pete with one of those
almost-but-not-quite nods that was the usual form of
address on Nashtoba.

"Oh, John, there you are," said Claire. "Could you
take care of Dapper, please?"

Forbes walked past Claire as if he hadn't heard her.
Even for Nashtoba, that was a bit much.

"John?" Claire said again. "Please?"

He stopped. She held out the reins. He lifted first
one foot and then the other as if his boots were mired
in quicksand. He took the reins and yanked the horse
around. The horse would have plowed into Claire if
she hadn't jumped.

Pete frowned. He waited for Simmons to say something, but apparently Simmons hadn't noticed. He
was looking at the small barn.

They returned to the house.

This time they found Rawling, Greg Hempstead,
and Lillian Bowles in the living room.

"Oh, good, you're back," Simmons said to Rawling.

"And so quickly," said Claire.

"That's the idea behind cars," said Rawling with
such venom that Claire Simmons stopped short, and
Pete found himself involuntarily taking a step forward to flank one side of her.

Pete looked down. The top of Claire's head came
level with his collarbone. Her bones were so fine he
was sure he could circle her waist with his hands. Pete
was used to Connie's height and heft, and standing
next to Claire made him feel as if he'd been pumping
iron for a year. *There's nothing to her,* he thought.
Anything could finish her. He thought of the beach
plums and the stairs and the hayrake. He thought of
John Forbes and those horse monsters. He looked

again at Rawling, standing with her back to her stepmother now, shoulders square, feet planted.

Claire Simmons collected herself, looked up at Pete, and smiled shyly. "So. Pete, is it? Won't you come in and sit down? You're going to do some work for us, I hear?"

"Yes," said Pete. "I am."

CHAPTER

4

The island of Nashtoba, like most islands, was surrounded by water. On the whole, the arrangement worked out well—the cold winter water might rob the island of most of its spring, but the warm summer water kept it temperate long into the fall. The first frost sometimes didn't come until November, but come it did, and knowing this, Connie Bartholomew was putting in a few late hours in the garden.

Connie didn't think of it as her garden. She'd inherited it—house, too, but she tended to think of the inheritance as involving the garden—from the elderly Bates sisters. The Bates sisters had hired Factotum to take care of the garden, and the garden had been Connie's job—at least until she'd found the sisters dead there. It had been easier to keep up with the garden when it was a job. Now that the garden fell under the category of a hobby, it seemed to get left to last.

Now, in October, the only things blooming were the chrysanthemums and a few snapdragons; other than planting next year's bulbs, the tasks ahead of her were housecleaning ones. She put in two hours pulling out gone-by annuals, then put away her tools, brushed the dirt off her clothes, and went inside to tackle a few bare essentials of the other kind of housecleaning.

The house had gotten away from her, too. It was the first time in years that Connie had lived in more than two rooms, and although she appreciated having some space to fly around in, she wasn't in the habit of having so many things to take care of. There were tiny Victorian tables to vacuum under; shelves full of dusty china to wash; thick, spidery drapes to be aired; and salt-crusted, mullioned windows to be sprayed down with the hose. Connie was lucky if on any given day she got as far as the dishes.

She was just finishing them when Pete knocked on her door. It was a strange system of divorce etiquette—he knocked, but he opened the door *before* he knocked and was therefore halfway across the kitchen by the time she hollered, "Come in." On the other hand, Connie never knocked on Pete's door; she just opened it and waltzed in.

But then again, so did everyone else on Nashtoba.

He folded her into his arms and held on a long time. They did that a lot these days. Then he kissed her. They did a lot of that, too. Finally he peered around her without letting go and looked at the clean dishes in the drain. "You've eaten?"

"No," said Connie. "These are from breakfast." Yesterday's breakfast. She'd eaten today's breakfast at Pete's. It seemed like a long time ago now; she could feel the roughness of his twelve-hour-old shave. Twelve hours ago he'd smelled of clean denim and shave soap. Now he smelled of . . . what?

Fresh hay. Horses.

Horses? Pete?

31

She pulled away. "Where have you been?"

"Heath Farm. A new job." He leaned against the edge of the counter and looked around Connie's kitchen the way he always did, as if something didn't fit. *Probably me,* thought Connie; other than removing the prunes from the refrigerator, she hadn't changed things much. She watched Pete's eye roam over the spoonrest shaped like a sunflower and the potholder shaped like a lobster, coming to rest on the eggcup shaped like a cat.

"What new job?"

Pete started talking. First it was about Heath Farm. Then it was about Anthony Simmons, its new owner. Then just when Connie figured she must have missed the part about what the job was, he started rambling on about beach plums and dry rot and how somebody was supposedly trying to kill this guy's wife.

Connie peered at him, looking for clues that this was a joke, but all she saw were solemn brown eyes and two frown lines she'd helped put in his forehead. "Are you out of your mind?"

"It's not me, it's him. He's the one who thinks—"

"So let him think it. Can't he dial a phone, call the cops?"

"No, he can't. His wife was raped by a cop when she was nineteen. She's scared to death of the police."

Connie had already opened her mouth to say something in response to the first half of Pete's answer when the second half sunk in. She closed her mouth. "Jesus," she said instead.

"Yeah," said Pete.

"But still—"

"And besides, Anthony Simmons isn't completely sure anyone's trying to hurt her. He just wants me to look into it and see what I think."

"Still," said Connie again.

"And fix the stairs." He had the look of somebody who had just repeated something that sounded better the first time he'd heard it.

"Give this to me again," she said. "I'm missing something. Somebody *might* be poisoning beach plums and sabotaging stairs with dry rot. And they want you to poke around and find out if it's so. If so, then what?"

"Then we call the cops."

"And then the cops come. All two of them. And meanwhile whoever did the poisoning or the rotting does what?"

"What do you mean?"

"I mean while you're cottoning on to him, what keeps him from cottoning on to you? And doing to you what he did to Claire? I'm talking about risk factors."

"You mean you want to know where the insurance industry places dry rot and beach plums on the actuarial tables?"

Connie couldn't help it. She laughed. "All right. All *right*. But I'm serious. Come on, Pete. Doesn't this sound a little . . . hare-brained to you?"

"Okay," Pete acknowledged. "Yes, it does. And that's why I can't believe there's anything to it. But if you think about it, what's the worst that can happen? They get their stairs fixed and I collect a decent check. By the looks of things, one that won't bounce."

"That's the *best* that can happen. And who needs it? We're busy enough."

Pete's normally straight jaw line began to take on a lumpy, set look. "That's not the point."

"It isn't? Then what is?"

Pete picked up the eggcup and examined it. "The point is, there are a couple of people over there who don't much like Claire Simmons. And you should see

33

her. She's like a toothpick going up against a couple of chain saws. I don't know, it made me mad, I guess."

Swell, thought Connie. *His Sir Galahad routine.* It wasn't one of her favorite bits, but she was careful not to let her thoughts appear on her face.

"Okay," said Pete. "What?"

"Nothing," said Connie.

"Come on. Remember the new rules? You tell me when something's wrong? I listen? We talk?"

Connie walked away from him, halfway around the table. "Okay. You want to know what's wrong? It's you. You do these crazy things. You'd jump off a bridge if you saw a *rat* drowning. Even if you couldn't swim! And there's something wrong about this job, too. I don't like the sound of it. I don't like the smell of it. And even if I did, I don't like the idea of you sticking your neck between a couple of chain saws and a toothpick."

Pete tossed the eggcup in the air and caught it. Once. Twice. Three times. "I'm sorry if this worries you," he said finally. "I'm not used to thinking of things this way, in terms of how it affects both of us. But this decision is made. I start tomorrow. And I'm not going to jump off any bridges." He grinned. "Besides, I can swim."

Connie snatched the eggcup when he tossed it again, went to the refrigerator, and opened the door. "I'm starving. Let's finish the spaghetti."

"I made the spaghetti, remember? It's at my house."

"Oh," said Connie. "Pizza?"

"Sure. What do you want?"

"I don't care," said Connie. "The usual." But was the usual what it once was?

Pete called Beaton's Pizza Shack and ordered

mushrooms, olives, and green peppers. Large, so there'd be enough left over for lunch.

Yes, that was the way they used to do it.

Later, on the couch, they entered phase two of divorce etiquette—The Formal Invitation.

"Staying?" she asked.

It was followed by the Formal Acceptance. "Staying. Yeah."

It sure wasn't how they used to do *that,* Connie thought.

CHAPTER
5

Pete woke tangled in warm limbs. Connie's limbs. It felt good, so good that he lay there thinking about nothing except how good it felt until a strange sensation came over him. It was an unfamiliar, uneasy feeling, and for a long time he couldn't place it. Then it dawned on him.

He was *happy*.

The shock of the discovery made him sit up, and once he sat up, he saw the clock. He was going to be late to Sarah's again. He sprang out of bed and jumped in the shower. He returned to the room, trying not to wake Connie, but as he opened one bureau drawer after another, it sounded like thunder.

Connie sat up. "What are you doing?"

"Looking for my clothes. I left some clean clothes right here on this bureau."

"Clean? I thought they were dirty. They're in the washing machine. Wet."

Pete went to the basement in his towel and threw the clothes in the dryer, but he didn't have time to wait for them. He went back upstairs, pulled on yesterday's clothes, and kissed Connie good-bye. He'd never perfected that perfunctory *Life with Father* kind of kiss good-bye. When they were through, he was even later.

Rita was already sitting at her desk, eyebrows in neutral position. "Good morning," she said.

"Good morning," said Pete.

"Coming or going?"

"Both," said Pete.

"From Connie's, I take it. Then to Sarah's. Then to the Hermitage?"

"Not yet," said Pete, still moving. "I have a few things to take care of out at the farm."

Rita's eyebrows left the neutral position. "The farm."

"I know," said Pete. "But it shouldn't take much longer. There have been some accidents——"

"What accidents?"

Pete told Rita about the accidents.

The eyebrows got worse.

"I'll hit the Hermitage this afternoon."

Rita's eyebrows didn't budge. He could have taken this as his second warning. Third, if you counted Connie's.

He decided not to count any of them.

He was only twenty minutes late to Sarah's.

"You're getting faster," she said. "Does that mean the honeymoon's over?"

Pete made a face at her but then remembered that she probably couldn't see it. "Very funny," he said instead. "I have ten minutes, so if you want to hear the newspaper, you'd better cut the lip."

Sarah waved a hand at the mention of the newspaper. "I'm sick of the news. You read it and tell me if we're still afloat. I have another job for you."

"If it's another one of these twenty-year deals—"

Sarah chuckled. "I've gotten my pound of flesh out of you with this newspaper job, haven't I? Connie, too." She smiled at the mention of Connie. It had been Sarah's pet project, getting Pete and Connie back on track. "I need a bat house," she said.

"A what?"

"A bat house. A house for bats. Do I have to spell it out for you? I heard about these bat houses over the radio. Like a birdhouse but different. If you hang one of these houses on your tree, the bats move into your yard and eat your mosquitoes. If the bats eat your mosquitoes, the mosquitoes don't eat you. See how it works? You can get the plans for them at Beston's."

Well, thought Pete, either he did all kinds of work or he didn't. A bat house it was. He promised Sarah he'd have a bat house for her next week, then he picked up the newspaper. He read her the headlines and let her pick what she wanted to hear. She selected a story on the new septic plant on the Hook, a feature piece on crickets, and, of course, the weather report. There was nothing more important on Nashtoba than the weather.

He was only eight minutes late to the farm, but Simmons was waiting on the lawn, checking his watch. He led Pete toward the old barn without preamble.

"I've been talking to Claire," Simmons said. "Although I'm more concerned with you taking a general look around, Claire is most anxious to get back to her studio, and since she thinks you've been hired to fix the stairs, I suggest this is where you start. I want

38

them rebuilt from the ground up. I don't want to take any chances."

"All right," said Pete. "I'll start with the stairs." But he really wanted to start with Anthony Simmons. "I take it a couple of people around here don't like your wife much?"

Simmons looked so surprised that Pete was surprised back. "Who? What are you talking about?"

Pete decided to attack it from the other flank.

"You said your daughter picked the beach plums?"

"Yes," said Simmons without blinking. "I suggested it. Claire likes them. I find them rather tart."

Rancid, most people would have said. "So this beach plum incident was the first suspicious incident. How long had your daughter been here by then?"

"Several weeks," said Simmons, still without flinching.

"And your daughter hadn't met your wife until this visit?"

Oddly, this was the question that seemed to make him uncomfortable. "Rawling was away at school. And then she left on a trip following graduation. Claire and I had left for Spain before she returned, and . . ." His voice trailed off.

"And her friend, this Greg Hempstead. He arrived when your daughter arrived?"

"Yes, he did."

"Where is he from?"

"New Hampshire, I believe. Yes, I recall my wife asked, and he said he was from Keene, New Hampshire. He said he'd been living there ever since he graduated from Keene State."

So if Hempstead was in his mid-thirties, as he appeared, he'd most likely been in Keene for over ten years.

"Had you met him before?"

"No, I hadn't. I believe the acquaintance is fairly recent."

"Okay. And who else is around? Your mother-in-law lives with you?"

"Yes. I suggested the arrangement. She's the nervous sort, she was alone, and I thought it might help Claire to have her mother here, since I'm often working late."

"Anyone else?"

"We have a maid. Joan Pitts."

The name was unfamiliar to Pete. "She's not from the island?"

"No. We brought her with us. She's been with Claire since before we were married."

"Okay. And the other help?"

"We hired two locals. John Forbes came around almost immediately on our arrival. We checked him out with the Heaths, and they assured us he was a hard worker, so we took him on as general handyman, but most of the actual work revolves around the stable, of course. We told them we needed an additional man, at least temporarily, what with all the construction going on, and the Heaths then suggested Scott Beaton. They had run into him recently, and he had mentioned he was looking for a position for the month of August. As it turned out, we continued to need him, and he has agreed, at least so far, to stay on. Do you know either of these men?"

Pete knew Forbes well enough to know about his variable temperament and his drinking habits, but the Heaths were right—he worked hard, at least when he wanted to. Scott Beaton he knew mostly from his parents' pizza shack, although now that he thought about it, Pete hadn't seen him around the shack in years. "Forbes does work hard," said Pete. "Scott's a good kid."

Simmons nodded, pleased but not surprised, as if he'd seldom found occasion to doubt his own judgment.

"What other contacts has your wife made on the island?" asked Pete.

"None," said Simmons. "My wife hasn't left the farm since we've arrived."

Pete turned, surprised. "At all?"

"Claire is not a person who adapts easily to the outside world. She will eventually venture out. At least I hope so." He cast an anxious look Pete's way. "That, in truth, is the reason I get her car ready to go each morning. I'm hoping to encourage her to test her wings."

They were in front of the house now. The door opened, and Claire Simmons came out. She stopped as if shy, an awkward few feet from them.

"Hello," said Pete.

She smiled. "Hello. Your secretary just called, Anthony. They were expecting you at eight-thirty for a meeting?"

"Oh, for heaven's sake! So call the cops," said a voice behind them.

Rawling.

But Pete kept his eye on Claire. At the word *cops,* she had frozen. No, that wasn't it—she hadn't been moving, so how could she have frozen? But she suddenly seemed to have gone somewhere else. Her eyes no longer saw him. Her lips separated, but she made no sound. One hand rose halfway in the air and stalled, trembling.

Simmons grabbed the hand between his. "Claire."

She didn't answer him.

"Claire."

She pulled her hand away and ran toward the house.

Simmons followed.

Rawling stared after them. *"Now* what's the matter with her?"

"Something upset her," said Pete. "If I were you, I'd—"

"And if I were you, I'd mind my own business," snapped Rawling.

Pete left her to simmer in her own juice. He collected his tape measure from the truck, then rummaged around for something to write on. He found a dry cleaner's slip for a jacket he'd forgotten he owned and a chewed-up pencil in the crack of the seat. He returned to the barn.

Despite the fresh paint, it was gloomy in there. He left the doors wide open. He didn't like what was going on around here. The stairs bothered him, Rawling bothered him, Forbes bothered him.

Pete heard a car pull out, probably Anthony Simmons. He didn't exactly hear footsteps or see her shadow, but still Pete knew when he turned around that Claire Simmons would be standing in the door.

She was backlit by the October sun, one hand on the doorframe, and because he couldn't see the details of her face or body, she again looked like a girl.

"Hello," said Pete. He had a feeling if he'd said boo, she would have run.

"Hello," said Claire. "I was about to go for a ride, but I thought I'd see if you needed anything."

"I'll find my way around. You were lucky about these stairs, weren't you? Your husband says there was a hayrake down there."

She let go of the door and came into the barn the way a wild deer would, giving him a wide berth. She

42

ducked under the stairs and stood under the gaping hole. "Before Anthony moved it, the old rake was right here."

Pete picked up one of the broken stair treads that was lying near her feet. "You never noticed these treads were rotten?"

"I never noticed the stairs."

Pete could believe it. He could see her floating down them weightlessly, eyes fixed on some point either inside her head or far away. He could also see her crashing through the stairs onto the hayrake, her small, pale form skewered on the tines.

Pete looked away.

CHAPTER

6

It had been a while since Connie Bartholomew had had to wonder what she'd been thinking of when she'd agreed to go back to work for Pete. True, working for your ex-husband was probably not high on the list of recommended reconciliatory techniques, but Connie had never done things the easy way, and she saw no reason to start now. Besides, she liked working at Factotum. Today, she arrived at the office in a positive frame of mind that lasted until she opened the door and saw Rita and Maxine.

For probably five and a half of the six days that Rita Peck manned the phone at Factotum, she was the model of efficiency. The problematic remaining half day arose whenever her teenage daughter, Maxine, appeared. When Connie saw Maxine sitting on her mother's desk and Rita standing in front of it with her hands on her hips, she groaned.

"What do you mean you missed the bus? I dropped you at that corner at—"

"So kill me. I missed the bus. I'm gonna walk, but I'll be late. I need a note."

Rita's eyebrows bunched. "What are you missing? Did you have a test? Is it *geometry* again?"

There was a crunching sound from the other room, followed by the appearance of Andy Oatley, a broken window box in his hands. "Gee, Rita, these things are, like, made of straw. It's the second one I busted. Hi, Connie. Hi, Max."

"Leave the window boxes," said Rita.

"There are two more out there. I can—"

"Don't *touch* the window boxes," Rita snapped. "Maxine, I don't know what you're up to, but it's not going to work. Connie, will you hold the fort here while I run Maxine to school?"

"Andy can drop me at school, can't you, Andy?" said Maxine.

"Sure, no problem."

"No," said Rita. But before she could solidify her defense, the phone rang, giving Maxine the edge she needed. She darted out the door, waving Andy after her. Rita dealt with her caller with dispatch, but it was too late. They were gone.

Rita frowned at the closed door. "What's she up to? This is all a scheme, I can smell it. But what's she scheming *after?*"

Connie decided to head off Rita's visions of doom before they escalated into full-blown disaster. "So where do you want me today?"

"The Hermitage," said Rita.

Connie could feel the remains of her morning's good mood leave her. "The Hermitage is a two-man job. At least."

"If I *had* two men, it would be a two-man job. Since I don't have two men, it's a one-woman job. Pete promised to get over there this afternoon. At least go in and look the place over so we know what to expect."

Connie gave up and left for the Hermitage.

Claire left the barn, heading toward the stable. Pete headed for his truck a minute or two after her, but he stopped halfway there. He looked at the stable instead.

There were things he wanted to be sure of, impressions he'd formed on his first visit that he needed to confirm. A trip to the stable would do it, but there was only one problem with the stable.

It had horses in it.

Pete looked at the stable again. The symmetry of the building, the gleaming fresh paint, the rolling pasture and pond in the distance seemed to imply a sense of order and control. So what was he worried about? Surely these horses would be well-behaved brutes, all locked up safe and sound in their stalls.

Still, he approached the stable the way John Wayne wouldn't, on the balls of his feet, ready to turn and run. And it was a good thing he did; when he rounded the door, there was the rear end of a horse in front of him, wild and free.

Well, not exactly free. Pete noticed with relief that the horse was secured from both sides of his halter to rings in the wall. At least his head was. His rump swung loose on top of the longest, most powerful legs Pete had ever seen, and Pete wasn't about to walk in back of them. He wasn't about to get between that well-muscled rump and the wall either. He went out the way he had come and entered from the other end of the stable. Now Pete and the brown monster were eyeball to eyeball. Pete blinked. The horse didn't.

Pete looked around.

The stable, like the rest of the farm, was immaculate. It was newly painted inside as well as out, and the wide doors at either end collected the sun and scattered it over freshly swept floorboards. Roomy stalls lined both sides of the corridor, and out of them gazed the soulful eyes of the other Simmons horses.

Next to the brown monster in front of him, Claire's palomino, which had seemed so huge yesterday, looked small. None of the horses looked mean, but then again, they didn't exactly look friendly either. It was more like they wanted to know what the hell Pete was doing in their barn. Pete examined the stall doors. It seemed to him that if any of them really wanted to, they could bust out easily enough. He decided to do what he came to do, then leave.

"Hello? Mrs. Simmons?"

This time Pete heard her steps, quick and light, before he saw her. Then her blond hair glittered as she stepped out of a side room behind the horse and into a square patch of sun. "Oh. Hello, Pete."

Claire laid a delicate hand on the brown horse's rump and to Pete's amazement, the horse moved aside. Claire walked toward Pete, between the horse and the wall, and emerged uncrushed.

Pete breathed. "I'm off to pick up the lumber. It occurred to me you might have some errands I could do in town. Your husband says you don't get out much."

She smiled. "No. I don't seem to. Thank you, but I think I'm fine. And please call me Claire."

Then Pete saw what he'd come for—John Forbes, coming out of another room, presumably the tack room, with saddle and bridle in his arms.

This time Forbes didn't even nod, but that was Nashtoba, too—they'd acknowledged each other once this month already. Pete watched carefully as

Forbes maneuvered around the horse the same way Claire had. He brushed past Claire. It didn't look like he touched her, but it seemed to Pete that Claire Simmons drew back as if she was afraid he might.

"Would you get Dapper ready, please?" she asked him.

Forbes ignored her.

Yes, there was something about Forbes or maybe it was about Claire that made Pete hesitate to leave them alone together. He backed up until he felt he was a safe distance from all hooves and teeth and watched as Forbes unclipped the big brown horse and returned him to his stall.

There were more footsteps behind Pete. He turned, and another man stepped into and quickly out of the patch of sun.

It took Pete a minute to realize this was Scott Beaton. He still thought of Scott as an awkward, stringy sixteen-year-old slinging pizzas in and out of his father's pizza oven after school. Now here he was, all fleshed out and surefooted and, what, eighteen or so? Yes, he remembered Rita telling him that Scott had started at Amherst. Unlike John Forbes, Scott at least began the day in clean clothes: crisp jeans and a thick turtleneck. He seemed surprised to see Pete. "Hi," he said. "What are you doing here?"

"Working on the barn. How's Amherst?"

"Okay, I guess. I graduated in June."

"Oh," said Pete, chagrined.

Forbes snapped his fingers in front of Scott's nose and pointed to the saddle and bridle.

"Okay, Amherst. Saddle up Dapper and get going on those stalls."

Scott Beaton flushed.

"I didn't know you went to Amherst," said Claire. "What did you study?"

"Horse dung," said Forbes from the door. He guffawed.

Claire acted like she hadn't heard him, waiting until Scott answered her.

"Environmental science," said Scott. He fetched Dapper and clipped his halter to the rings in the wall. He smoothed the saddle blankets over Dapper's back, then tossed the saddle on and cinched it. He lowered the near stirrup as far as it would go, unfastened the halter, and, with brazen disregard for a bunch of inch-long yellow teeth, worked the bit deep into Dapper's mouth. He buckled on the bridle, handed the reins to Claire, and walked away. He returned with a wheel-barrow and a shovel and yanked them through the door to Dapper's stall.

Pete walked slowly to the barn, wondering if he'd found out what he'd come for. He was pretty sure his suspicions of yesterday had been correct, that John Forbes didn't much like Claire. And what else had he learned?

That small people can move big horses.

That Scott Beaton graduated from Amherst in June with a major in environmental science.

That Forbes and Beaton might work together, but they probably didn't go out together Saturday nights for beers.

Before entering the old barn, Pete paused to watch Claire Simmons. Outside the stable she stopped and checked the cinch on Dapper's saddle. Then she passed the reins over Dapper's neck, slid her foot into the lowered stirrup, and vaulted into the saddle. She lifted her near leg, shortened the stirrup, and nudged Dapper with her heels. Dapper moved off sedately, apparently having no clue that he outweighed his tiny rider by a thousand pounds.

Once they were past the corral and into the pasture,

Claire lifted the reins, and they broke into a lope, heading toward the pond. Again, the scene struck him—the woman and horse, the picture-postcard serenity of field and pond. It was like something out of *National Velvet,* Pete thought.

Pete turned away and got to work. The first thing he did was to give the stairs another careful once-over, and he was even less pleased this time with what he found. Not only did the treads appear to be in disparate condition, but the nails in the stronger treads appeared to be more corroded than the nails in the rotten ones.

Pete did his measuring. Then he pried off one of the new treads, picked up one of the rotted treads, and returned to the truck. Before he got in, he looked again for Claire Simmons. They seemed to have reached the pond safely. The horse stretched his neck to the water, one foreleg extended gracefully, apparently taking a drink, and Claire Simmons sat on his back, small and straight and still.

Pete got in his truck and headed for the Shearsons.

To leave Nashtoba Pete had to travel over a wooden causeway that was at best shaky, and at worst not there. He turned up the radio to drown out the hollow sound of his tires on the planks, made it safely across, and cut onto the highway. He sped past mile after mile of scrub pines and golden marshes until he exited at Bradford. At Bradford he ran into things they didn't have on Nashtoba: strip malls, hotels, parking meters, timed traffic lights. Even traffic.

The Shearson Brothers were big enough to have a real office. It was tucked in on Bradford's Main Street between a bank that actually had two stories and a restaurant that had a dress code. Yeah, Bradford was big time. Pete parked his truck, put a quarter in the meter, took his stair treads up the brick walk, and laid them on the counter in front of a woman who had that distinctive Bradford look in the eye—a look that said she'd been around the block and then some. She eyed the stair treads warily.

"May I help you?"

"I don't know," said Pete. "My name is Peter Bartholomew. I'm doing some work for a fellow named Anthony Simmons."

The woman's face went deliberately blank.

"The Shearsons were working for him before me. I'm in need of some information. About these." Pete pointed to the treads.

"What kind of information?"

"What they looked like before I got to them."

This time the blank look was real.

"So I'd like to talk to whichever of the Shearsons was in charge of the Simmons job."

The woman behind the counter must have decided to pass the buck. She pushed back her stool, left the room, and returned with a stocky man dressed in twill pants and a chamois shirt that looked fresh out of the box. "This is Charlie Shearson. Charlie, this is Peter Bartholomew. It's about the Simmons place, like I told you."

Shearson looked at the stair treads first, Pete second. Then he looked at the treads again. He picked up the rotten one. "This isn't from those stairs," he said. "I don't care what line of bull you're selling. This tread was not on those stairs when I was there, and I'll tell Simmons that and I'll tell his lawyer that."

"He doesn't have a lawyer," said Pete, but the minute he said it, he knew he was wrong, that Simmons probably had twenty lawyers. "That is to say," he amended, "he doesn't have a lawyer on *this*.

At least not yet. He hired me to fix the stairs. I took one look at them and didn't much like what I saw, but I figured I'd better check it out with you first. So you never saw a tread like this on the stairs in the old barn?"

Charlie Shearson picked up the newer tread. "Every tread on those stairs was as solid as this when I was last there. We went up and down those stairs fifty times setting up the studio. The stairs were the first thing we checked out, and this tread"—he put down the good one and picked up the bad one—"this tread was not on 'em."

"That's what I figured," said Pete. "Any ideas on why it was there now?"

"Damned if I know," said Shearson. "If somebody put it there to get rid of us, it worked. You tell him if he's got anything else in mind, he's picked the wrong boys."

"I don't think he has anything in mind," said Pete. "He was worried about his wife. She fell through the stairs, and there was a—"

"Hayrake underneath! You think I didn't have to listen to a twenty-minute tirade on it all? And that's another thing—the boys hung that hayrake on the wall."

"Yes," said Pete. "Only I guess it fell off."

Charlie Shearson moved his face six inches closer to Pete's. "My boys put that rake up good and solid on the wall. You tell Simmons that. You tell him the hayrake was on the wall tight, and the treads were solid." Shearson slapped the stair tread down on the desk and pointed a fat finger at Pete. "And you tell him next time he decides to pick up the phone and mouth off like that, he'll be hearing from *my* lawyer! With a libel suit." Shearson walked back through the door he'd come from.

The woman behind the counter got busy shuffling papers.

"Thank you," Pete told her. "You've been very helpful."

The woman looked up, wary again, as if she weren't sure being helpful was an asset.

CHAPTER

7

The Hermitage was tall and narrow. It rose straight on four sides for three stories and was topped with a shallow roof. The shingles were old and curling, both on the house and on the roof. It was surrounded by overgrown lilacs that were half strangled by honeysuckle and abandoned rambler roses. Its nearest neighbor was the swamp. As Connie got closer, she could see that the windows were fogged and rounded with accumulated dirt. As she crossed the sunken porch, she made a mental note to find out who the idiot was who had agreed to this job. Pete or Rita? Probably Rita. Rita was the type who would have been itching to get her hands on the Hermitage just so she could clean it up.

Or just so *Connie* could clean it up. Connie jammed the key into the lock, but unfortunately, it turned. She pushed open the door and a thick web straight out of Miss Havisham's house trailed along with it. She poked her head in and backed up.

Miss Havisham's place couldn't hold a candle to this.

There were webs. There were webs that stretched from the corners of the ceiling to the tops of the lamps and then sideways to each other. There were unwashed dishes and cups on every horizontal surface. There were dust bunnies mixed with dead bugs blowing around the middle of the room. There were rips in the overstuffed sofa and chairs and batting dripping onto the floor. Behind and between the furniture, everywhere except in a central, clear corridor in the middle of the room, were piles of newspapers, magazines, empty bags, tin cans, and cartons.

And it smelled.

Pete had no reason to think Shearson was lying, but he wanted some confirmation. Simmons said the stairs had been rebuilt. Pete decided to find out who did the job and what he had to say about the treads. Pete mulled over the method for finding out this information and reluctantly came to the conclusion that Beston's was his best bet. Not the quickest, maybe, but the best. He picked up his lumber and returned to the island. When he pulled up in front of the store, the old men practically sucked him out of his truck and up the steps.

"So!" said Ed. "Back again! And looking a mite worn out, I don't mind telling you! But you're working for Simmons, I hear. That'll slow you down some. What's the place look like? I hear it's pretty smart."

"It's plenty smart," said Pete. "I've got a question for you. When the Heaths had the place—"

"What I want to know is what *she's* like," said Bert. "Heard he doesn't let her off the place. Is she a juicy number or what?"

"She can come and go as she pleases," said Pete.

"She just pleases to keep to herself. And she's very nice."

"Oh! *Nice.*" Bert looked at Ed and winked.

Pete turned to Evan Spender. "I'm trying to find out who worked on the old barn for the Heaths. Simmons has asked me to do some work, and I've got a few questions."

"Pimental," said Evan. "Cliff Pimental. He's working over to the fish market now, doing the roof. So what did they do to the farm, Pete?"

"They cleaned it up," said Pete.

"Oh, lah-dee-dah!" said Bert. "They cleaned it up. And the rest of us are too filthy for the likes of her, is that it?"

Pete had about a five-second tolerance for Bert these days, and he'd already heard Claire picked on enough. "Yeah, Bert," he said. "That's it."

Pete tracked down Cliff Pimental on the fish market's roof. On Nashtoba, time was money, and there wasn't a whole lot of either. Pete climbed up and balanced himself on the ridge pole, talking to Cliff Pimental as he worked. He'd laid the tar paper and was about to start shingling.

"Heaths?" said Cliff. "Sure, I worked for the Heaths." He tacked a chalked string on one end of the roof and, walking bent-kneed, crossed to the other side and tacked it again. He returned to the middle, picked up the string, and snapped it. A white, true line stretched across the roof to mark the first row of shingles.

"I'm curious about the stairs in the small barn," said Pete. "The ones going up to the loft. I'm told you rebuilt them a few years ago."

Cliff slapped a pad of shingles down just above the scaffolding on the roof and pulled one out. "Sure, I

built the stairs. Funny job, though. Usually, going up
to a hay loft, a ladder would do. But they wanted
stairs. Nothing fancy, just open treads, but still, a
ladder wouldn't do."

"Why?"

"Damned if I know. I built 'em the stairs, though."
Cliff hammered in three shingles in a row. Then he
looked up and saw that Pete was holding out the stair
treads he brought with him to the roof. "What's with
those?"

"These are from the stairs. A couple of treads like
this one rotted out and tore loose. This other one
looked newer. How many of the treads did you
replace?"

"What treads? I told you. It was a ladder before I
got there. I built new stairs. With all new treads." He
resumed hammering.

Pete raised his voice. "All new treads? All new
wood?"

Cliff stopped again, sitting back on his heels. "What
are you getting at? You think I put a tread like that on
there?" He pointed to the rotted one.

"No, I don't. I—"

"And what *do* you think then? Spit it out, why don't
you?"

"I don't think anything. It just seemed strange to
me that one pair of treads would rot out like this,
that's all."

"Around here it's what doesn't rot."

"True," said Pete. "Still—"

"Bad wood. Carpenter ants. Leak in the roof. No
big deal."

Different nails, Pete wanted to say, but he was
starting to feel like a fool. Anyone could reach in his
carpenter's apron and pull out an odd nail or two.

"What's with you, Pete? Don't you have enough to do? I'll put you on the other side of this here roof if you want."

Pete swung a leg over the ridge pole. "Thanks, no." He had one foot on the ladder when Cliff Pimental hollered after him.

"Hey, wait. I just remembered something. One of those Heath boys got stepped on by their Percheron. One mother of a horse. Got flown to Boston and still lost all his toes. Now that I think of it, must be why they wanted those stairs put in."

"Must be," said Pete.

Cliff looked up at the sky and squinted the way every old Nashtoban did before giving some pronouncement they felt to be of particular worth. Usually it was about the weather. "I'll tell you something," said Cliff. "There's no dumber animal than a horse."

Pete couldn't agree with him. It seemed to him the dumber animal was the one who allowed his foot in the vicinity of the horse in the first place.

Pete returned to the farm, his mind racing, and the closer he got, the greater a queer sense of apprehension grew. Still, when he came in sight of the neat buildings, the green pasture, the glistening pond, the process reversed itself. It was hard to imagine there could be any real trouble here.

Pete got to work on the stairs, and even though he kept his eyes open, he saw nothing to disturb him further, probably because he didn't see John Forbes. He didn't see Scott Beaton either, but he heard him, and from the noises coming out of the stable, it sounded to Pete like Scott was taking out a few things on the wheelbarrow.

* * *

Andy arrived at the Hermitage at nine-thirty, and Connie met him on the porch. "Rita sent me to see if you need help."

"A little," said Connie. She waved him toward the door. He walked in, gagged, and backed up.

Connie laid a ruthless hand between his shoulder blades and pushed him in front of her through the living room, into the kitchen.

She had barely made a dent. She'd opened all the doors and windows to let in some of the antiseptic October air, and she'd piled the dirty dishes she found in the living room on the kitchen floor. She would have piled them on the kitchen table and counter, but the table and counter were already full. With other dirty dishes. Even the floor had been shaky going. There was a pile of rancid dish towels in one corner and empty cereal boxes full of mouse cards in another. There were sour-smelling milk cartons under the table. There were greasy paper bags on the chairs. There were empty, moldy cans and bottles everywhere.

And flies.

Oh, well, thought Connie, she'd take flies over maggots any day. Then she lifted the lid on a cardboard pizza box and found the maggots.

At three-thirty Claire Simmons came out to the barn with a round metal tray containing a can of Coke, a can of Very Fine grapefruit juice, and a bottle of Beck's. Beside the cans were two frosted mugs, one full of crushed ice and one without. Beside the mug was a basket of thick pretzels crusted with salt.

"Could you use refueling?" she asked. "You've been working awfully hard. I wasn't sure what you'd prefer."

Pete preferred beer, but he was working. He put down his tools and took the Coke and the mug full of ice. Claire removed the basket of pretzels and set it down on one of the stairs.

"Thank you," said Pete. "This is perfect. Thank you."

"You're fixing my stairs. It's the least I can do. I can't wait to get back to work."

"Your husband says you sculpt. What kind of stuff?"

"Horses," said Claire. "People. It's all very boring. The horses look like horses. The people look like people."

Pete smiled. "My kind of art."

Claire smiled back but said nothing else.

Pete went back to work. He expected her to leave, but to his surprise she put down the tray, found a seat on an old oat bin, and opened the can of juice.

"Have you lived on the island long?" she asked.

"All my life."

"Always? Every day? You've never left?"

Pete turned around, surprised. "Sure I've left. I went to college. I traveled some. But I'm like Scott, I guess. I'd rather stay on the island. I have to go to the mainland from time to time, but I'll admit I don't go more than I can help."

"So you like it here."

"Sure. Don't you? Not like Connecticut, I guess?"

"No, but in some ways Nashtoba reminds me of the place I lived just before I moved to Connecticut. A little town in Vermont. Swippingsdale. Have you heard of it?"

"No," said Pete. He grinned. "But I've heard of Vermont."

Claire Simmons didn't smile. She seemed to be gazing at something on the floor. "I think it would be nice to have never left here. To have been born here and never to have left. What do you think the world would seem like to you if you had never left?"

"About the same as it seems now. We do get newspapers over here, you know. Radio, TV even."

"I'd never look. I'd never listen. I'd pretend this was the whole world, this place. I'd avoid all the suffering."

Pete looked at her in surprise a second time. "Oh, we have our share of suffering, all right."

She looked up. "Are you married?"

It was an oddly timed question. It seemed to Pete that he'd been asked it a lot, though. He remembered how he used to answer it, too—*very.* But the *very* hadn't worked out so hot. After nine years of marriage Connie had run off with someone else. Pete had divorced her as fast as the papers could find her. A year later she'd come back to the island alone. For a long time Pete had kept his distance, but slowly and by no means steadily they had again drawn close. And now . . . what *were* they now? But that wasn't the question. The question was whether he was married. Easy enough. "No," said Pete. Still, the bald *no* didn't sound just right. "Not really," he added, but that sounded worse. "Actually," he said, "I'm sort of divorced." It wasn't getting any better. He picked up a pretzel and shoved it in his mouth.

Claire pulled her feet up and hugged her knees to her chest. "Sort of divorced," she repeated. "Yes. It's like that, isn't? You hear people say that divorce is final, but somehow I doubt if it's that neat." She looked up and seemed to notice Pete's discomfiture. "I'm sorry," she said. "I didn't mean to pry. We blissful newlyweds do that, I guess."

"How long have you been married?"

"Three months."

Three months. Pete remembered those three months. He remembered the nine years that came after them, too. And sometimes, on bad days, he remembered every detail of what came after that.

Pete said nothing more. Neither did Claire. Still, she sat there on the oat bin until he tapped the last nail into the last tread and straightened up.

"Okay," said Pete. "There are your stairs. Now I'll just clean this up and be on my way."

He wanted her to go so he could stop at the bog before its owner, Jasper Sears, quit for the day, but Claire slid off the oat bin and returned with a dustpan and brush. As Pete cleaned up the larger mess, she swept the sawdust off the stairs, starting at the top.

"I'm so pleased to have the stairs done," she said as she worked. "I'll be able to begin work again tomorrow. Will you be able to start the exterior in the morning?"

Pete straightened up. "The exterior?"

"We have the paint, but there is still some scraping to be done."

"I'm sorry," said Pete. "I promised your husband just this one day. He didn't mention painting the barn and I have some other commitments."

"Oh," said Claire. "I see. I assumed when he hired you it would be for everything, but I understand, of course. It's just that now he'll have to hire a complete stranger."

"Like me, you mean?"

Claire smiled. "That did sound foolish, didn't it? It's just that now you don't seem like a stranger. I've never done well with strangers, and lately . . ." She looked down. All Pete could see was the tip of a small nose and the fine blond hair fringing her face. "I don't know," she said. "Sometimes I feel surrounded by them."

Having met the people who surrounded her, Pete could see why. He could also see where somebody who'd been through what she'd been through wouldn't "do well" with strangers. Come to think of it, that probably also explained why she wasn't too anxious to leave her house.

Pete looked at his watch. It was past five o'clock. Since Jasper wasn't harvesting yet, the odds were he'd already left. And there wasn't much point in involving himself with the Hermitage this late in the day.

The Hermitage. True, there was still the Hermitage, but how bad could it be? It was just one house.

"Show me what you want done," he said to Claire. "I could work it in, I guess."

CHAPTER
8

At four-thirty, Connie looked at the clock. Still no Pete. She wondered what he was doing. For that matter, she wondered what Andy was doing. She'd sent him out an hour ago to get more garbage bags and hadn't seen him since.

Not that she could blame him.

Connie went out to the porch to grab some air. The view was not pleasant. It looked like the house had thrown up on the lawn, and the porch was piled high with full garbage bags. Connie figured that overnight the racoons would rip all the bags open and they'd be back where they'd started, but by the time they'd bagged enough garbage to see where they were going, it had been too late for the dump.

Connie was back inside and elbow deep in moldy newspapers when Andy showed up. With Maxine.

"Pee-yew!" said Maxine when she stepped in the door.

"Yucko," said Andy. "I think it's getting worse."

"What are you doing here, Maxine?" asked Connie.

"I didn't have any money," said Andy. "So I stopped at Factotum and ran into Maxine. I told her about the place, and she didn't believe me. She wanted to take a look."

"I can help," said Maxine. "That's why I had Andy bring me. To help."

Connie eyed her suspiciously. On her best day you couldn't pay Maxine to do Factotum's *cleaner* work. Maxine was after something, all right, but what?

"It'll take you *years,*" said Maxine. "You'll be gassed in here. You'll *choke.*" Connie opened her mouth to respond, but as she looked at Maxine, she realized it wasn't Connie Maxine was so worried about. She was looking up at Andy with large, brown, earnest eyes, and suddenly the light dawned.

What was she after?

Andy, of course.

Connie tried to look at Andy Oatley with the eyes of a seventeen-year-old instead of the eyes of someone he accidentally almost killed once a week. He had the streaky blond hair of a surfer, deep blue eyes, rose cheeks, white teeth. He drove his truck to the Hook three times a week and worked out. The muscles in his thighs were rubbing the color out of his jeans, and there wasn't much extra room through the shoulders of his shirt. He was Gidget's dream date, but up to now, at least, Maxine had run more toward the black-leather–motorcycle set. And although most mothers would consider Andy a vast improvement, Connie had a feeling Rita wasn't going to go for the idea of Maxine and Andy rummaging around together in possibly rat-infested muck.

"You can't help," said Connie. "You have school. Andy, help me toss these bags back inside so the raccoons don't get them."

By the time they'd flung about twenty garbage bags

back inside, Connie was beat. It took a lot of energy to run back and forth between rooms without breathing. "Okay," she said. "Let's call it day. Andy, meet me here tomorrow at eight, all ready for about ten trips to the dump." She followed Andy and Maxine out and shut the door, but she left the windows open.

Connie pulled into her driveway, got out of the car, took one look at the bedraggled garden, and kept going. She was too tired to move. The first thing she did when she got inside was strip off all her clothes and throw them in the wash. The second thing she did was hop in the shower. When she got out, she put on a clean pair of jeans and a new sweater in a color the catalog had called oyster. Then she remembered they were eating spaghetti. Fond as she was of red sauce on oysters when they were in the half shell, she didn't want it on her new oyster-colored sweater. She pulled off the sweater and put on a flannel shirt instead. She ran a comb through her hair and looked in the mirror, not something she did often since a scalp laceration had cost her half her hair and her attempts to even it off had cost her most of the rest, but it seemed to be growing out okay—it was starting to lie down in wisps of pale brown around her face and neck. She picked up her leather jacket and stepped out the door to walk to Pete's.

Their two houses, Pete's Cape cottage and Connie's Victorian inheritance, were accessible to each other by an isolated stretch of beach. At six o'clock the sun had just gone, but the sky was still gold and the sand was full of deep shadows. Still, to the north Connie could see a row of gray black clouds that looked runny with rain. She licked a finger and held it to the wind. Yes, they were coming this way. She gave up on the beach walk and took the long way around by car instead.

Pete's truck was not in his driveway. But Connie opened the cottage door and said "Hello?" anyway.

No answer.

She walked down the hall to the two rooms he lived in—one a kitchen–dining room, the other a bedroom–living room—rapped on the kitchen door, and went in. "Hello?"

Again, no answer.

Connie went out on the porch, sat down in the rocker, put her sneakers up on the rail, and watched the rain roll in.

At six Pete and Claire Simmons walked toward the farmhouse. "I can't help feeling that somehow I've pressured you into this," she said. "You mentioned other commitments."

"The barn won't take long," said Pete. "A week, maybe, tops. I can fit it in."

"Still," said Claire, "I'd like to express my gratitude somehow. Do you ride?"

"No," said Pete quickly. He looked at his watch. "Gee," he said. "It's later than I thought. I'd better run. See you tomorrow." He veered off for his truck.

Pete called Connie's house from the store. No answer. He called his house. On the fourth ring he wondered. It was his phone, his house. Even if she were there, would she answer?

She picked up on ring six. "Hello?"

"Oh, good, you answered," said Pete. "I'm at the store. I can't remember if I have tomatoes."

"Wait a minute, I'll look." She came back to the phone. "No tomatoes."

"Okay," said Pete. "I think that's all we need. Maybe I'll pick up some wine."

"And some beer," said Connie.

How could he forget? Connie didn't like wine. "And some beer." He said good-bye and went to the wine section. He picked out a bottle of Merlot, but then he put it back. He felt stupid buying wine just for himself. He picked up a six-pack of Ballantine Ale, Connie's favorite. He liked Ballantine. He'd drink that.

When he walked into the kitchen Connie was stirring the sauce, and when he kissed her, her face felt dewy from the steam rising from a second pot. He turned toward the sink to wash his hands and stopped. Three ripe tomatoes were sitting on the window sill. "I thought you said I didn't have tomatoes."

Connie pointed at the fridge. "Look for yourself. You don't."

"They're here. On the windowsill."

Connie turned around. "Oh, Christ. Sorry."

Pete picked up a knife to make the salad but Connie waved her spoon at him. "Hey. Put that down. I'm cooking. You're cleaning up."

Yes, that was how they used to do it—one cooked, one cleaned up. It felt good to be back on the old track.

Pete lined up the new tomatoes next to the old ones, took a beer for himself and one for Connie, and put the rest in the fridge. He sat down at the kitchen table and put his feet up on the chair across from him.

"Were you at the farm all this time?"

"More or less. I fixed the stairs. Drove to Bradford and talked to Shearson. Talked to Cliff Pimental, the guy who built the stairs in the first place. Something's fishy, I'm just not sure what."

"So you're calling the cops?"

"Not yet. I have to talk to Jasper Sears. He owns the bog near the beach plums. And I agreed to paint the barn. A few more days at most."

Connie didn't say anything. Pete had a pretty good idea what it cost her to do that. He got up and put his arms around her. Then he backed up.

"Hey, isn't this my shirt?"

Connie looked down. "It was in my closet. You could at least *talk* to Will McOwat."

"Not yet."

"Why not?"

"I'm still not sure what's what. And I got a chance to watch Claire Simmons when her stepdaughter mentioned the police. She was rattled, all right. I've never seen anything like it. Rawling said the word *cop,* and she fell apart. Simmons is a nervous wreck."

"Hmm," said Connie.

"Meaning?"

"Meaning I don't trust this nervous wreck act. So what if she was raped by a cop? To me, that makes it worse. If *you* thought your wife was in danger, would *you* circumnavigate the cops? And hire some—" Connie stopped.

"Idiot like me? No, maybe not. But the fact remains that Simmons did, and I agreed to it, and I'm not prepared to back away from that yet. I feel sorry for her. I think she's lonely. Here she is stuck on this farm in the middle of a bunch of strangers—"

"Strangers? Her husband and her mother?"

"I wonder if her husband isn't half a stranger, too. They've only been married three months. And her mother looks like a pretty cold fish. Claire's nice, though. She brought me soda and pretzels at three-thirty."

"Soda and pretzels. Whereas at three-thirty I was

checking out the house number to make sure I wasn't at the dump."

"Bad?"

"I'll save the details till after you eat." She went over to the windowsill and took down one of the new orangy pink tomatoes. *Thwap* went the knife. Pete tried not to look at the older, riper tomatoes she'd left on the sill to rot. She put the two salads and the two steaming plates of spaghetti on the table.

Pete was starving. He speared a mouthful of spaghetti, and then he looked at the beer.

I should have bought the wine, he thought.

CHAPTER
9

Pete tossed and turned all night. Early on he dreamed about stairs, hayrakes, small pale bodies spattered with blood. He woke up and fumbled around for Connie until he remembered she hadn't stayed—after dinner it had started to pour, and she'd remembered her windows weren't shut. She'd left Pete with his dishes and driven home, worried about Clara Bates's hooked rugs. Pete had half expected her to come back, but she didn't. By now Pete was getting used to having her in bed with him. He felt unanchored, cast adrift. As soon as the sun came up, he got up, too.

He was out of Wheaties, but he managed to find a banana that was still yellow in spots. His food shopping had gone down the tubes since he'd been eating at Connie's a lot. He ate the banana as he wrote Rita a note. "Off to Sarah's. Then straight to farm. Have a few more days' work there, but we've still got time. Don't panic. Pete."

He got to Sarah at seven-thirty.

Sarah was in her chair, listening to the radio. When

she saw Pete, her face lit up. "You're early. What happened, has she kicked you out?"

"I don't know why I keep coming here," said Pete. "Do you want to hear the paper or not?"

"I suppose so. But nothing about the election. I'm sick to death of the election. Have you made my bat house?"

"Not yet. I've been busy."

"I bet. They sell the plans at Beston's, did I tell you?"

"Yes, you did. Mosquitoes don't hatch till spring, you know."

"I know that," said Sarah. "But it said on the radio that bats don't take kindly to change. It takes them a while to settle in."

"It takes everyone a while to settle in."

"So get going," said Sarah.

Pete snapped open the paper and read.

Pete arrived at the farm early, but still, Simmons answered the door in his camel hair coat. "Another early meeting," he said.

"Ask Pete if he'd like breakfast," Claire called from inside. "Hot waffles, fresh fruit, coffee?"

Hot waffles. Fresh fruit. Coffee. The banana was sitting in Pete's stomach like a small, lonely lump.

"Yes, do," said Simmons. "Go right in. That was a most efficient job on the stairs. And Claire tells me you'll be starting the exterior today." He winked and went out.

Pete went in.

They were lined up on the long benches at the kitchen table, Claire in the corner seat nearest the stove, her mother and Greg across from her, Rawling on Claire's side of the table but separated by a gap.

The gap must have been caused by Anthony leaving. Or was it?

Pete sat next to Lillian Bowles.

"You've met my mother?" asked Claire.

"Yes. Hello, Mrs. Bowles."

Claire smiled at him. "Oh, you're allowed to call her Lillian. Isn't he, Mother?"

Lillian Bowles nodded. At least Pete was pretty sure she nodded. Her eyelids drooped and rose again, like a doll's.

Pete was so entranced with Lillian's doll trick that he didn't see the other woman until she was at his elbow, pouring coffee. Like all the women in the house, her age confused him. She had the muddy, deeply creased skin of a heavy cigarette smoker, and she wore her hair in an old-fashioned clip, but something in her eye told him she was younger than she looked.

"This is Joan Pitts," said Claire. "Joan, this is Peter Bartholomew. Joan, would you bring Pete some fresh waffles? These are cooling down. Here, Pete." Claire handed him a platter covered with neatly arranged melon, grapes, strawberries, and kiwi.

Pete took a couple of grapes. "Thank you. I hadn't expected to be served breakfast."

Rawling stood up. "You'd better watch out, you'll get served all kinds of things around here. Ready, Greg?"

Greg tore his eyes away from the stack of steaming waffles Joan Pitts had just deposited on the table and followed Rawling out.

"They're going riding," said Claire. "Everyone rides but Mother." She looked at Pete. "And you. Don't you like horses, Pete?"

Pete didn't answer.

For one thing, Claire was watching him too closely, and for another, his mouth was full of waffle. Also real butter. And Vermont maple syrup, the kind in the metal can that meant it really was maple syrup and really was from Vermont. Pete took a swallow of coffee. It tasted like real coffee, not like Mocha-Nut-Swiss-Mint-Something, and by the time he got to the bottom of the cup, Joan Pitts was at his elbow with more. "Thank you," said Pete.

Joan Pitts ignored him.

Lillian Bowles waited politely until Pete had swallowed his last swallow and then took her leave.

The maid cleared the dishes. Pete stood. Claire balled up the tablecloth and carried it into the kitchen. When she returned, she said, "Let me show you where we keep the paint."

Pete followed her.

The rest of the house was no surprise. Claire led Pete past what she called Anthony's room. It had cherrywood file cabinets, bookshelves, and desk and an Oriental rug. There wasn't a paper unfiled or a book out of place. The next room she called the sunny room. It was full of plants and glass and wicker. Pete wasn't much with plants, but he could see some time had been taken to group these to the best advantage of their colors and height.

"Here we are," she said finally.

She led him into an unheated ell at the back of the farmhouse, the room that the old-timers on Nashtoba called the back kitchen, a cool place that they used to store fruit, vegetables, drink, sometimes meat. Nashtoba's back kitchens tended to collect whatever junk wasn't fit to be seen in the main part of the house, but in the Simmons back kitchen there wasn't a piece of junk in sight. Neatly painted cupboards and spotless countertops faced them. The shelves were lined with blue-checked shelf paper and filled with rows of neatly labeled containers that said things like "tacks" or "screws" or "tape." There was a box marked "rags" on the counter, but it was unlike any rag box Pete had ever seen. All the rags were white, so white they looked as if they'd been bleached.

Claire opened a cupboard. "The paint is in here."

"Okay," said Pete. "I'll come back for it when the scraping's done." He headed for the outer door, but something as light as a hummingbird landed on his arm, stopping him.

Claire's fingers.

"I would like to explain about Rawling."

"You don't have to."

"I would feel better if I do. She didn't mean to be rude when she said that about watching out for what we serve you. I would like to explain why she said that."

"It really isn't necessary."

"I know. But I want to. It . . . it will help you to understand her. Rawling picked some beach plums that were contaminated with some sort of pesticide. I ate some and got sick. My husband was quite upset, and I'm afraid poor Rawling took the brunt of his alarm. She tries to joke, but she's quite defensive about it. She idolizes her father, and she hates to upset him."

But doesn't mind almost killing you? Pete wanted to ask. "I see," he said instead. "What kind of pesticide was it? Do you know?"

"I don't remember the name of it. Anthony knows. He had the beach plums tested. That's how upset he was. The pesticide came from the cranberry bog nearby. Poor Rawling seems to persist in feeling to blame. Of course, it was nothing but a harmless chain of accidental circumstances."

Of course? She looked like a child who knew her watch was broken but kept thinking she could hear it tick.

"But actually," Claire went on, "the blame was all mine. I should have known better than to eat unwashed fruit. It's just that it was already in the bowl, and I assumed it had been washed."

Right. Claire's fault, all the way.

"You see how it is, don't you?" said Claire. "It's been difficult. For Rawling, I mean. And again, I feel to blame. Anthony and I decided to marry rather suddenly. He didn't tell Rawling about me until after we were married, and I had my reservations about this plan, but I didn't share them with him. I believe now it was wrong of me to do that."

Again, Claire's fault? "It couldn't have been too easy on you either," said Pete.

"Oh, I didn't mind," said Claire. "That is to say, I minded more for Rawling than for me. Anthony and I have each other. Rawling has already lost her mother, and she's Anthony's only child. I'm sure you see how hard that could be. Since she's come, I've done my best to make sure she feels welcome in our home, but I'm afraid it's going to take something more than that."

"Time helps," said Pete. As soon as it was out of his mouth, it sounded trite, but Claire didn't seem to look at it that way. The faint smudge of worry between her eyes disappeared, and she smiled up at him.

CHAPTER
10

By ten o'clock Connie was covered with sweat. Andy, on the other hand, still looked pretty crisp. Connie wasn't sure if it was because of his relative youth or because she was the one who'd been lugging all the bags out of the house and tossing them *up* into the truck. All Andy had done was to fuss around with a bunch of ropes, drive to the dump, and throw them *down*. Besides, he was out in the sharp, clean October air. Connie was inside in the stink and the hot.

"Next trip bring me back a Coke, will you?" she asked.

The next trip took a long time, longer than could possibly be justified by the purchase of one Coke. The light dawned when Andy returned with Maxine sitting beside him in the cab of the truck.

"What are you doing here? Why aren't you in school, Maxine?"

Maxine pointed to her neck and mouthed the words "Sore throat."

Connie decided against suggesting that the reason

her throat was so sore was because her sweater was so tight.

"Here's your Coke, Connie," said Andy. "Boy, do you look hot. Why don't you sit down and drink it? I'll take care of this junk."

Connie pulled off her protective rubber gloves, the thick kind used by shellfishermen. She took the Coke and dropped onto the porch steps. Despite their day's efforts, the porch still seemed full of garbage bags.

Andy picked up two and headed for the truck. One bag snagged on the pillar to the porch and ripped open, but he didn't see it. He trailed putrid food containers in a foot-wide swath from the porch to the truck.

Connie watched Maxine, hanging out the window of the truck, gazing at Andy as if he were constructing objects of art instead of screwing up. "Does your mother know you're here, Maxine?"

"The school nurse called and told her I was walking home. I mean to Factotum. That's what I was doing when Andy saw me and picked me up in the truck."

Hmm. Connie considered the lay-out of the island of Nashtoba. The quickest route from the school to Factotum, by far, was down a short stretch of beach. Of course if Maxine knew Andy was going to be making multiple trips down Shore Road from the Hermitage to the dump, it might cause her to take an alternate route.

"Maybe you could call her from here," said Maxine. "Tell her I'm okay. I'm just kind of resting in the truck?"

Right. Connie debated her options. Call Rita and report her truant daughter. Pick up the spilled garbage. Shoot Andy. Shoot herself. She stood up and pulled on her gloves.

"No, wait. I'll do it." Maxine scrambled from the

78

cab, took Connie's gloves, pulled them on, and started scooping up garbage.

What was going on around here? Then Connie got it. Maxine wanted Connie to call her mother and say it was okay for Maxine to stick around here with Andy. Connie was being bribed, that's what it was.

Connie sat back down on the steps. "Maybe you should see Hardy Rogers about that throat."

"Oh, I think it's getting better," said Maxine. "I think even in another couple hours—"

"About when school gets out?"

Maxine grinned sheepishly. "Really. It's okay. Andy's dropping me off at Factotum next trip. We just didn't want you wondering where he was."

We didn't, did we? Connie doubted Andy had worried about it much. She also doubted he had a clue what Maxine was up to. But God only knew when they'd see Sir Gallahad again, and time was running out. "Okay," she said. "Here's the deal. Andy, you clean up this mess and get it to the dump. I'll run Maxine back."

Maxine's face fell.

"I'll talk to your mother," said Connie. "Maybe she'll let you help us. *After* school gets out."

Pete was glad the unfinished side of the barn was on the south side in the sun. There wasn't much Pete liked better than the sun in October, when the air was crisp enough that you needed a little sun to keep you warm. He had it all planned out. He'd scrape till noon, and then on the pretext of lunch break, he'd leave to talk to Jasper about his bog. He'd just hauled the extension ladder out of his truck and had climbed up to start at the peak, when Claire and Dapper came out of the stable.

She waved her feathery wave, and Pete waved back.

He watched her repeat the routine of the day before—checking the cinch, gathering the reins—but from up here the perspective was different. Claire seemed even smaller. Somehow, though, the horse seemed bigger. Maybe it was because this time Dapper danced around skittishly as Claire fitted her tiny boot into the lengthened stirrup, and when she threw her other leg over the horse, she was off balance, landing hard in the saddle. At least that was what it looked like from high up on the ladder. At any rate, the minute she came down into the saddle, Dapper bolted.

Pete remembered a scene just like it in *Duel in the Sun*. The horse took off on a dead run, straight for the pond, with Claire clinging like a tiny blond burr, still off-kilter in the saddle. Pete did his best Gregory Peck. He scrambled down the ladder and ran, but he had only reached the far end of the corral when Dapper planted his front legs and shot out with his hind ones.

Claire sailed over his head and landed in a heap by the edge of the pond as still and as limp as a half-stuffed scarecrow.

It occurred to Pete that Gregory Peck had been on a horse when he rescued his distressed damsel, and he'd gotten there a lot sooner. Pete was on foot.

And he got there too late.

Claire's body was still, lifeless. Yes, he was too late. It didn't seem possible. Nobody died just falling off a horse. Then he remembered *Gone with the Wind*. He also remembered Anthony's conviction that Claire was at serious risk. Risk. Pete of all people should have sensed that it would happen when she was on a horse.

He was still twenty feet from Claire when she sat up.

She was propped up on her hands, her legs splayed

in front of her, when Pete puffed up. "What happened?" she asked.

"He bucked you off," said Pete as soon as he could breathe again. "He took off like a shot and almost dumped you in the pond. Are you all right?"

"I don't know. Yes, I . . . I must be. I've fallen before, but not for some time. It was careless of me. He was skittish from the start."

Leave it to her to take the blame for this, too, thought Pete. "Here." He helped her up and supported her by an elbow while she dusted off the seat of her pants. He was so relieved he almost hugged her. "You're sure you're all right?"

She smiled up at him shakily. "I'm fine. It's easier if you go limp."

"You were limp, all right. I don't mind telling you, you scared the pants off me. I thought you'd snapped your neck in two. You're sure you're all right?"

Claire took three steps. "See? I'm fine. Let's go back."

Still, she didn't remove her elbow from his hand as they set out for the house. Ahead of them Pete could see two figures coming their way—the jerky trot had to be John Forbes's, the more nimble one, Scott Beaton's.

When they got within earshot Claire said, "Do you have Dapper?"

Pete had forgotten about the horse.

"He's in the stable," said Scott. "We tied him and came running. Are you okay?"

"Yes, fine. I wonder what's wrong with him? He fussed when you saddled him, didn't he, John?"

Forbes jerked his head, possibly assenting.

"The minute I hit the saddle he ran," said Claire. "I've never seen him do something like that."

They were approaching the stable, and suddenly

her knees buckled. Pete grabbed one arm, and Scott grabbed the other. They helped her to the house, while John Forbes went into the stable.

They were met on the porch by the maid and Lillian. The women steered Claire straight for her bedroom, even though she continued to insist she was fine. Pete headed back to the old barn; Scott headed for the stable.

There were angry voices coming from it.

First a woman's voice, loud but unclear. Then a man's, just as loud, but more brief. The woman came back at him uncowed. The man's answer was briefer still and clearly audible this time—two words, one four-lettered. It had been Pete's experience that this particular response didn't, as a rule, defuse things much. Scott Beaton was twenty feet from the stable, but he hung back, looking at Pete. Pete moved toward the voices.

Slowly.

It was Rawling and John Forbes.

"And I'm telling *you*," shouted Rawling, "that you have no business being around horses! When I talk to my father—"

Pete rounded the stable door. "Anybody need any help in here?"

"No," said Forbes.

"Yes," said Rawling. "I want this man removed from the premises. Immediately. You work for my father, don't you? I want you to—"

"Want him to what?" asked Forbes in a voice that convinced Pete he might not want to do much of anything.

"Look," Rawling said to Pete. *"Look."*

Pete looked. Rawling was pointing at Dapper. He was standing in the middle of the corridor, tethered as usual on both sides to the rings in the wall. He was

wearing the blanket that went under the saddle, but
the saddle itself was now on the floor. Dapper looked
a little wild-eyed, but then again, so did everyone else.
The blanket had been flipped up over Dapper's neck,
and Rawling was pointing to the middle of Dapper's
back. Pete leaned in cautiously, keeping his toes at a
distance. In the middle of Dapper's back he saw what
looked like a small puncture wound. Rawling pointed
to the blanket. What looked like the point of a nail
was sticking through it.

"This man saddled this horse with *that.*"

"I see," said Pete.

"Oh, no you don't," said Forbes.

"Get away from that horse," said Rawling. "Here!
You! What's your name?"

Scott Beaton had come up behind them. When he
saw the horse, his face went through a series of grim
changes, starting with shock and ending with something less well defined but more resolute.

"Here," said Rawling. "Take care of this horse."
Then she seemed to remember something they must
have taught her at Smith. "Please."

Forbes stomped out of the stable. Scott disappeared
into the tackroom.

Pete backed a safe distance from Dapper and
turned to Rawling. "What happened?"

"I walked into the stable and found Dapper, all in a
lather, tied up and trembling. I managed to get the
saddle off but he was dancing around like crazy. Then
Forbes came in and yelled at me to get away from the
horse, but I'd already lifted the blanket and seen it."

"The nail?"

"The nail. That man put a blanket with a *nail* in it
on this horse."

Scott returned. He ignored Rawling and moved in
on Dapper, whisking off the blanket. As he cleaned

out the wound, Dapper's hind end sashayed back and forth. Pete moved toward the tethered end.

"Easy, old man," said Scott. He put ointment on Dapper's wound.

Rawling fussed and fumed around them for a minute or two, but it seemed clear even to Pete that Dapper was now in good hands, and finally Rawling left the stable.

Pete picked up the blanket. "Funny place for a nail."

Scott capped the ointment tube. "This place has been under construction all summer."

"Yeah, but I wouldn't think you'd see too many nails in a spot like this." Pete held out the blanket. It was actually two blankets. The nail had entered from between the two blankets and had pierced the bottom one. "Why two blankets?"

"No saddle sores that way."

"You always use two blankets?"

Scott nodded. He still looked a little grim around the mouth.

"Dapper is Claire's horse?"

"Yes."

"No one else rides him?"

"I haven't seen anyone else on him."

"Who usually saddles Claire's horse?"

Scott said nothing. He started to walk toward the tack room. Pete followed.

"Do you?"

"I do what I'm told." Scott heaved the saddle onto a rack protruding from the wall, next to a lot of other racks and a lot of other saddles. The blankets, Pete noticed, were stored on top of the saddles. Scott went down the rows and checked all of them.

"How long have you been here, Scott? At the Simmonses?"

"Since they came. August."

"Forbes, too?"

"Yeah."

"Any plans?"

Scott turned around. "Plans?"

"Something in environmental sciences?"

"I had plans. They fell through."

"You like it here at the farm?"

"Sure," said Scott.

"About Forbes," began Pete, but Scott cut him off.

"I'm not talking about Forbes."

"Okay then, about the Simmonses—"

"Look," said Scott. "I have nothing to say about these people, all right? I do what they tell me, that's it."

He walked out of the tack room. Pete followed. He looked at the wheelbarrow full of smelly straw waiting for Scott.

"You must like this place a lot," said Pete.

Scott picked up the wheelbarrow and pushed it out into the sun without answering.

CHAPTER
11

Pete returned to scraping the barn, but it was another hour before he felt recovered from the sight of what he had presumed was Claire dead. And it was another hour after that before he saw John Forbes return to the stable.

At one-fifteen Claire Simmons came out of the house and stopped at the foot of Pete's ladder.

"How are you?" he asked.

"I'm fine. I'm giving up on today's ride, though. I'm going to do a little work in the studio. Thank you for your help this morning."

"Any time," said Pete. "Although I'd rather you didn't do it again."

He expected Claire to smile, but she only blinked up at him, her brown eyes troubled. Pete could see why. Even the most cockeyed optimist would have to start wondering after accident number three.

After fifteen minutes, Pete climbed down the outside of the barn and up into the inside, to Claire's studio. The door to the studio was open. Pete rapped on the doorframe and walked in.

The studio was as orderly as the rest of the farm. There were shelves filled with blocks of stone arranged by color and size along one wall by the door. There were other shelves for tools and completed works of art. Claire was sitting on a stool in front of a highly organized worktable, kneading a lump that looked almost grotesque under her delicate hands. She was wearing a taupe-colored smock that barely showed the splotches of wet clay. She looked up, and this time she smiled.

"It's so good to get back to work," she said. "Thank you for the stairs. Anthony wouldn't hear of me hopping over the hole and coming up."

"Good," said Pete.

"And I'm most anxious to see the outside done. It's been such a bone in my throat. You have no idea."

Considering the impeccable state of the rest of Heath Farm, Pete could see where the old barn would be a bit of bone. "What are you making?" he asked her. As he said it, it didn't sound right—it was the kind of question you'd put to a three-year-old mucking around with mudpies.

"Anthony," she said. "Again. I just can't get him right." She draped a wet cloth over her lump of clay and slid off the stool. She went to the sink, rolled up her sleeves, and washed her arms to the elbows. Then she led Pete to a shelf behind her. "This is the very first one I did, soon after we met. I did this one a month ago. Anthony didn't care for either of them; that's why I started this. I thought I might give it to Rawling. Do you see Anthony's point?"

Pete wasn't sure that he did. All he could tell was that the first one seemed the best somehow. He tried to analyze it. The lines of neck and jaw stood firm but less than perfectly defined—a man facing middle age, still strong but beginning to weaken. The peaked eyes were sad but curious. In the second head the eyes were wider, the face happier, but that intriguing sense of the conflicted man was gone.

Claire returned to the worktable and pulled the cloth off the current work. It was only a head and neck so far, but the positioning seemed wrong—stiff and lifeless.

Claire tilted her head at it critically, and that smudge of a frown Pete had seen before reappeared. "Of course, it would help if I could get him to sit." She turned away and pointed to the opposite wall. "Here are the others."

They were all there. Only Lillian Bowles, probably because she was the one person Claire had known long enough, was done in stone—her fine features painstakingly carved out against a background of rough-hewn rock. Rawling had been done in clay, almost a caricature with her hair spiraling out from her head like a Medusa, but the features were clear and strong and very Rawlingesque. Greg Hempstead's head seemed poorly proportioned—the neck dominated the head and the eyes were unfinished, blank. The base of the neck was circled by a man's heavy neck chain that from a distance looked like rope. Scott Beaton's classic features took better to clay than John Forbes's lumpy ones. The eye wanted to linger over Scott. Forbes's head was all Forbes—raw, rough, intrusive.

Pete turned to Claire and found her watching him. "What do you think?"

"I wouldn't insult you by offering my opinion. I know nothing about art. The people are here, that's all I know."

Claire laughed, a ripple of sound, full of delight. "That's all you need to know about art. And that's all you need to tell the artist. Did you see the horses?"

Pete hadn't noticed the horses. He turned to them now. There were a half dozen or so, some in motion, some standing still, but all of them minutely executed down to the finest nostril and tendon. He liked them better than the real things, that was for sure. "They're perfect," he said.

Claire smiled again. "You really don't know anything about art, do you? But I'm pleased that you came by."

That brought Pete back to business. "I wanted to touch base with you. I'm off for lunch."

"Won't you eat with us? Joan has cold chicken, hot chowder, potato salad."

Pete tried not to listen to his stomach's opinion. "I can't. Thank you, though. I have an errand to run."

Claire nodded, her clear eyes watching him, not asking.

So why did Pete feel like telling her everything? He was going to report to Anthony about the incident with Dapper. He was going to visit Jasper's bog. He was going to try to have a talk with Forbes, possibly a talk with Rawling. Beach plums. Stairs. Nails in saddles.

As if she could read his mind, Claire's face clouded. "Rawling told us about the nail. She seems to think Anthony should fire John Forbes because of it. I don't think so, do you? It would be easy to miss a nail in a saddle blanket, wouldn't it?"

"It would have been easy to miss this nail. It was between two blankets."

"Poor Dapper." She turned away from him, picking up one of the clay horses, running a finger along its back. The horse was unglazed, and it left a residue of

89

clay dust on her finger. She returned to the sink and washed her hands again.

Pete said good-bye and left the studio.

First Pete went to the house. He knocked on the door, and after a delay that seemed longer than the size of the house accounted for, the door was opened by the maid, Joan Pitts.

"Hi," said Pete.

"Good afternoon," she replied primly.

"Is anyone home?"

"Mrs. Bowles is in her private chambers. Mr. Simmons is at his place of employment. Mrs. Simmons is in her studio. The younger Ms. Simmons and her gentleman friend have gone out for a drive."

She was too good. At breakfast she'd seemed merely efficient, but now she seemed almost a parody—the professional maid done up to a shine. He felt like clapping or laughing, but he did neither. "I see," he said solemnly. "In that case, maybe you could guide me to a phone."

She turned crisply. Pete followed her down the hall and into Simmons's study. She pointed to the phone on the desk, bowed herself out, and shut the door behind her. Pete looked up the phone number of the Wequassett Trust and dialed.

When Simmons picked up the phone, his alarm was electric. "What's wrong? Is there something wrong? What has—"

"Nothing's wrong. No one is hurt. Your wife got tossed off her horse, but apparently she's not even black and blue. I'll tell you all about it later."

"*Dapper* tossed her? That's not like Dapper."

"There were extenuating circumstances. Somehow a nail got caught between his saddle blankets, and it pricked him and made him jittery."

"A nail? *Between* the blankets? Good God. Is this
... This isn't an accident, is it? It's like the others,
isn't it? Like the beach plums and the stairs?"

"Since I haven't had time to decide about the
others, I don't know. I should know more when I talk
to you later. I'm off to the bog now, but I need to
know the name of the pesticide the lab found on the
beach plums."

A sigh like a wind sailed over the wire. "You're sure
she's all right?"

"She's fine. She's working in the studio."

"All right. But I want to see you later."

"The pesticide," Pete reminded him.

"Pesticide. Of course. Of course. Malathion. It was
a pesticide called malathion. I asked, and they told
me it is commonly used on bogs mid- to late August,
just when the beach plums could have been affected.
Good. I'm pleased that you'll be able to get to the bog
today. And as I said, I'd like to speak with you later. I
anticipate arriving at the farm around six-thirty.
Perhaps we could talk then."

"Sure," said Pete.

"I'll see that Claire expects you for dinner."

"I don't—" began Pete, but then he thought again.
He wouldn't mind observing the household longer,
this so-called maid in particular. As far as Pete could
tell, this "maid" was as phony as a three-dollar bill.
"All right," he said, and then he remembered *The
Man Who Came to Dinner*. Monty Woolley had been
invited for dinner and had ended up trapped there for
what, a week? A month?

"I'll call Claire," said Anthony. "I'll tell her we've
spoken. But wait. Why have we spoken?"

"The trim on the south window," said Pete. "It
needs replacing."

"Excellent! Excellent. By all means, replace the trim. Very good. So, you've called me about the trim, and I've invited you for dinner, and now I'll call Claire. This is working out quite nicely. I'll see you at six-thirty then."

Working out quite nicely? Pete wouldn't say that exactly.

And as he drove off, he thought about it. It seemed to him there was something unreal about Simmons's reaction, but he couldn't decide what. He knew what Connie would say, though. That any man in his right mind, after getting a call like this one, would call the cops immediately. But Connie hadn't seen Claire's face when the subject of the police had come up, and she didn't know Claire Simmons. Or Anthony.

As Pete approached the bog, he could see from down the road that harvesting had begun. The bog looked striped—in the middle it was still full of the dark red berries, but along the edge where the picking machines had already cut a swath, it was a speckled green.

The Sears family had been in the cranberry business since before the Civil War, back in the days when every man, woman, and child was expected to get down on their hands and knees and pick berries at harvest. School closed, and household chores were done after dark or not at all. As the Sears family got smaller, so did the bogs, until this was all that was left. It was managed by the aging Jasper and his last child by a second marriage, Edwin Sears. As Pete got closer, he recognized both Jasper and Edwin pushing Furfords, the picking machines, contraptions that looked like lawnmowers with escalators attached. The bog was already dotted with full burlap bags, and a truck waited on the far side for the bags to be loaded. Jasper wore a wide-brimmed, floppy hat to protect him from the sun. Edwin wore a baseball cap with the brim facing where it did the least good—backward.

Pete holloed from the other side of the drainage ditch that outlined the bog, and both heads came up. Jasper motioned to Edwin to keep going, then cut across the bog toward Pete.

"What the heck, Pete," said Jasper, whipping off his hat and swiping at the sweat. "Come see me some time in January, why don't you? We got work to do here."

"I know, I know. I'd wait if I could Jasper, but I can't. I'm doing some work for the Simmonses up the road. They had a problem with some beach plums from along the way over there, and they wanted to know what the odds were of some of the pesticides from the bog—"

"And how many times do they want to know it, will you tell me that? We've been over this once already. 'Bout beach plum time this year all I used was Round Up."

"How does that go on? By spraying?"

Jasper snorted. "I haul a cart around this here bog on my own two feet. Passes right over the tops of the weeds and wipes the stuff on 'em. Those beach plum bushes are chin high. That wasn't any of my Round Up on anybody's beach plums. Now mind if I get back to my business?"

"So you only used this weed killer, Round Up? You've never used something called malathion?"

"Sure I have, when I have fireworms. Didn't have any this year."

"So you didn't use malathion this year?"

"Nope. Now stop holding me up here on shore."

On shore. It was an old expression dating back to the days when the sea captains were the main cranberry cultivators—they had the capital to buy the land

and the available crew in the off-season. "On shore" was the land on the other side of the drainage ditch that surrounded the bog.

Pete backed away, raising a hand in thanks.

Jasper hopped the ditch, back to his sea of cranberries.

Pete went to Factotum first. He walked in to find Rita gaping in astonishment at Connie.

"Maxine wants to *what?*"

Connie snuck a look at Pete and grinned. "Work on the Hermitage after school. She could come by on the bus. I don't mind telling you I could use her, at least until Pete comes back to the fold."

"Why?" said Rita. "This isn't like her. Why?"

"Andy," said Connie.

"Andy?"

"I think."

"Of course," said Rita. "Andy. I should have known."

"What do you mean, Andy?" asked Pete.

"She's after him," said Rita.

"Maxine? After Andy?"

"Yes. And I don't like it. He's *twenty-two.*"

"Going on ten," said Pete.

"And Maxine is seventeen going on *six.*"

"It's okay," said Connie. "Andy hasn't noticed she's after him."

"That's even worse," said Rita. "Now she'll go into high gear."

"If you do something to stop her, she'll just try even harder," said Connie. "I say let them be."

"And how many children have you raised, Ms. Know-It-All?" asked Rita.

"Just me," said Connie.

"I see. And of course your parents were no help."

"No," said Connie, grinning at Pete again. "No help whatsoever."

Rita rubbed her temples with the pads of her fingers. "This is all your fault, Pete. If you hadn't taken this *insane* job at Heath Farm ..." She dropped her hands flat on the desk, squared her shoulders, and looked up. "Okay, Pete, what do you suggest? Do we send the poor kid to the wolves?"

"Andy's no wolf."

"I'm talking about *Maxine*. Oh, go ahead, Connie, take her. You deserve each other. But I'm warning you, if I end up an illegitimate grandmother, it'll be on your head!"

Pete turned to Connie. "How's it going over there anyway?"

Connie shuddered.

CHAPTER

12

Pete followed Connie back to the Hermitage. He hadn't much cared for that shudder when he'd asked her how it was going. Once they were inside, however, he understood it.

It was hard to believe they'd been working in here for a day and a half already. The room was full of . . . stuff. Newspapers, magazines, bags, boxes, and a mishmash of chairs, tables, and torn upholstery.

And dust.

Pete could see that the dust wasn't untouched dust. There were dark, blank circles here and there where things had recently been removed, and judging from the lingering smell, the things that had been removed had probably had food on them. Very old food. Pete opened his mouth to say something, but he couldn't think what. Connie gave him a baleful look and led the way to the kitchen.

The kitchen was considerably cleaner than the living room. There were boxes everywhere, but the kitchen counters had been cleared off and washed down and were filled with row after row of clean dishes. Still, he said nothing.

Connie led him upstairs, batting at cobwebs as she went. On the second floor, dust was the main thing. Dust and more baskets and boxes and bins full of junk than Pete had ever seen in his life. In the first room she showed him, the junk rose around them on four sides till it covered the windows, only stopping six inches shy of the ceiling.

Connie took off her jacket, ran her fingers through her hair, and for the first time he saw how dirty she was. There were dark streaks along her hairline, the kind of streaks you got when you mixed sweat with dust. Wisps of her hair stuck to her face and her T-shirt was decorated with dark, wet circles.

Connie picked up a shoebox, and clouds of dust jetted upward. She started to cough. "So what are you doing for lunch? You want to stay and help?"

Pete shook his head. "I have to get back. There's been another accident. And besides, I'm eating dinner at the farm, so I can't get too dirty. They don't have things like dust at the farm."

Connie glared at him. "You *are* obnoxious, do you know that? What kind of accident?"

"Her horse tossed her." Pete explained about the nail in the saddle blanket.

Connie straightened. "A nail? In a saddle blanket? That's a pretty dumb way to try to kill somebody."

"Yeah," said Pete. He looked at Connie thoughtfully. "Yeah."

"Is she all right?"

"Apparently. She rested a bit and then went back to work in her studio."

"And what did her husband say when he saw her?"

"He hasn't seen her. I called him and told him what happened. He was plenty upset." He hadn't meant it to sound defensive, but Connie gave him an odd look anyway.

"And he still won't call the cops?"

"No," said Pete. "He appears to want to stick with this idiot who runs an odd-job company."

Connie grinned. "Your words, not mine, kiddo."

Pete grinned back, and suddenly he realized how much he needed this—seeing her, talking to her. In the old days he might have kept that thought to himself. Now, he said, "You know what's weird? How much I miss you. I see you more now than I have in a long time, but it seems like less. What happened to you last night anyway? I waited for you to come back."

"You did? I didn't know I was invited."

"What do you mean, 'invited'? You don't have to be invited." But even as Pete said it, he realized that up to now they had exercised a certain amount of caution in this regard. Excess caution, Pete decided. "You're always invited," he said. "I thought you knew that."

"Okay. And ditto for me, too."

They grinned at each other. Another bridge crossed.

"So come by after dinner," said Connie.

Pete took a step back and looked Connie up and down. "Are you planning to shower?"

Connie planted both hands in the nearest layer of dust and came at him.

Pete grabbed a sandwich at Hall's Market and ate it on the way back to the farm. The first thing he did when he got there was to track down John Forbes, and the first place he looked was the stable. He heard Scott Beaton banging around in a stall somewhere. He found John Forbes in the tackroom, straddling a box, polishing a bridle.

Pete looked at the racks of saddles on the wall, each

one carrying its blankets on top. He looked up at the ceiling. It didn't look new, but the saddle racks did, and Pete supposed it would have been easy enough for a loose nail to have gotten caught in a blanket. But *between* blankets?

"Which one is Dapper's saddle?" asked Pete.

Forbes didn't look up from his bridle. "Depends who wants to know."

"Me," said Pete. "And don't ask me why. I don't know why. Rawling's accusation just struck me as a bit farfetched."

Forbes looked up, got up, walked to the wall, and kicked a saddle in the middle row. Then he returned to his box.

"Who cleans up around here?"

"I'm no janitor."

"So Scott does it? Sweeps up, picks up?"

Forbes nodded.

"When did Shearson finish this stable?"

"Dunno."

"Take a guess."

"Mid-September."

"A couple of weeks ago. And you're still finding nails around the place?"

"Found one, anyway."

"Yes," said Pete. "I saw that one. How do you think it got there?"

"Dunno."

"What did you do when you saddled Dapper? Do you pick up both blankets together?"

Somewhat to Pete's surprise, Forbes got up off his box for a second time and approached Dapper's saddle. He picked up the blankets, both at once, and threw them onto the box. Then he squared off the corners and smoothed them down. Then he returned for the saddle. Before he could put the saddle on top of the blankets, Pete felt them. The material was thick and solid, almost like felt. Pete could see where a nail could have been missed in there.

Pete straightened up. He didn't like Forbes. He liked him less and less every day. But he wasn't so foolish as to underestimate him. If Forbes was doing all this, it was going to be hard to catch him. "So how do you think that nail got in the blanket?" he asked.

"Beats me," said Forbes.

Pete had been back on the ladder for several hours before anything else happened, and when it happened, it dawned on Pete that from up on his ladder he had an ideal bird's-eye view of the Simmons clan machinations.

Not that he necessarily wanted one. The first thing Pete saw was John Forbes knocking into Scott's wheelbarrow and sending manure and dirty straw spewing across the walk. It could have been an accident, but Pete would have bet it wasn't.

"Amherst!" Forbes shouted. When Scott appeared, he pointed.

As far as Pete could tell from high above them, Scott said nothing. He turned on his heel, collected a rake, and proceeded to clean up the mess.

The next thing Pete saw was Claire Simmons leaving the studio. She reappeared moments later at the foot of the ladder with today's beverage assortment and cheese, fruit, and crackers. "Anthony says you're staying for dinner," she said. "I'm glad. We eat at seven. Do you know, they say when you fall off a horse it's important to get right back on? If you'd like, when you're through working, we could go for that ride. You can have Buster, the one in the corral. See?"

Pete looked at the corral. Oh, he'd seen Buster before. It was that brown monster he'd run into, almost, yesterday in the barn. He took a bite of cracker in lieu of answering.

"I could show you the basics in the corral, then we could ride to the pond. It's lovely out there at the end of the day."

Pete looked at the pond. There was a breeze, but a soft breeze for October, and the surface of the pond barely rippled. It looked like an oasis—promising, peaceful. Then he looked again at Buster. "Gee," said Pete. He balled his fists into the small of his back and leaned into them. "I'm pretty stiff today. Maybe some other time."

Was it his imagination or did Claire seem almost annoyed with him? She said a brief good-bye, collected her tray, and left.

The next thing Pete saw was Hempstead's Toyota pulling in. For a while no one got out. What was it, a heavy clinch in the front seat? No. The passenger's side door burst open, and Rawling came out running. Hempstead barreled out the opposite side and caught up with her. Rawling shrugged him off. Hempstead returned to the house. Rawling took off across the field, toward the pond.

Pete worked till five-thirty.

Then he climbed down from his perch and struck out for the pond.

On foot.

He found Rawling face down on a bed of caramel-colored pine needles twenty feet from the pond. Her arms were twisted under her cheek, and her legs were spread-eagled. It was an awkward pose, so awkward that . . . Suddenly Pete's face and hands tingled. He leaped forward, and a twig snapped under him. Rawling bolted to her feet.

"Who . . . oh. It's you." She turned away.

Pete walked around until he faced her again. He

might not have if he'd gotten a better look at her face the first time—she appeared to have been crying.

Hard.

"I'm sorry I scared you," said Pete. "I saw you lying there and thought something was wrong."

Rawling busied herself picking pine needles out of her sweater. "You'd think this farm was big enough that a person could find a place to be alone."

"Yes," said Pete, "you would. It's just that we both picked the same place to do it."

For the first time, Rawling looked at him. Pete tried to look like he hadn't noticed she'd been crying. He watched Rawling try to look like she fell for it.

"I haven't been in these woods in years," said Pete.

"You used to live here?"

"Not *here* here, no. But I had a good buddy who lived on the other side of these woods. We used to play here all the time. Look at this." Pete looked around, orienting himself. Then he began to walk. Rawling followed him. Fifty yards in he found it—the old tree and the tattered remains of the kind of tree house two eight-year-old boys might make. Pete touched one of the boards, and it came loose in his hands. He grinned at Rawling. "I guess I'm older than I thought."

Rawling studied him. "You're not as old as my father."

"No."

"But older than Claire."

Pete sensed some sort of a dig there, but whether at Claire, himself, or her father, he couldn't tell. "Yes," he said. "Older than Claire."

"I had a tree house. My father had it built for me. It had real stairs, real windows, and a shingled roof. It had everything."

Pete reached up and touched the nearest branch in the old tree. "So did this one. Stairs, windows, roof.

Or sometimes sails and a gangplank. Once it was a submarine, and all these trees were battleships. We made up more—" He stopped. Rawling's eyes had burst into flame, like an angry cat's.

What had he said? Or more to the point, what had she heard? *My tree house is better than your tree house?* It had to be more than that. But what? He decided to try to find out. Her father had given her the tree house. Maybe that was a clue. He'd start with her father.

He turned, leading them back the way they had come. "So your dad likes it here?"

He watched her struggle to master herself. When she spoke, she sounded half strangled. "Yes, he does like it. God knows why."

"You don't like it?"

"No," said Rawling fast, but as she said it, she looked around, and her eyes lingered on the pond. She repeated it, but this time with more resentment than conviction. "No. And neither should he. It's not the kind of place he likes at all."

"He must have had a farm before, what with all those horses."

"Not a farm, a stable. And it wasn't out in the sticks like this. He needs his museums, his theater, his fancy restaurants. He needs to be close to Metropolis."

"So what happened this time? Claire?"

In a flash the angry cat was back, but this time she didn't struggle to subdue it. Instead, she let fly with a rush of unchecked words. "Yes, Claire. And I'd like to know how she worked it, too. Until Claire he was oblivious. Completely oblivious. After my mother died, Marilyn Monroe could have walked down the street and he wouldn't have turned around. For ten years he's been like that. Then all of a sudden, poof! First, Claire comes. Then he's gone."

So, thought Pete, it was much as he expected, and it was nothing new. But wasn't Rawling a little old for the wicked stepmother routine? He thought of Claire, intimidated in her own home by this young tyrant, and his annoyance with Rawling grew. "People do move on, you know. And your father has a right to—"

He doubted Rawling heard him. She was walking fast on a track of her own. "Crying his eyes out over my mother's grave one day, honeymooning in Spain the next. He hardly knew her! Next thing you know I get a phone call from Madrid. *Madrid.* 'Hello, Rawling dear, how are you? By the way, I've something to tell you . . .' The whole thing was so *underhanded.* Of course she wouldn't want him to tell me ahead of time. She knew I'd talk him out of it."

Pete didn't bother to argue with her, even though he'd recently heard a different set of facts. He decided to let Rawling run and see how far she'd go. "So what's your theory? She's after his money?"

Rawling stopped walking and peered at Pete. Slowly, she regained control. "No," she said. "Oddly enough, I know it's not that. Claire has money out the ears. My father said she couldn't spend all of it if she tried, and he says she doesn't try very much. Besides, he's worked it out so she won't get much of his."

At first it struck Pete as odd that Simmons would have told his daughter all about Claire's financial arrangements, but seconds later he could see the sense of it. Rawling's resentment of her new stepmother was obvious, and Simmons probably didn't want to give Rawling any more fuel. The least he could do would be to assure his only child that her inheritance remained intact. But even so, there was an ugly, gloating tone to Rawling's voice when she talked about her father's money, and Pete's annoyance with her turned to something stronger. "So you've got your money. So what's your beef?"

The rage returned. One of her hands rose, and for a minute Pete thought he was in for a face-rake, but she looked at her own hand as it crossed her peripheral vision, as if she'd temporarily lost control of it, and yanked it back. She let fly with words instead.

"My beef is my father, *my father,* a person I used to know better than I know myself, has *overnight* married someone he doesn't know, and she's turning him into somebody else! *God,* you sound just like Greg. 'Don't make waves,' he says. Well, why shouldn't I? They met last *November.* They got married in *July.* He knows nothing about her!"

"So let him get to know her now. Plenty of people don't get to know each other until after they're married." Or after they're divorced. "And how long have you and Greg known each other?"

Rawling exploded. "Greg Hempstead and I have known each other for three months, and I wouldn't marry him if I'd known him my whole *life!*" She broke away from Pete and ran toward the house, hands to her face, crying.

Pete turned around and wandered back into the white pines, troubled and thinking. He thought about the beach plums and the stairs, about the nail in Dapper's blanket. Could Rawling Simmons have done those things to Claire? What had he seen just now? A young woman with a near uncontrollable temper, childish emotions, a tendency to physical violence, and a deep, possibly pathological devotion to her father.

Yes, Pete decided, Rawling might well be capable of trying to hurt Claire, possibly even kill her. But if she had tried it, would she be talking about her feelings so openly to a complete stranger? Wouldn't she make every effort to conceal her feelings about Claire? Pete almost smiled. Rawling conceal her feelings? He doubted if it were possible. Or that she would even feel it necessary. Rawling was obviously used to having her own way and unused to being discommoded. She might think it was her right to get rid of Claire—by any means necessary—that it was even her right to gloat about it. And there was no denying that she felt intense jealousy, possibly hatred, for her stepmother.

Pete looked around. He was still in the woods, and the soft pines were nothing but dark shapes and shadows. It was almost time for dinner. He turned for the farmhouse, still thinking. He remembered how he'd found Rawling and, again, how he'd left her.

True, Rawling might be distraught over her stepmother, but today it was Greg Hempstead who'd gotten her crying.

Twice.

CHAPTER
13

___

Pete was barely on time for dinner. When he slid into his place at the table, everyone but Rawling was already there.

The greetings he received were assorted. The host and hostess formally expressed their pleasure at his company. Lillian Bowles gave him another doll's nod. Greg Hempstead glared. That was all Pete needed, the meeting in the pines to be misconstrued.

Anthony, it seemed, had also just arrived. "Where is Rawling?" he asked.

"I'm told she won't be joining us," said Claire. "She's experiencing . . . What is it, Greg? A headache?"

The muscles in Greg's jaws bulged and subsided. "Yes, a headache."

"I ran into Rawling out by the pond," said Pete. "I don't think she felt well then either."

"No," said Greg, still glaring. "She didn't."

"Perhaps I should go up," said Anthony. "Has she any aspirin?"

"I don't think—" began Greg, but he stopped.

It was Claire who rescued him. "She has aspirin in her medicine cabinet. I've told her it's there. We'll check on her after dinner, shall we?"

"Very well," said Anthony. He turned to Claire. "And how are you feeling, darling?"

"I'm a little stiff, that's all."

As she gave her husband the details, Pete watched him closely, trying to see if Connie's suspicions had any basis, but Anthony's eyes hovered over Claire with genuine concern and anxiety. Still, it was Lillian, rigidly controlled Lillian, who burst out emphatically, "You must be more careful, Anthony. You can't have this kind of thing."

"Of course not, Lillian," said Anthony. "Rest assured, I'll be speaking to Forbes about it in the morning."

"Excuse me, Anthony," said Lillian. "I don't mean to imply you don't have the matter in hand. It was only—" But she stopped, unable to finish, still shaken.

Again, Claire saved it. She gave a soft laugh. "My mother has a strong distrust of horses, nails notwithstanding. I'm afraid we're scaring her to death. Can't we change the subject please, Anthony?"

"You're absolutely right, darling. Let's change the subject. And are you sleeping better, Lillian?"

"Yes, thank you." She smiled, thawing slightly.

"Mother? What's this?" Claire asked.

Lillian didn't answer.

"Your mother confessed to me earlier that she wasn't sleeping," said Anthony.

Claire raised her eyebrows. "Why, Mother, you should have told me."

"No need," said Lillian. "You had also stocked *my* medicine cabinet with aspirin. I suffered for two

nights and then did something drastic. I took one."
She smiled again, but one good smile was apparently
all she could muster per evening. This one didn't go
from start to finish without refreezing.

Simmons appeared to notice the weak smile, too.
"All the same, I think you're still a bit enervated. I'd
go whole hog and take *two* aspirin this evening." But
even as Simmons forced his attention to Lillian, Pete
saw that his eyes kept wandering back to his wife.
Connie is wrong, thought Pete. *And so is Rawling.
Anthony might have been oblivious to Marilyn Monroe, but he turned around fast enough when he found
what he'd been wanting.*

Dinner was lamb, new potatoes, salad, and a squash
casserole that contained whatever it was that squash
was usually lacking. Joan Pitts waited on them without speaking and, in Pete's case, without looking.
That was okay with Pete—it made up for Greg
Hempstead, whose eyes had barely left him. Between
the main course and dessert, Claire had Joan whisk
off the used tablecloth and replace it with a pristine
white one. This, thought Pete, was fancy dining. Then
Joan brought dessert—homemade apple pie and ice
cream. After dinner, Anthony asked Pete if he'd like
to join him for brandy and a cigar.

Brandy and a cigar? No one had ever offered brandy
and cigars to Pete seriously. He managed to accept
without laughing and followed Simmons into his
study.

The minute the door closed Simmons accosted
him. "So what else do you have to tell me about this
nail situation?"

"Not much. I got there when Rawling and Forbes
were arguing. Rawling thought it was careless of
Forbes not to see the nail."

"And I should say it was. Rawling is absolutely

right. For that matter, so is Lillian. I've tried to keep my fears from her, but Lillian confided to me that she'd been having nightmares since those stairs collapsed." Simmons walked to his desk, picked up a humidor, and handed it to Pete. Pete took out a long, smooth cigar. Simmons took one, picked up a tool that looked something like a small guillotine, and snipped off the end. He handed the machine to Pete, who did likewise. Carefully. They lit up. As if on cue, Joan Pitts came through the door with snifters and brandy on a tray. She continued to avoid Pete's eyes.

Pete and Simmons sat down in matching armchairs. Leather, of course. Just like *Witness for the Prosecution*. Well, maybe Pete would have better luck at Charles Laughton than he'd had at Gregory Peck. He leaned back in the chair, sucked on his cigar, took a sip of brandy, and studied Simmons carefully, thinking about something Connie had said earlier. After a while the smoke, or maybe it was the brandy fumes, seemed to clear his head. "So this is the third incident."

"Yes," said Simmons. "And I must now take this most seriously. A third attempt on my wife's life."

"Funny. I'm suddenly inclined to lean the other way."

"The other way?"

"To be less worried, I guess I should say. Three accidents? That's at least plausible, if not probable. But three completely botched murder attempts? That's absurd. Jasper Sears said there was no malathion used on the bog this year. All he used was something completely unrelated, something for weeds. It wasn't even a pesticide. So if someone was trying to kill her and wanted to make it look like an accidental poisoning from the bog, they didn't do their homework very well. And speaking of homework, why didn't you tell me you'd already talked to him? We don't need to do everything twice."

"Me? I didn't talk to him. But I don't see how you can be less worried. These three attempts—"

"At what? One raw beach plum goes a long way. What were the chances that your wife would eat enough to actually kill her? And I looked carefully at those stair treads. I admit this one worried me more. The rotten treads didn't match the others. Neither did the nails. The treads were older, but the nails were newer. Both Shearson and Cliff Pimental denied leaving old treads on those stairs, and it started to sound to me like someone had purposely replaced solid treads with rotten ones. But really, what were the chances that a fall down the stairs would kill her?"

"The rake was there."

"Shearson insisted the rake was on the wall. It *could* have fallen, couldn't it? And even if it had been deliberately left under the rotten treads, who's to say your wife would have fallen on it? People grab onto things when they fall. She could have swung herself out of the way. Or do what she did do—grab onto something and save herself from falling at all. And then there's this thing with the horse. She was bucked off, but she wasn't hurt. No one in their right mind could plan with any certainty that a fall from a horse would kill her. Not unless she landed on her head just right or snapped her neck or—" Pete stopped at the expression of alarm on Anthony's face. "Sorry," he said. "But you see what I'm driving at. Pretty dumb way to murder somebody, isn't it?"

"Dumb," Simmons repeated but without conviction. "So what then? I find three *accidents* equally hard to swallow."

111

"So let's discard the accident theory, too. Now what do we have? We have someone making three purposeful attempts to *not* murder Claire."

Claire.

For the first time, Pete had used her Christian name between them. It did something strange to him. It suddenly made *him* seem part of all of it, of the place, of the family. He took a sip of brandy and admired his cigar ash as the liquor burned through him. No, he wasn't Charles Laughton. More like Montgomery Clift, starting to feel at home in *The Heiress's* library.

"Is someone trying to frighten her then?" asked Anthony. "But why? To what end? I don't understand. Who in the world would want to frighten Claire?"

"There are those who might," said Pete, thinking for the moment of Rawling, but all of a sudden something else occurred to him. If someone were trying to frighten Claire, so far there was no visible proof that it was working.

Connie's suspicions to the contrary, the one who was frightened was Anthony.

CHAPTER
14

Connie heard the token knock. She heard the door open, and she heard his footsteps, loud as he came in, then as they reached the hall and saw her light was out, quieter.

"It's okay, I took a shower."

"Ah. You're awake. Good." He went into the bathroom, came back out, and stripped off his clothes, outlined by the glow of Annabel Bates's hall nightlight. He slid under the covers. "So how was—" he began, but bare skin had touched bare skin, and his words floundered. "Ah," he said again, and for some time they were involved with things besides talk.

So some things hadn't changed, thought Connie. They still remembered all the old joys and secrets. But there were a few things that were new and strange— another scar, this one on the inside of Pete's thigh. And this trick he'd picked up, God knows where . . . Connie decided it was best not to think about it. But there was also a new intensity in him that she felt in herself, a desperation, or maybe fear, fear that they'd come so close to losing this. There was also a new *smell* to him, something that wasn't horse farm. She rubbed her nose in his hair and breathed. "Cigar?"

"Yes. And a good one, I might add. With brandy."

"Tough job."

"You'd better believe it. My head is splitting."

"So now he's buying you off with expensive cigars and brandy."

Pete shifted onto his elbow. "Okay, out with it. What's your theory? You think Simmons is trying to murder his wife?"

"Well, it's possible, isn't it?"

"No."

"Why not?"

Pete dropped back into the pillows and yawned. "Because he loves her. He really loves her. I may not be able to recognize it when I'm doing it, but I can recognize it when I see it. And besides that, I don't think anyone is trying to kill her. I think you were closer to the mark today when you said that a nail in a blanket is a crazy way to try to kill somebody. I think this is a scare tactic, and I told Simmons that."

"Did he agree with you?"

"Maybe," said Pete. "And he's been scared plenty." He changed the subject. "So how was your afternoon?"

"Not so hot. Maxine arrived."

Pete raised his head. "Isn't she helping?"

"Yes and no. It's this curse Rita's put on my head. I can't get anything done, I'm too busy worrying about what they're doing."

"What else did you do? Did you get to the garden?"

"Finished off the annuals, that's it. My body started complaining."

Pete readjusted himself so he could reach her neck and began to rub.

"Mm," said Connie, her muscles and tendons melting slowly. "Glad you stopped by."

Pete's hand had slowed to making dreamy circles on her skin and Connie was close to sleep when her last words reverberated in her head. "Hey, Pete."

"Right here."

Connie raised up. "Yes, sometimes you are. But why not all the time?"

Pete stopped rubbing.

Connie turned over. "You know what you said at the Hermitage? About missing me? I miss you, too. When you're not here, I miss you like crazy."

Pete shifted beside her. He must have been near sleep himself—she could almost feel him trying to switch gears, to come awake.

"And the food," she said. "We never have the right food in the right refrigerator. And our clothes. We can't find our clothes. I had your shirt, remember? And the clothes in the washer? It's no way to run a railroad."

"What railroad?" said Pete, still struggling.

Connie pushed on. "You could stay. Move in."

For a second, a long one, Pete said nothing. "Move in here?"

"There's plenty of room. And you could turn the cottage over to Factotum. It makes sense, doesn't it?"

"I don't know. It never occurred to me."

"What did occur to you?"

Pete shifted again. "I don't know. Nothing. I hadn't thought about it."

"Oh," said Connie.

"Let's talk about it in the morning. My head is killing me." Pete rolled away.

Connie lay on her back and stared at the ceiling.

* * *

She woke to the sound of Pete swearing. She looked around. By the faint hall light she could see him sitting in the caned chair next to the door, holding his toe. She looked at the clock. Two-thirty. "What are you doing?"

"I was looking for aspirin. I stubbed my toe on this damned horse. What is it anyway?"

"Annabel's doorstop. It's cast iron."

"No kidding! Well, you're out of aspirin."

"No I'm not. It's in the downstairs bathroom."

*"Down*stairs?"

"I'll get it."

"No. I'll do it." Pete limped out.

When he came back, he said, "Claire Simmons keeps aspirin in *all* the bathrooms."

Claire Simmons. Connie started to retort, but some stray dust that had settled in her lungs rose to her windpipe and instead she started coughing.

When she woke again it was to gray light, and the bed beside her was empty. She sat up. Pete was at the door. Dressed. Leaving.

"Where are you going? What time is it?"

"Early. Go back to sleep."

"Wait a minute." Her eyes wouldn't focus. Neither would her mind. But weren't they in the middle of something? Ah, yes. She remembered. And so did Pete, apparently.

"Listen," he said. "About what you were saying last night. I'll see you after work, and we'll talk more about it."

"Okay," said Connie. "If you want to eat, pick up a pizza."

"We just *had* pizza," said Pete. He sounded cranky. Too much brandy. *Maybe.*

* * *

Pete thought about it as he drove home. It had taken him by surprise, this idea of moving into the Bates house. *Connie's house,* he corrected himself. *Their* house, maybe. So what was the big deal? It made sense, he told himself.

Really it did.

When he opened the door to his cottage, he walked around, looking at the old living room that was now Foctotum's office, the former dining room that now served as a newspaper morgue, the two bedrooms that more closely resembled a tool shed and a garage. Of course, it made sense.

He went into the kitchen, made himself a bowl of Wheaties, and sat down where he always sat down, at the kitchen table, facing the marsh. It was green gold now, in October. In summer it was a lush green and dotted with wild flowers. In January it would be the color of straw. But Pete could be living in the Bates house by January. He could be living in the Bates house by next week if he wanted to.

And you couldn't see the marsh from the Bates house at all.

Pete's mind was still on a track of its own when he got to Sarah's.

"Do you have it?" she asked him.

"Have what?"

"My bat house."

"Oh," said Pete. "No, not yet. I'll get to it."

"Oh, will you? Still a little busy, aren't we? Although you're getting here earlier and earlier. Don't tell me the honeymoon is over already."

Pete was suddenly tired of this joke. "I am not on any honeymoon," he said crossly.

"I see," said Sarah. "Well, you'd better read me the paper and cheer yourself up. See if you can find something about a murder. That usually does you nicely."

Pete snapped open the paper. "Ed Brock ahead in polls," he read.

"Oh, Ed Brock can go jump in the lake," said Sarah darkly.

Pete's mind was still on other things when he topped the first steep grade to Heath Farm and caught a glimpse of something through the trees. It was just a flicker in the sunlight, far off, a flash of white. Or was it yellow? Yes, it was yellow. Pete could tell when it took the next turn and swept out of sight again, traveling downward. It was a yellow car, and it was going fast. And the next time it shot into view it was going faster, careening around the bend like it was on a roller coaster. *Idiot,* thought Pete, slowing his truck, looking for a place to pull off so he could avoid this lunatic, but then he saw it again clearly, a small yellow car. A convertible. And it was still plunging downward, going even faster now. Pete started to sweat. The car was coming into the worst turn on the road and it was going way too fast. It was cutting too wide! It was . . . gone.

Pete slammed down on his own gas pedal and bucked forward, straining his eyes toward the few bare patches of road he could glimpse through the trees, watching for the yellow car, seeing nothing. Where was it, dammit? He rounded a turn and saw a cloud of dust, a whole explosion of dust, billowing up from God knows where. The gully? The floor of the gully? It must be. The gully was screened from Pete's view by thick trees and sharp grades, but the dust was there. The dust was still rising. Pete forced the old truck into speeds and turns it couldn't make without groaning, until finally, finally, he was at the hairpin turn. He plowed off the road into the soft sand at the edge of the bluff, jumped out of the truck, and looked down at the floor of the gully.

It was Claire's Mercedes.

And there was someone small and blond crumpled behind the wheel.

Pete scrambled over the rocks and down the grade, banging his already swollen toe on a boulder, sliding down the slope, making more dust, until he hit the gravel bottom of the gully.

The car had careened into a wall of boulders, and it's right side was jacked up on one of them. Claire's body was still in its seat belt but canted sideways, her head by the door, one leg skewed up almost in the passenger seat. The windshield was a starburst of cracked glass, as if Claire's head had struck it. Pete hit the gully floor on the passenger side of the car and found himself facing the sole of a small white sneaker, with gravel wedged in the treads. *Move,* he said silently to the sneaker. *Get up. Get out.* Daisy Kenyon *did, didn't she?*

He scrambled around the car until he could see Claire's face. Her skin was the color of paste. Her eyes were closed, her mouth slightly open, with the smallest trickle of blood in the corner. Internal bleeding. He'd been wrong, and Anthony had been right from the start of things. Someone *had* wanted to kill her. And someone had done it, too. He was wrong, he was so wrong . . .

But there were things to do. He opened the car door with heavy hand and heart, and Claire's body swayed toward him. With one arm he supported her, with the other he undid the belt, and he had her halfway out before it dawned on him.

She was breathing.

"Claire."

She opened her eyes. "Oh," she said and closed her eyes again. Then she opened them and said, "Pete?"

He picked her up and kept going, fast, away from the car, afraid of an explosion. He set her down on a slope covered with wild cranberry vines and knelt over her. "Are you all right?"

"I think so. My head hurts. And my knee. My knee hurts. I . . . I'm a little out of breath. Let me—" She struggled to sit up, but Pete pressed her gently downward. "Stay still. I'll call rescue."

"No. Really." This time she persisted and sat. "I think I'm just frightened." She took several deep breaths. She pressed her hand to her mouth, and it came away with the blood on it. Her eyes grew round. "Oh," she said.

In the movies the man always carried a spotless white handkerchief. The best Pete could do was the tail of his shirt. "You're bleeding. You need a doctor."

Claire explored inside her mouth. "It's a cut lip. I'm all right, really. I feel better already. What happened?"

"The car went off the road. Don't you remember?"

"I don't know. I . . . Wait, it was the brakes. That's it. There weren't any. I pressed down, and they wouldn't go. They wouldn't . . . *go*. I . . ." She started to shake.

Pete stood up. "I'm calling rescue."

"No. Please." Claire got to her feet. "See? Everything works. Rescue will make this all so much worse for me. Couldn't we just go home? I'm able to walk. I'm all right, really."

Pete thought. He didn't think he should move her, but if he didn't, that meant he'd have to leave her here alone while he went for help, and he didn't want to do that either. Besides, the procedure on Nashtoba was if the rescue came to a scene of an accident, the police came, too. Had Claire figured that out already?

"My truck's right there." Pete pointed up to the road.

Claire smiled. "See? The best kind of ambulance, ready and waiting."

Pete helped her up the slope and into the truck. Once settled in the seat, she put her head back and closed her eyes, and again Pete noted the pasty color. "I think I'd better take you to the doctor."

Claire opened her eyes. "Not yet. Please, not yet. I want to go home first. If I feel odd after I've rested, I'll see the doctor."

Pete had to admit that with her eyes open she looked better. And he certainly knew how she felt about strangers. He'd take her home, call Anthony, and let *him* argue with her.

It was almost a routine now. Lillian Bowles and Joan Pitts again greeted Pete at the door when he helped Claire in, but this time Claire didn't seem to want to let go of him, and it was Pete who guided her up the stairs and into the master bedroom, with Lillian Bowles and Joan Pitts following. The room was light yellow, like the car, like Claire's hair, like her horse. Long windows that reached the floor looked out toward the pond. Joan Pitts folded back the light yellow bedspread and massed light yellow pillows edged in white lace at the head of bed. Pete helped Claire to lie down, covered her with the spread, and turned her over to the care of the women. As he left, Joan Pitts was fetching ice and Lillian Bowles was hovering ineffectually.

Pete called Anthony Simmons from the den. Simmons agreed to come right home. Pete waited in the living room, listening to the sounds from upstairs, until Simmons arrived, wild-eyed. Pete told him what had happened and kept him there until he'd calmed sufficiently for a sick room, then sent him upstairs to see his wife.

Pete let himself out and went back to the gully.

His second trip wasn't much more graceful than the first. He scrambled down the hill and struggled over the gravel on the gully floor to the car.

It looked the same as when Pete had left it. It must have plunged down the hill, spun around, and hung up on the boulder to the right. He began to check it over, expecting but not finding anything amiss under the hood or with the brake fluid.

When he finally found it, it was so simple he couldn't believe it. A triangle of raw wood, the kind left when a two-by-four had been mitered at the corners, was jammed under the brake pedal.

CHAPTER
15

The Hermitage crew settled into a routine. Andy picked Maxine up at school and brought her home to change into more practical clothes. In Connie's opinion the clothes Maxine changed into would have been practical only as tourniquets. Still, their effect seemed to be wasted on Andy. There might have been more conversation than work, but from what Connie overheard there was nothing, so far, that would cause Rita to break into a sweat.

Connie's first hint of unease came that day at four-thirty. They had finished with the roomful of boxes, and the three of them decided to make a cursory sweep through the Hermit's bedroom.

It was stacked high with mounds of sour-smelling laundry.

"Aagh," said Maxine. "What a *pig*. You go first, Andy," but she followed closely, clinging to his shirt.

Maxine's clinging didn't bother Connie. It was

Andy squaring his shoulders and inflating his pectorals that did.

"I don't like it," said Pete.

"For God's sake, do you think I do?" asked Simmons. He knocked around two gold pens in a penholder and looked at the chief of police, who had planted his massive frame in one of Simmons's leather chairs. "But you see my concern? If she even knew you were here—"

"There were wood fragments and sawdust all over the place," said Will McOwat. "In the backseat as well as the trunk. I spoke to Forbes. He said your wife asked him to clean up the scrap heap the Shearsons left in back of the stable, and he used her car. He piled the scraps into it, drove across the field, and unloaded it in the woods."

"Her car? He used Claire's car? The Mercedes?"

"I asked him about that," said Willy. He looked around Simmons's den and let his eyes come to rest on its owner. He squinted. Pete was used to that trick. "He says you were gone in your vehicle, and his assistant was using the wheelbarrow, and he was damned if he was going to walk back and forth from the woods twenty times with an armload of junk. He walks to work. He lost his license over an OUI. When your wife asked him to clean up the wood, she made it sound like it was a big rush, so he used the Mercedes."

"He used the *Mercedes?*" said Anthony again, and then, as if he hadn't already made it obvious, "I find that behavior incomprehensible. Why didn't he wait for the wheelbarrow? Or for me to get home? Or simply explain to my wife that he lacked the necessary conveyance to do the task properly?"

The chief looked at Pete without the squint. "Odd,"

he said. "But offhand, I'd say he doesn't like your wife much."

"Doesn't like—"

"Which would explain why he used the Mercedes, which might, in turn, explain how that block of wood came to be wedged under the brake."

"By accident, you seem to say."

"Maybe," said Willy.

"And the matter of the beach plums?"

"I looked around Jasper's shed. He's got malathion, all right. He says he didn't use it this year, but maybe he's a little reluctant to admit he poisoned your wife."

"By accident."

"By accident."

"And the stairs?"

Willy shrugged. "Not much to go on there. But if someone's trying to frighten your wife—"

There was a knock on the study door, and Lillian's head appeared. "I'm sorry to disturb you, Anthony, but Claire is asking to speak with you."

Anthony jumped up and strode to the door. "Of course. Excuse me, gentlemen, please."

After he was gone, the chief grimaced at Pete. "You have a weird way of making a living, you know that?"

"Yes," said Pete. "So Jasper has malathion?"

"He has a bunch of stuff in that shed that he says he doesn't use anymore. He keeps it because it's too hard to get rid of it."

"But he *could* have used it."

"Sure, he could have used it. How's your sister?"

"She's okay," said Pete. "And you're right about Forbes. He doesn't like Claire. Neither does her step-daughter."

Willy didn't seem too excited about this news.

"So what do you do next?" Pete prodded.

"Not much. When's Polly coming back?"

Pete eyed the chief suspiciously. Willy had met Pete's sister Polly that September. He had, as a matter of fact, extricated them from considerable red tape surrounding the murder of Polly's fiancé. The chief, Pete, Connie, and Polly had shared a car ride from Maine to Nashtoba, but that was the last Willy had seen of her. Granted it had been a long car ride, but still . . . "Thanksgiving. She's coming for Thanksgiving. But what about keeping an eye on Claire? This is the fourth accident." And as far as Pete was concerned, this one changed everything. Maybe you didn't die eating fruit or falling down stairs or off a horse, but you *did* die in car crashes, and Pete had seen her unconscious at the bottom of the gully. Now he believed as never before that someone wanted Claire dead and that someone had come very, very close to succeeding.

"Maybe it's the fourth accident," said Willy. "Maybe not. Thanksgiving, huh?"

"I think some sort of a guard should be posted."

"Right. And if I send out Ted Ball, my only cop, to post a guard on Claire Simmons, who's going to man the school crosswalk? And sit at Knackie's Saturday night to corral the drunks before they kill somebody on Shore Road? And chase Mrs. Potts's phantom prowlers? Not to mention all the other mundane yet necessary chores our department—"

"All right." Pete had to admit he had a point. "But what's Simmons supposed to do, just sit around waiting until somebody accidentally breaks his wife's neck?"

"He could send her away for a while."

Pete didn't know why he didn't much like that idea. All he knew was that he didn't.

* * *

They tied the last garbage bag over the last rank, threadbare shirt at six o'clock.

"Boy," said Maxine. "Could I use a Coke."

"Come on," said Andy. "I'll buy you one."

Nobody offered to buy one for Connie. She went home alone, bone tired, coughing chronically now, not even giving a thought to the garden, thinking about dust-free homes with aspirin in every medicine cabinet.

And Pete.

Had she rushed things last night, suggesting they move in together? She didn't think so. How could anything they'd done be called *rushed?* But she knew the idea had caught him by surprise and that he needed a day to think it over before they talked about it. Okay. So they'd talk about it tonight.

Connie took off her clothes and got in the shower, thinking about tonight. Okay, so they'd just had pizza. So maybe they should go out to eat. But not Lupo's, that was for sure, not with everyone within a twenty-foot radius listening as she and Pete mapped out their plans for the future. And Martelli's would be no better. It was roomier, true, but every time she and Pete showed up, Jean or Alton Martell seemed to make a point of sitting down with them for a little chat after dinner. And wasn't Anna Pease, a kid she'd taught in high school, waitressing there now? Connie didn't want to share her personal life with Alton or Jean or Anna.

So why didn't she make dinner here? Granted, there was *still* no food in her refrigerator, but that was because it was such a waste to shop when she never knew half the time if they'd be eating together and if so, where. But tonight she knew she and Pete were eating here.

Connie got out of the shower, changed, and went to

the store. She came home with French bread and swiss cheese and white wine for fondue, one of Pete's favorites.

She was making the salad when the phone rang.

"Hi," said Pete.

"Hi," said Connie. "How's it going?"

"So-so. Have you eaten?"

Eaten? "No, I haven't eaten. You said we were—"

"I know. It's just that it's late."

Connie looked at the clock. "It's only seven-thirty."

"Claire Simmons serves dinner at seven."

Oh, really, thought Connie. *And what does she serve, individual bottles of aspirin?* But instead she said, "You mean you've eaten?"

"No," said Pete, "I haven't eaten."

"Well, the Bartholomews eat when they feel like it," said Connie. But as she said it, it sounded funny. *The Bartholomews.*

It must have sounded funny to Pete, too. There was an awkward silence. Come to think of it, the whole conversation was awkward. Connie was sometimes slow on picking up a nuance, but once she got there, she dealt with it. "What's going on?"

"Claire was in a bad car accident. She's all right, but Willy just left here, and Anthony and I have to talk strategy. It doesn't look like I'll be back anytime soon. Not for dinner anyway."

"Okay," said Connie. "No big deal. So who was driving? Anthony?"

"No," said Pete. He sounded annoyed. "Claire was driving."

"Is she in the hospital?"

"No. I tried to take her to the doctor, but she refused to go. Anthony's with her now. I'm sure he'll persuade her."

"I'm sure."

128

Another silence.

"I have to go. I'll talk to you later."

"I'll wait up for you."

"You don't have to."

"I know. I miss you."

"Me, too," said Pete. "I'll talk to you later."

After he hung up, Connie sat, thinking about all the things that were wrong with that conversation. The *Have you eaten?* when he knew she was waiting for him. And *Claire Simmons serves dinner at seven,* as if anybody cared. And *The Bartholomews,* of course, but that wasn't the worst part. The worst part had been the *Me, too. I miss you,* she'd said, and he'd said, *Me, too.* Pete wasn't a me-too-er. But so what? It sounded like a tough day at the races. There'd been another accident. And this Simmons character . . . But at least now, thank God, the police were in on it. Connie shrugged off the subject and stood up. Whatever was on his mind, they'd talk about it later.

Then she spied the French bread. Well, she wasn't about to make fondue for one. She rummaged around in the cupboard until she found a dusty can of tuna, mixed it up, cut off a six-inch section of French bread, and stuffed the tuna in. She put the wine and cheese in the refrigerator, fished out a Ballantine, and sat down to eat.

Pete was alone in the study when Simmons returned, looking worn out.

"The chief left?"

"Yes," said Pete. "He said he'd be in touch."

"Oh, did he? And did he have any suggestions in the meantime?"

"He thinks you should send her away for a while."

In a split second Simmons looked worse. "I see." He made an effort to collect himself. "Claire would like to speak with you, Pete. I believe she'd like to thank you. She wanted to come down, but I felt it would be better if you went up if you wouldn't mind. She looks terrible."

"Sure," said Pete.

Simmons followed him out of the room. Standing just outside the door was Joan Pitts. She began to hurry away, but Simmons stopped her.

"Pete and I could use something to eat. Here in the den, please, in about fifteen minutes. I take it the others have eaten?"

The perfect maid was in top form. "Your daughter and Mr. Hempstead were out for the day and have not as yet returned. Mrs. Bowles has refused to eat anything. Mrs. Simmons took some soup and crackers."

"All right. See that Lillian eats something, will you?"

"Yes, sir." The perfect maid left.

Pete and Simmons climbed the stairs and went into Claire's bedroom. Her hair may have been the yellow of the pillow cover, but her skin was the white of the lace. Still, Pete wouldn't have said that she looked terrible.

"Hello, Pete," she said.

"Hello. How are you?"

She smiled at him. "I'm perfectly fine. You're all making a fuss over nothing. I do feel things stiffening, but nothing of any concern. I wanted to thank you. Again. You wasted your whole day over me, and I believe I've caused you some anxiety. My apologies and my thanks."

"It was nothing."

"I'm afraid I can't agree with you. It cost you an entire day on the barn."

Pete would like to have thought she was kidding,

but as he looked at her, he doubted it. In Claire's mind, the tragedy of her accident took a distant second place to the tragedy of a day missed sprucing up the barn.

As Pete watched her, the slender fingers tightened around the coverlet and her chest heaved once. "And what did the police have to say about this little accident?"

Pete and Simmons exchanged a look.

"I'm sorry, darling," said Simmons. "I know how you feel about the police, but it was just too much, another accident."

"Yes," said Claire. "Another accident. Were they helpful?"

Simmons cleared his throat. "Yes, as a matter of fact. They feel convinced this is nothing but a series of accidents, but at the same time they made a very sensible suggestion. They thought you should leave here for a while. Perhaps you and Lillian could take a short trip."

"No," said Claire. "I won't leave you, Anthony. I can't."

"Just for a while, Claire. Just until—"

"Until what? Until someone comes forward and confesses to trying to hurt me? They won't. You know they won't, Anthony. This is all foolishness. A series of accidents. That's all."

"Perhaps we should both go," said Anthony. "I'll speak to Hugh James at the trust in the morning. You and Lillian could go on ahead while I tidy up the loose ends."

"No," said Claire. "I'm not leaving, Anthony. I won't. I can't. The police only said that because they had to, in case they're wrong. They're not wrong, Anthony."

"I won't leave you alone here all day."

"I'm not alone. Everyone is here—Mother, Rawling, Greg, Joan. And we have two strapping men working right nearby in the stable."

Pete and Simmons exchanged another look.

Claire watched them. Before Anthony could speak again, she said, "And Pete. Don't forget we have Pete."

Anthony's face brightened. "Ah, yes," he said. "Pete."

Connie's phone rang again at eleven-thirty. The minute she heard Pete's voice she knew he was done in and what was coming.

"Were you asleep?" he asked.

"No, not really."

"I didn't want to leave you hanging if you decided to wait up. It's been a hell of a night."

"Really?"

"Really." He said nothing more.

"Are you through now? Are you leaving?"

"I left ten minutes ago. I'm at home."

"Oh," said Connie. She started to cough.

"Are you all right?"

"It's all that damned dust," said Connie. "It's coated my lungs. So how's Claire? Did her husband get her to the doctor?"

"No. But she insists she's all right, and he seems to feel he can believe her. He didn't . . ." Pete's voice trailed off.

He didn't try, thought Connie. "So what happened?"

"There was a block of wood wedged under the brake pedal. Willy's making all these excuses about how it could be an accident, but Simmons doesn't want to take any chances. He's extended my shift."

"Till eleven-thirty at night?"

"No, just till he gets home every night. Just to cover the bases."

"Except for home plate?"

There was a distinctly unamused silence on the other end of the line, but Connie chose to ignore it. She was seriously worried now. Willy was dismissing the whole thing, and if Anthony *were* trying to harm his wife, and Pete tripped him up, Pete would be next.

"Really, Pete. Suppose he's trying some funny business and using you as a sort of an alibi. Who would believe he was trying to hurt his wife if he hired you to prevent that very thing from happening?"

Silence.

"I see," said Pete finally. "So either way, someone thinks I'm a pretty big schmuck. You, of course, obviously. And if you're to be believed, then Simmons must think either I'm dumb enough to fall for his tricks or that I'm too inept to catch him."

"That's not what I meant," said Connie.

"It wasn't? Good. Obviously, it's not my favorite theory."

Connie gave up. She was tired. "So you're at home?"

"It's late. I'm beat. I know we need to talk. Tomorrow, okay?"

"Sure," said Connie. "No big deal."

"Okay," said Pete. "Good night."

Connie tried not to notice the other things he could have said but didn't.

CHAPTER
16

As tired as he was, Pete couldn't get to sleep. The minute he closed his eyes and let his mind empty and his muscles go loose, the subject that had been kept at bay by the events of the day came crashing home to roost.

Moving in with Connie. To the Bates house. Annabel's bed. Clara's spoonrest. No marsh.

Be fair, Pete told himself. There'd be no mess either. At least none of Factotum's mess. And they'd each have a closet, and all their possessions would be under one roof. And best of all—and, of course, the whole point—was that they'd know, for sure, that at the end of every day they'd be together in one place.

But when Pete finally slept, he dreamed he was living at the Bates house with Connie. They had bought a huge refrigerator. He opened it up and saw that it was full of orangy-pink half-ripe tomatoes. He turned, and there on the windowsill was one rich, ripe red one. He grabbed a knife and cut it open.

It was full of worms.

Pete woke late. He might not have woken at all if he hadn't heard tires churning up the gravel in his road. He looked out the window and saw Scott Beaton standing uncertainly in his drive.

Pete threw on some clothes and went out. "Scott, what brings you here?"

"A job."

"You have a job for Factotum?"

Scott shook his head. "I'm looking for a job. I hear you've got a lot to do. I thought you might need someone."

Pete studied Scott. Week after week with John Forbes and a wheelbarrow full of manure, and Pete could see why he might be looking for a different job. But still, the things Factotum did weren't glamorous, and Pete doubted they paid Simmons-type wages. He told Scott so.

Scott looked away. "I'm looking for a job," he repeated.

"Okay," said Pete. "Let me talk it over with Rita. She's half of this place. I'll get back to you. Where can I reach you?"

"I'm still at the farm," said Scott. "At least for a day or two." He returned to his Jeep, got in, and drove off.

When Rita arrived, Pete told her about his early caller. "What are you trying to do to me?" she asked.

"What do you mean?"

"Andy's bad enough. You want to throw in Scott Beaton, too?"

"We need the help. You keep telling me—"

Rita rolled her eyes at the ceiling. "Number one," she began.

Pete groaned. He hated it when she got counting.

"Number one," said Rita again, "what we need around here is *you*. Number two, why, of all the people you could pick from, do you have to latch onto *Scott Beaton?*"

"I don't see what's the matter with Scott Beaton. He's a hard worker, and he happens to be looking for a job."

Rita rolled her eyes at the ceiling again. "Okay. *Fine*. Do whatever you want to do. Now what's going on at that farm? Aren't you through?"

"As a matter of fact," said Pete. "There's quite a bit still to do. And I'm late. Is there someone who could read to Sarah this morning?"

"Did you ask Connie?"

"I haven't seen Connie this morning."

Rita looked at him curiously. But all she said was, "I'll look after Sarah."

When Pete finally got to the farm, Scott's Jeep wasn't there, and Anthony was just leaving the stable. Claire was holding his arm. Pete walked toward them, not at first picking up on the tenor of the scene.

"Please, Anthony," said Claire. "I know he didn't mean it that way. He has a funny sort of chip on his shoulder, that's all. I'd feel awful if this one little thing cost him his job."

"Hello, Pete," said Anthony. "We're off to a poor start this morning, I'm afraid—I've been forced to fire one of our stable crew. He was absolutely out of line."

So this explained Scott's visit to Factotum. "Is there something I could do?" asked Pete. "I'd be happy to talk to him. I've known Scott and his parents for a long time."

Claire and Anthony looked at him with surprise.

"Forbes," said Anthony. "I fired Forbes, not Scott. I accosted him about this business with the Mercedes, and he was arrogant and insolent. Worse than insolent. He behaved most rudely to Claire. There's no need for it, and I won't stand for it."

"Oh, Anthony," said Claire. "I feel this is my fault. A mixed communication, that's all it was. Please. Ask him to stay."

Neither spoke again, but some sort of silent communication must have passed, because Anthony returned to the stable.

"Was Scott mixed up in this?" asked Pete.

"No," said Claire. "Why do you ask? As a matter of fact, he's not here. He's late today."

Simmons came up behind them. "I'll see you both this evening. And, Claire, you remember what you promised?"

"I'll be in the studio all day. Don't worry, darling. And Pete will be working right outside my door."

"All right. Pete, I'll see you this evening."

Simmons stooped low and kissed his wife good-bye.

Claire watched him go until his car was out of sight.

Connie took Sarah by surprise.

"You?" said Sarah. "Where's Pete?"

"And nice to see you, too," said Connie, kissing Sarah on the forehead.

Sarah reached up and squeezed her hand. "It's lovely to see you. As long as Pete hasn't died."

"No," said Connie. "Not dead, just preoccupied."

"It seemed so," said Sarah thoughtfully. "You don't, by any chance, have anything to do with it?"

"You always want to blame me for everything, don't you? But it's Heath Farm mostly. He's out straight with it. Claire Simmons has experienced a run of accidents, and Sir Gallahad is right in the thick of it."

"Oh, dear," said Sarah. "Sometimes I wish he'd do something more *ordinary*. But I am glad you're here. I wanted to say something to you."

"What?"

Whatever it was, Sarah took her time over it. Finally she said, "Nothing, really. Just that I wish you could see how foolishly he grins whenever your name is mentioned."

"Oh, I'll soon put an end to that."

Sarah put up her free hand, making a sandwich of Connie's. "No," she said. "I don't think you will. Not this time. But he just might, and that's what I wanted to say to you. Don't you let him. And one more thing. You tell him I want that bat house before I have to use it for a coffin. Now sit down and tell me what's going on out at the farm."

"Ah, the farm," said Connie. "The plot sickens."

The barn was now ready for the paint. Pete started at the peak, near the window to Claire's studio, intent on keeping an eye on her, as Anthony requested. But as he painted, he also turned and twisted on his ladder, intent on keeping his eye on as many other people as he could.

Scott Beaton arrived late and walked by Pete without speaking. He got royally chewed out by Forbes, as could have been expected.

Rawling and Greg left early in the Greg's Toyota.

Joan Pitts remained out of sight.

Soon after ten Pete was surprised to see Lillian

Bowles cross the lawn and approach the foot of his ladder. Pete climbed down.

"Good morning," said Lillian. Her face seemed so tight she could barely move her features. "Is my daughter in the studio?"

"Yes," said Pete.

"I'm surprised. She said she felt quite stiff this morning."

"I bet. That was a good bouncing she got."

"Yes, it was. Her third one of late."

Pete said nothing.

Lillian raised her eyes to the face of the barn, then returned to Pete and peered at him intently. "Forgive me for intruding, but it seems to me things are not just as they appear."

"Oh? In what regard?"

"In regard to you, for one. A factotum, is it?"

"I'm just here to paint the barn," said Pete, but he knew he didn't sound convincing, and Lillian didn't look convinced.

"Who hired you?"

"Your son-in-law."

Lillian's face changed suddenly, loosening with relief. Then almost at once it changed back.

Pete had a feeling he knew what she was thinking. It was one thing to know that your son-in-law was trying to protect your daughter. It was another to know that he thought she needed protection.

Claire appeared at the foot of Pete's ladder at lunchtime. "Care to join me?" she asked.

Pete started to say no but then thought better of it. It would be the best way to keep an eye on her. He climbed down and walked to the house with her. He could see things operated on a strict schedule here.

There was already a tray of sandwiches and a tureen of some sort of soup on the table. But it was only Pete and Claire and Lillian who assembled, and it soon became evident that the two women expected Pete to lead the way conversationally.

Pete turned to Lillian. "How do you like Nashtoba?"

"It's lovely," said Lillian. "Although a little out of the way for my liking."

"Mother prefers city apartments," said Claire. "With bars on the windows and dead bolts on the doors. Don't you, Mother?"

Lillian didn't answer.

Joan Pitts appeared. She collected empty sandwich plates and soup bowls and returned with a platter of delicately sliced pound cake surrounding a mound of strawberries. But before she could put it down, Claire stopped her.

"The tablecloth, please, Joan?"

Something in the maid's face flickered, something dark and dangerous. Then it was gone, and a clean cloth appeared. The platter was set down, followed by coffee mugs, and an urn of steaming coffee.

Yes, thought Pete, he could get used to this. He held up his cup. "Thank you," he said to Joan Pitts.

She dipped in a half curtsey. Then, for the first time, she met his eyes full on, and Pete could have sworn she was laughing.

After lunch Claire went straight up to her studio, and Pete went straight to his paint can. He didn't know what happened to Lillian or Joan, and he saw nothing of Greg or Rawling. Occasionally Scott or John crossed his peripheral vision, but no one approached the studio.

Claire appeared at the foot of Pete's ladder at four-thirty.

"I'm hardly stiff at all now," she said. "I think I'll go for a ride after all."

Swell, thought Pete. *Out of sight and out of earshot. Alone.* "Didn't you tell Anthony you'd stick to the studio?"

"Yes," said Claire, and for the first time since Pete had known her, she sounded close to defiant. "But you have no idea how lonely it gets up there." She brightened suddenly. "Why don't you come with me? Anthony won't mind if he knows I have company."

"Maybe some other time."

"I admit it's silly of me," she said, "but Anthony aside, I think *I'd* feel easier with the company."

"I'm sorry," said Pete.

Claire's face fell. She looked so small from up there, so fragile, so expendable. She reminded Pete of a small yellow bird. A canary, maybe, or a finch. Next to her Connie would look like a chicken. And speaking of chickens . . . Pete looked across the field to the corral where Buster was grazing. *He* looked like a dirigible.

"I'm sorry," he said again, more firmly this time. "I don't think so. Not today." He said a few more things, things about how far he had to go on the barn, things about her promise to Anthony, things about the late afternoon chill, the damp, the nonexistent rain clouds. Finally, when she continued to gaze up at him hopefully, he said plain old "No." He was proud of how forceful he sounded. That's what happened when you were talking to a finch instead of a chicken.

"Give him a kick," said Claire.

Was she out of her mind? Here he was on top of the

Empire State Building, on top of *King Kong* on top of the Empire State Building, and the only thing that was maintaining this particular order of ascendancy was that nobody was moving. And she wanted him to kick him?

Claire swung Dapper close beside him. "It's okay," she said. "You won't hurt him. He's just waiting for you to tell him what to do. Tell him you want him to get going."

Pete looked at the velvety backs of Buster's ears. "Get going," he said. Buster's ears swiveled backward, but he did nothing.

Claire laughed. "Good," she said. "It's important to talk to him. But when you tell him to go, tap your heels into him."

There was no way around it. Unless Pete wanted to sit up there all day, he was going to have to kick Buster and get them going. *Going,* Pete knew, meant Buster forward and Pete downward, but he decided if he did it here in the soft dirt of the corral, the chances were less of his cracking his head open on a boulder or something.

Pete wiped the back of his hand across his beaded upper lip, and keeping his eye on his future handhold, the pommel, he touched the heels of his sneakers to Buster's gleaming sides. Buster picked up one foot and followed it with another. And another and another. Pete looked at Claire and grinned.

Claire circled the ring beside him. She showed him how to tell Buster to stop, first, and then how to turn. Then she rode Dapper to the center of the ring and stood still, watching.

Pete weaved back and forth across the ring, first turning when Buster decided to, once in a while doing it when it was his own idea, until finally he was weaving figure eights like Roy Rogers.

John Forbes came out of the barn. *Hey, look at me!* Pete wanted to holler, but Forbes gave one disgusted look and disappeared. Scott Beaton, too, stood half hidden in the shadow of the stable door. What was *he* doing? Laughing?

"Very good, Pete," said Claire finally. "Are you ready to go?"

Go?

She opened the gate and guided Dapper through.

Buster hung a right and followed Dapper out of the ring. Pete tried to look like he'd suggested it. The minute he was out of the ring he fully expected Buster to take off at a dead run for Wyoming, but Buster didn't seem inclined to do anything more strenuous than walking. Claire reined Dapper in a circle until she was beside Pete, and they were off.

Riding.

They walked their horses, side by side, along the pasture fence, toward the white pine forest and the pond.

At first they said little, Pete concentrating on where Buster was putting his feet, Claire gazing around her happily.

"I'm glad we're doing this," said Claire finally. "Not just for the sake of the ride, but because I've wanted to talk to you. You don't believe in these 'accidents,' do you?"

"I don't know what I think about them."

"Anthony doesn't believe in them. That's why he hired you, isn't it? I asked Scott Beaton about you. He told me about some of Factotum's old jobs. Anthony thinks you'll find out who's doing this, doesn't he?"

"Not really," said Pete. "He just hired me to ask some questions."

"So ask them."

Pete started to say that the questions weren't for

her, but then he changed his mind. He did have questions for Claire, and all of a sudden he saw no reason not to ask them. Claire had finally brought it into the open. There was no pretense anymore.

They reached the pond, and Pete returned his attention to Buster, but without any direction from Pete, Buster began to circle the water. A familiar route, apparently. Now that they were closer to it, the silver light on the surface of the pond gave way, and Pete could see into the black below. The water was so still that the edge against the sand never wavered. Buster plodded along the perimeter, as placid as the water. Pete relaxed a little. He smiled at Claire, and she returned his smile with a broad one.

"The beach plums," Pete began. "You're the only one who liked them. Who knew that?"

"Everyone," said Claire. "Anthony made it a joke at dinner about a week before Rawling picked them. They are odd tasting, aren't they? He teased me about it."

"So at dinner Rawling and Greg and your mother and Joan Pitts would all have been able to hear your husband tease you about your fondness for beach plums."

"Oh, and John Forbes."

"Forbes?"

"The next morning Anthony and I went for a ride, and when Forbes brought out the horses, Anthony told him we were going to find beach plums. He told Forbes I was the only true Nashtoban, the only one who liked them."

"And where was Scott Beaton?"

"Scott? I don't know." A clump of Dapper's mane had fallen to the wrong side and she straightened it. "Next question?"

"The stairs. What time of day did that happen?"

"Late morning. On my way up to the studio after my ride. It's my usual routine."

"You ride every morning, then you go to the studio."

"Yes."

So while Claire went on her usual morning ride, someone could have fiddled with the stairs, sight unseen.

And the horse was easy. Maybe.

"Do you ride the same horse every day?"

"Yes," said Claire. "Dapper."

"Does anyone else ever ride him?"

"Dapper? Never." She patted his neck affectionately.

Pete patted Buster's neck, too, his confidence growing. "And what about the car? Who knew you were going out driving yesterday?"

"I announced it at breakfast. Anthony was pleased. I hadn't felt . . . It takes me a while, sometimes, in a new place, to feel . . ."

"Sure it does," said Pete. "And once again, everyone was at breakfast?"

"Everyone."

"But the stable crew wouldn't have known?"

Claire looked up at Pete and blinked. "I told John Forbes before breakfast. I had to. I needed to postpone my ride."

"And Scott?"

Claire shook her head. "I didn't see Scott."

Didn't see him, maybe, but it seemed to Pete that Scott was always nearby, within earshot, lurking.

"So after breakfast you went straight to your car?"

Claire shook her head. "First I went upstairs to change."

"And the Mercedes was in the driveway ready to go?"

"Yes, facing out. I'd been a bit anxious about venturing forth, and Anthony tried to make it easy for me. But what it meant was that when I did finally go out, I didn't need to apply the brakes until I was on that terrible hill, and when I finally tried the brakes, they didn't . . . they wouldn't—"

"No," said Pete. "They wouldn't."

They had reached the far side of the pond. Now, as they rode, they could look ahead and see the farm. The shadows had grown long. Pete saw Greg Hempstead's Toyota pull in. Scott Beaton's Jeep pulled out, and then Forbes appeared on foot, heading down the road toward home.

"And now tell me what *you* think," said Pete. "Do you seriously believe in these 'accidents' as accidents?"

They rode in silence for twenty yards.

"They were accidents," said Claire finally, but she said it like a question.

"Okay," said Pete. "But let's not make it easy, just in case. How many of the horses can you ride?"

"I could ride all of them but Buster," said Claire. "He's too big. Do you think I should mix it up some?"

"Yes," said Pete. "And let's not stick to the old routine. No riding unless you're with me or Anthony. Ride at different times, and don't go announcing it. Don't announce anything. And as a matter of fact, don't do anything at all without me or Anthony. And don't eat anything someone else isn't eating."

"You say don't do anything without you or Anthony," said Claire. "But once the barn is done, you'll be gone."

"I think I can stick around for a while."

Pete was surprised at the relief that filled Claire's eyes. He thought of the Hermitage, but only briefly. After all, he had a double job here now: to find out about the accidents and also to watch over Claire. Clearly, that took precedence. He couldn't possibly leave yet, and no one could possibly expect him to.

They rode in silence around the far side of the pond, and when they approached the turn at the near end, Claire said, "What do you think? Have you had enough? Shall we go in?"

"Sure," said Pete. He guided Buster out of his track around the pond, feeling cocky.

"Watch out," said Claire. "As soon as he knows we're heading home, he'll want to run." She said something about sitting down harder, about short pulls on the reins, about saying whoa, but Pete hardly heard her. He was looking ahead at the farm. There were too many vehicles there. Pete's truck. Greg's Toyota. Anthony's Range Rover. And two others, one big one, mostly white, and one smaller one, mostly red. The big one's light was red. The smaller one's light was blue.

Pete didn't have to use his heels this time. He loosened his grip, and Buster flew.

Yes, it was the rescue truck, and the police chief's official all-terrain vehicle. Pete slid to the ground and found he had no knees. In the second it took him to regain his land legs, Claire caught up to him.

"What . . . Oh, Pete, what?"

"Take the horses." He shoved Buster's reins at her and headed for the old barn.

Nobody was moving. They stood helplessly around the door to Claire's studio, the rescue squad volunteers, the police chief, all looking down. It told Pete most of what he needed to know. What he didn't know was who.

But it wasn't Claire. That much he knew. He pushed his way into the room. He saw the camel hair coat, the legs in tan trousers, the soles of the shoes. He saw a huge block of marble on the floor. Between the marble and the collar of the coat was what was left of Anthony's head.

"Pete!"

He could hear her on the stairs. He turned around to block her way, to stop her, but he was too late and the rest of them were too much like the Red Sea—they parted, and she saw him.

She pitched her face into Pete's chest and screamed.

CHAPTER

17

Connie heard the truck and looked at her watch. One-thirty A.M. She was just struggling up from a fetal position on Pete's couch when he opened the door and turned on the light.

He jumped. *"Jesus,* what are you—"

"I heard."

"About Simmons?"

"Kay told Evan and Evan told Rita. Rita called me at eight."

"Kay?"

"Kay Dodd. From the paper. Didn't you see her?"

"Yeah. I don't know. I guess so." Pete sank onto the couch, his legs splayed in front of him. He rubbed his eyes and let his head sink back. He smelled more like horse than usual. "So that shoots your big theory about Anthony."

Yes, thought Connie. *It did that.* And it also shot Pete's big theory about these accidents being nothing but scare tactics, but she decided this wasn't the time to mention it. "What happened?"

149

"A new variation on the old water-bucket-over-the-door trick, only this was a block of stone instead of a bucket. It was on the shelf over the door, tied to the inside door handle by a piece of monofilament fishing line. When the door opened far enough for Simmons to move forward, the block crashed down. It was obviously meant for Claire. It was in her studio. It would have been waiting for her when she went in tomorrow morning, only when we were out riding Anthony got home and went into the studio looking for his wife. He caught the block instead. It crushed his skull. Hardy said it killed him in two seconds flat."

Riding? Pete was out riding? It explained the strong scent of horse, but that was about all it explained. And Pete, head still back, eyes fixed on the ceiling, didn't look like he was about to clarify things any.

"How is she?" Connie asked finally.

"In shock. She talked to Willy for an hour and didn't even put up a fight. She's doing whatever they tell her. Eat this. Take this. Sit down. Get up. Go to bed."

"And the daughter?"

"Alternating between crying her head off and yelling at Willy. Claire's poor mother just collapsed into a chair and didn't move or speak all night. Thank God for that Greg fellow. Between him and the maid, we were finally able to pack everyone off to bed and call it a night."

"Did you talk to Willy?"

"Yeah. He's decided Claire was in danger, all right."

"Was?"

"He thinks this will scare him or her from trying it again. The state lab crew is crawling all over the place, and he and Ted Ball intend to make their presence known from here on out."

"What about you? Does this mean you're out of it?"

Pete lifted his shoulders and let them drop. He closed his eyes. Connie touched his face, but he didn't seem to feel it. She stood up.

Pete opened his eyes. "You're not going?"

"No," said Connie, although a second before she thought she might.

It was cold. Connie borrowed a T-shirt, and they got into bed. Pete lay curled around her for half an hour. Then she felt him back away gently and get up. She heard him rummaging in the tiny closet, pulling on clothes. She saw him go out through the kitchen to the screen porch.

Connie knew what Pete was doing; in the old days she'd put in enough time on the porch in the middle of the night. She knew what he was seeing, too. There was a half-moon out. The marsh grass would look like silver fur. The creek would glimmer in spots, but in other spots it would look like ink. This time of year Orion would be hanging low in the east, arm raised, dagger handy, looking for a fight.

Connie started to cough. She sat up. Through the open door she could see Pete, sitting in the porch chair, rocking in the cold night. She sat there, coughing and watching for a while, but sometime before he came back to bed, she fell asleep.

Connie woke to the sound of keys dropping. She opened her eyes and saw Pete, jacket in his hand. "Where are you going?"

"The farm. I told her I'd be back first thing this morning."

"What for?"

Pete shrugged. "I told her I'd be back. She might need some help."

"Do *you* need any? Want me to come?"

Pete's face lightened. Then uncertainty crept in. "I don't know. Claire doesn't take well to strangers. I'd better get a feel for things first. You'll be at the Hermitage?"

"Until I die."

"I'll try to stop by later. But there is something you could do. Until things calm down at the farm, could you take over reading to Sarah?"

For some reason, Connie didn't much care for that suggestion. It wasn't that she didn't want to read to Sarah, it was the fact that Pete didn't want to that bothered her. But she nodded.

Pete hesitated. Then he crossed to the bed and kissed her. He straightened up, hesitated again, changed his mind, and sat down next to her. "About this thing with us. About moving in. It makes sense. It's just—" He stopped.

"It's okay," said Connie. "No big deal. It was just a thought. Since I have so much room at the Bates house."

"But that's it," said Pete. "That's the problem. It's always the Bates house. It's not *your* house."

"That's because—"

"That's because you haven't changed anything. If I move in and start taking those lace things off the furniture—"

"Antimacassars," said Connie. She heard the edge in her voice and said it again. "They're called antimacassars," but it came out worse.

"I don't care what they're called. I liked Annabel and Clara as much as you did, but I don't want lace things hanging all over my furniture."

152

"No, you didn't," said Connie.

Pete frowned. "Didn't what?"

"Like them as much as I did. You liked them a lot, I know that, but not like I did."

Pete stood up. "Okay. Have it your way. You liked them more. And that's the whole point. You want to keep their lace doilies lying around the house and I don't."

"I *don't*—" Connie took a deep breath. "I think we're missing the point. The point is, do we make a move forward or not?"

Pete made a move forward, all right. To the door. He looked back at her from a safe distance. "This is obviously not the time to discuss this. If I can, I'll come by the Hermitage."

He walked out.

Maxine and Andy were already at the Hermitage when Connie got there. She climbed the stairs, calling, but no one answered. When she got to the second floor, she saw the stairs to the attic had been pulled down. She called again, but there was no response. Connie climbed up.

"Help, I've been webbed!" That was Maxine.

"I'll save you." That was Andy.

"Yucko," said Max. She stood close to Andy with her head bowed and her hands on his chest. Andy ran his fingers through her hair, combing out webs.

"It's everywhere," said Maxine. "I can feel it in my eyelashes." She tipped her face up. Andy's fingers brushed her lashes, her cheeks, her chin.

Her lips.

Connie backed up. Then she remembered Rita and the curse that had been hung on her head. She reclimbed the ladder reluctantly.

Now lips were touching lips.

"Hi, there," she said.

Greg Hempstead was leaving the farmhouse as Pete was arriving. He looked tired, nervous, and, for the first time, relieved to see Pete. Pete decided to take advantage of the opportunity, and fell in beside him as he walked toward the pasture.

Pete looked around. "The police are gone?"

"The state crew left in the early hours this morning. The big guy left about an hour ago, but he left some kid lurking in the barn."

Pete was sure Ted Ball wouldn't enjoy being called "some kid." "The chief's coming back?"

"He'd better. He left the kid."

Pete nodded toward the house. "How's everyone?"

Hempstead made a thumbs-down motion. "Rawling is very upset. I haven't been able to calm her."

"And Claire?"

"No one's seen her. She hasn't gotten up."

Pete frowned. "Someone should check on her. Maybe you should send the maid up."

Hempstead gave Pete a withering look. "If I could find the maid, I'd do so. I knocked on her door and got no answer."

"What about Lillian?"

"Sitting in a chair, staring into space. I don't think she'll be much help. She was fond of him, I think."

Pete looked at Greg, surprised that he'd noticed. "Yes, I think she was. Are you going to be around for a while?"

"I wasn't supposed to be. Now, I don't know. I don't feel comfortable leaving Rawling."

Pete could see that it was an awkward situation. Hempstead might not feel right about leaving, but if their relationship was still undefined, it could be just as uncomfortable staying. For the first time Pete felt sympathy for Hempstead. "You haven't known her long?"

"It seems longer, now."

Pete wasn't sure what he meant by that. At any rate, Hempstead didn't seem to be picking up on Pete's vibes of sympathy. "I'd like to know what *you're* doing here."

"Who knows. But I'd like to help if I can. I'll tell you what, you do what you can with Rawling. I'll hunt down the maid."

Greg nodded, seemingly relieved by the lessening of his responsibility. He headed for the house, then stopped. "If she's not in her room, call me."

"I'll find her. She's probably in the cellar, doing the laundry."

"Not the maid, Claire. If she's not in her room—" He didn't finish.

Involuntarily, Pete's eyes slid to the pond.

The maid's room was on the first floor, in the back of the house, tucked in behind the stairs. Pete knocked and got no answer. "This is Peter Bartholomew," he said. "We have an emergency. Are you there?"

No answer. Pete had turned away when he finally heard her.

"Oh, come in. It's open."

Pete opened the door. The room was small, with a sharply angled ceiling, but comfortable, with a single bed, a table, a bureau, a closet, and its own bathroom. Joan Pitts sat cross-legged on the bed, leaning over an ashtray that was full to bursting. The air was so thick with smoke it was strangling. The perfect maid was gone.

Her eyes flicked insolently over him. "What."

"It seems Claire hasn't appeared this morning. We were wondering if you could go up and see how she's doing."

"You call this an emergency?"

"We don't know if she's all right. We want to know—"

"If she's tossed herself on the funeral pyre?"

"Possibly," said Pete evenly, or as evenly as he could. He wanted to yank the mattress out from under her and give her a boot toward the door as she went sailing.

"I'm sorry, but I can't help you. The household is on its own today. The maid is in mourning."

"There are others here in mourning."

"Ah, yes. But not for the same reason. It's *me* I'm mourning."

Pete gave up. He went back to the living room. Lillian Bowles was sitting next to the fireplace, holding her hands out toward the flame, but there was no fire going.

"I'm cold," she said. "Anthony always made a fire for me in the evening."

"This is morning," said Pete. "You know that, Lillian? This is morning?"

She looked at him blankly.

Damn that maid. Pete made a fire for Lillian and then went up the stairs two at a time to Claire's bedroom.

He knocked.

"Who is it?"

"Pete."

"Pete! Come in." The answer was quick. Relieved. But now that Anthony was dead and her mother was crumbling, who else could she count on?

Pete went in.

"Shut the door."

Pete shut the door, feeling as if he were breaking some ancient rule of Victorian etiquette.

All in all, she didn't look too bad, he decided. Sure, she was pale, but he'd seen her paler. Her eyes looked too bright, as if she were feverish, but other than that . . .

"Come here. Sit down." She patted the bed beside her.

Pete sat. There went rule number two.

Claire straightened the coverlet around them until there wasn't a wrinkle showing.

"You didn't come down," said Pete. "It's late. We were worried about you."

"I just can't . . . I don't . . ." She turned her face away. She was crying.

"It's okay," he said, God knows why, since everything was far from okay, and they both knew it. "Why don't you get dressed and have some breakfast? I'm sure I can scrape up something in the kitchen."

Claire bolted upright. "Where's Joan? Is she gone?"

"No, she's here. She's not feeling well, that's all. Will you come down?" Claire looked doubtful. Pete decided to try an old strategy that had worked in the past—get the helpless to feel useful. "To tell you the truth, your mother isn't doing so hot. It might be a good idea if you checked on her."

But it didn't work on Claire. She turned away again. "I can't face it," she said. "I just can't."

Pete shifted uncomfortably on the bed, but before he could come up with another stategy, she spoke again, her voice so hollow it alarmed him.

"This is my fault. Anthony's dying is my fault. If only I'd gone away as he asked me to. He begged me to go, but I wouldn't do it."

"Because he didn't really want you to. You should have seen his face when I first suggested it. He may have asked you to go, but his heart wasn't in it. He was glad you stayed. Really."

Claire gave Pete a weak smile. "You know just what to say, don't you? All right. At least I can do what *you* ask me to. I'll be down shortly."

Pete stood up, vastly relieved. Claire held out her hand, and for a second the Victorian era was with him so strongly that he almost kissed it. Instead, he gave it an awkward squeeze and walked to the door.

"You'll be at the barn?"

"No," said Pete. "They've been very thorough. They don't need me interfering."

"I meant," said Claire, with the ghost of a real smile, "will you be *painting* the barn."

"Oh," said Pete. "Right. Painting."

CHAPTER

18

When Pete returned to the living room, he found Lillian gone and the police chief waiting for him. The chief jerked his head at the door. They went outside and climbed into his Scout.

"So what have you got?"

"Nothing," said Willy. "Not much anyway."

"Prints?"

"The ones you'd expect. The wife's, the daughter's, the Hempstead fellow."

"Rawling? And Hempstead?"

"The daughter found him. Then she fetched her boyfriend. There were a few of their prints where you'd expect to find them—the marble block where they pushed it off Simmons, the doorjamb. The monofilament line that pulled the block off the shelf turned out to be from one of those fishing rods hanging in the rafters. There were no prints on the rod."

"So somebody wiped it off or used gloves on it."

"And on a few other things, too." The chief opened

his notebook and flipped pages. "I want to back up and go over this. You say Claire Simmons left her studio at four-thirty. You think around five you saw Hempstead's car, the blue Toyota, drive in and Beaton's Jeep go out. Then you saw Forbes head down the road shortly after."

"They were all there at some point," said Pete. "After Claire left the studio and before Anthony entered it. The booby trap wasn't that sophisticated. Any one of them could have done it. Where was the maid?"

Pete didn't think he sounded particularly revealing, but Willy looked up when he said it.

"So what's with the maid?"

"I don't know," said Pete. "She's too good, that's all. At least she was until this morning. It's like a role she's playing. But could she lift that heavy block?"

"Why not? It's no heavier than some of the furniture she must be moving." Willy looked at his notes. "Joan Pitts," he read from somewhere. "She says she was lying down in her room from four until six, before she began to prepare dinner."

"She's back in her room now. She said the house was on its own today because she was 'in mourning.'"

Willy squinted. "Mourning? For Simmons? Was something going on with her and Simmons?"

"She said it was herself she was mourning."

Willy groaned. "I guess I'll have another talk with her." He made a note. "And what about this Hempstead? Where's he from?"

"New Hampshire. I don't know about him. He's fairly newly acquainted with Rawling." Pete thought about Hempstead. "I don't know about him," he repeated.

"Okay. Now tell me what you know about these Simmonses."

Pete told Willy what he knew. After a second's hesitation, he told him about the rape.

The chief didn't like it. "Is the guy out of jail?"

"I have no idea."

"So I guess I go back to the station and talk to— Where are they from? Briar Hills?"

"That was their last address. But Simmons told me the rape occurred in Claire's hometown, a small town in New Hampshire called Millburton."

The chief made another note. "What about Beaton and Forbes?"

"Forbes is an old sot," said Pete with enough force to draw another look from Willy.

"He contributes to our Policemen's Fund rather handsomely."

"Forbes? *John* Forbes?"

"Yes," said Willy. "But you don't care for him, I take it?"

"No, I don't. He tortures Scott Beaton. He treats Claire rudely. Anthony Simmons tried to fire him, but Claire felt sorry for him so they kept him. She feels sorry for everybody."

Willy looked at Pete strangely. "And Beaton?"

"He's looking for another job. He asked me about Factotum. I was planning to hire him, but now that Simmons is dead, I'd kind of hate to see him bail out on them."

"Them?"

"Well, Claire. Forbes is no help to her. Neither is anybody else for that matter. What are you doing about all these accidents anyway?"

"All what accidents? We're talking about one thing now. Murder."

"It was almost *Claire's* murder," said Pete.

Again, Willy looked at him strangely.

* * *

Scott Beaton intercepted Pete as he walked to his truck. "Have you decided?" he asked. "About the job?"

"Not yet," said Pete. "But do you still want to leave here, considering?"

A deep flush spread across Scott's features. "I'm leaving," said Scott. "It doesn't matter if you hire me or not. I'm leaving."

"Okay. I'll talk to Rita. But do me a favor. Don't do anything for a couple of days."

Scott turned away without answering.

It was official. They were a couple. They walked around the Hermitage glued to each other, and Connie walked around looking over her shoulder for Rita or Rita's curse. She finally managed to pry Maxine loose from Andy while he made the last dump run before lunch so she could have two more hands for furniture moving.

On his return, Andy came hollering into the room Connie was currently disinfecting. "Where's Maxine? She was right here when I left. I want her to go to lunch with me. You said if I could manage the dump alone, we'd break for lunch when I got back. You didn't let her go without me?"

"She's right behind you," said Connie.

Andy turned around and gazed at Maxine. "Oh. I couldn't find you."

"I was in the basement." Maxine turned away.

Andy followed her.

Connie could hear him still, halfway down the stairs. "I thought you left without me."

Connie's lunch was a sandwich on the road to Sarah Abrew's. They assembled in the usual formation—Sarah in her thronelike chair, holding her cane like a septre, Connie horizontal on the couch with her feet on its arm. Anthony Simmons's death hadn't yet reached the newspaper, but that didn't surprise Connie. The *Islander*'s editor closed up shop Friday at five, and whatever news cropped up after that was left for Sunday's paper.

Connie explained Pete's absence with the gruesome news from the farm.

Sarah seemed to wilt slightly. "That poor man," she said, but Connie wasn't sure if she meant Pete or Anthony.

Connie picked up the paper and began to read, but after she'd stumbled over her fifth word in as many sentences, Sarah lifted her cane and pointed it at her. "What the devil is eating you? It's more than this Simmons fellow."

Connie snapped the newspaper onto Sarah's coffee table. What the hell. "It's Pete," she said. "I told him he should move in with me and turn his cottage over to Factotum. You know what he said?"

"What?"

"That he didn't like lace doilies."

Sarah peered at Connie through thick lenses. "Lace doilies. That's all he said?"

"What he *said* was he didn't like lace doilies. What he *meant* was he doesn't want to do it. He said if he moves in, he's going to want to get rid of all the doilies, and if he does that, I'm going to get upset."

"Are you?"

"No, I am not." But as Connie said it, she pictured Clara's gray head leaning back against the web of lace. "Anyway, that's not the point."

"I didn't think it was."

"He says it's not my house."

Sarah released her grip on her cane and rubbed a gnarled hand over her forehead. "Perhaps all Pete means is that it isn't *his* house. You know how he loves that cottage."

Sure Connie knew it. But that wasn't the point either. Or was it?

"So you have two choices, don't you? You could run away again, of course."

Connie shot up.

"Or you could sort through this. Come here."

Connie reluctantly crossed to Sarah's chair. The old woman reached out and gripped her hand. "I know how much you loved Clara and Annabel. But do you love their house? The way Pete loves that cottage?"

"That's not the point either. There's no *room* in that cottage. You should see it. You can't walk from the bed to the bureau without falling over some birdfeeder he's making for Fergy Potts or twelve years' worth of *National Geographic*s he's supposed to look through for Jimmy Swenson or a broken radio he was going to fix for somebody back in the year dot. And you should see the closet. The half that used to be mine is full of somebody's *refrigerator.*"

"So perhaps it's time Factotum moved out."

Right. Move Factotum out. Connie pulled her hand away. "I have to go."

"Give him time," said Sarah. "Whatever his problem, it's not you. Since you've gotten back together, this is the happiest I've ever seen him."

Connie snorted. *"That's* his problem. Being happy. He doesn't know how to do it. The minute he feels the first twinge, he sharpens a stick and pokes himself in the eye with it."

Sarah tipped back her head and laughed so hard her eyes watered.

Pete left the farm, uneasy. He didn't like the way Willy had pooh-poohed all those previous "accidents." True, someone had murdered Anthony, but it had been meant for Claire, and that put the previous incidents in a new light. He decided to start at the beginning with the poison. So Jasper had malathion in his shed, but he said he didn't use it. Maybe that was true, and maybe it wasn't. But someone else could have used it, right? Pete had seen Jasper's shed. It wouldn't take five minutes to break into it. Still, if it looked like the shed had been broken into, wouldn't Willy have mentioned it? Still, again, there must be other malathion on Nashtoba. Pete decided to try to find it.

The murder was the subject of the day on Beston's porch.

"I knew it," said Bert. "I knew something was fishy with those Simmonses. They kept to themselves too much."

"Oh, pshaw," said Ed. "You'd been married only a couple months, you'd keep to yourself, too."

"Speaking of keeping to himself," said Bert.

"Hi, Pete," said Evan.

"Hi," said Pete.

"And speaking of being *married*," said Bert.

Pete kept walking.

Yes, there was malathion on the shelf. Pete poured over the fine print and felt himself begin to sweat. You could poison yourself in all kinds of ways—you could breathe it in, you could absorb it through your skin, and yes, you could ingest it. There were warnings all over the place. There were instructions on inducing vomiting. There were orders to contact a physician immediately.

Pete took the bottle up to the counter and showed it to George Beston. "Sell much if this, George?"

"Here and there," said George.

"Do you remember selling any to anyone from Heath Farm? Sometime back in September?"

"Sure," said George. "I sold a bottle to that fellow. What's his name?"

Pete opted to remain quiet, not wanting to lead his witness.

George Beston shook his head, struggling. "I know his name as well as I know my wife's. Middle-aged fellow, swarthy-complected, knobby nose. What the devil is his name? You know who I mean."

Pete couldn't stand it. "John Forbes?" he asked.

"Yes," said George Beston. "Good for you, Pete. That's the fellow I sold it to. John Forbes. Some trouble out there, I hear. Quite some trouble. Seems you're mixed up in another one, aren't you, Pete? I swear I don't know how you—"

Pete backed away. "Thanks, George."

"And for no extra charge my wife's name is Edith," said George. "My current wife, that is. No telling what the name of my next wife will be." He chuckled gleefully. Pete was almost at the door when George called after him, "Bet I could tell you the name of *your* next wife, Pete!"

Pete found the remark highly annoying. Somewhere in the recesses of his mind it occurred to him that he found the remark *too* annoying, but that was as far as his self-examination took him.

CHAPTER
19

Pete returned to the farm to look for John Forbes, but when he pulled into the drive, he hesitated as he got out of the truck, looking around him.

There was something about the air in October on Nashtoba that made everything seem clearer. The sun was so bright it was blinding. It shot back at Pete from the neat white buildings, skipping over the half-painted barn as a building not worth illuminating. It danced across the surface of the pond, moving as the water moved, rippling.

Nothing had changed. All was orderly and serene.

At least on the surface.

Pete had some trouble finding Forbes. He finally found him sitting on the oat bin in the old barn, staring at the old harness on the wall across from him. When Pete asked him his question, he barely moved.

"I bought malathion in September. What of it? There were Japanese beetles on the roses."

"The roses by the porch?"

167

Forbes nodded. "She said there were beetles on the roses. She asked me to buy something to treat the roses. I picked up some malathion and took care of the beetles and that was the end of it. I didn't do anything to any beach plums, and I put the stuff on the shelf in the back kitchen when I was through with it. Somebody crushed his skull. I don't see where malathion fits into it."

"Show me where you left it," said Pete. He expected Forbes to argue with him, so he was surprised when Forbes got up meekly and led him to the back kitchen.

Everything was much as Pete had last seen it—the neat containers, the pristine rags, the immaculate cupboards and counters, but they couldn't find any malathion.

Pete wasn't surprised. Forbes didn't look surprised either. He was too busy trying to look matter-of-fact.

When they returned, Claire was alone in the stable, brushing down Dapper.

"Where's Amherst?" snapped Forbes. His tone toward the recent widow hadn't softened any, and Pete bristled.

"Running an errand," said Claire. "Apparently we ran out of tape. He wanted to rewrap that front leg on Medallion."

"Are you riding?" asked Pete.

Claire shook her head. "I needed to do something. But to go out riding—" She didn't add "alone," but Pete could hear it, lurking. She rubbed Dapper's nearest ear and whispered to him, too low for Pete's smaller ears to catch the words, but still, he could catch the sense of it. She was in the barn brushing down Dapper because she was lonely.

That didn't mean Pete had to push his luck on horseback again. There were other ways to share someone's company. "Let's go for a walk." He turned to Forbes. "Take care of the horse, will you?"

Forbes's head snapped around. He glared at Pete. Pete ignored it. He unclipped Dapper's halter from the ring in the wall, handing the horse to Forbes. Claire washed her hands in the tackroom, and she and Pete left the stable. When they got outside, Claire frowned at the half-painted barn. "I'm wasting your precious time. You could be painting."

"Not now," said Pete. "I have some questions."

They struck out for the pond, walking side by side in silence until they were well out of earshot of the buildings. "So tell me about the roses," said Pete.

"Roses?"

"The Japanese beetles on the roses. Forbes says you asked him to get something to kill the beetles. Did you suggest that he get a specific pesticide, or did he come up with malathion on his own?"

"I didn't suggest anything. I don't know about those things. I just knew there were Japanese beetles on my roses."

"And did you see him using it?"

Claire looked at the ground, concentrating. "I think so. I remember one day he came around the house with a small sprayer. But I was on my way to the studio. I assumed he was going to spray the roses, but I didn't notice."

"And how soon after this did you eat those beach plums?"

"I don't remember." She looked up at Pete, eyes round and half liquid, as if tears were imminent. "You don't mean—"

"You're often in the back kitchen?"

Claire nodded. "Fairly often."

"Do you recall seeing the malathion stored there? A brown bottle with a bright orange and yellow label?"

"No. I don't recall seeing anything like that. As I think about it, I don't recall seeing the sprayer again either."

They walked in silence a few more yards. "From what I've seen of John Forbes, I'd say you were right when you described that chip on his shoulder. I'm surprised he took on the rose job so willingly."

"Yes," said Claire thoughtfully. "He didn't quibble at all. That's odd, isn't it?"

"Come on." Pete turned her around with a hand under her elbow.

"Where are you going?"

"To report in."

"To the—"

He could feel the tremor through her elbow.

"Yes," said Pete. "To them."

Willy and Ted arrived, with men and equipment from the state police barracks. They tracked down George Beston, then John Forbes and every other household or stable member. Everyone except John Forbes denied seeing a bottle of pesticide, and John Forbes denied disposing of it or the sprayer. They turned the farm upside down and found no bottle of malathion and no sprayer.

"What now?" Pete asked Willy.

Willy ran a tired hand through his hair, what was left of it, anyway. "We tackle the dump."

Pete looked out across the pasture, following the sun again, his eyes coming to rest on the water's silver surface. "Or the pond, maybe?"

Connie rung out a gray sponge in grayer water and looked at her red, chapped hands. Enough. If she quit now, she might have an hour or two of daylight to muck around in her garden. She raised her voice to call to Andy and Maxine and started coughing. She wiped her hands on her jeans and walked down the hall to the room they were supposedly washing.

They should have heard her coming. She was coughing so much she sounded like the Little Engine That Could. Still, when she rounded the corner, Maxine was leaning against the footboard of the hermit's bed and Andy was eating away at the various parts of her face and neck as fast as he could find them.

Maxine saw her. "Oh, hi. Time to quit?" She pushed Andy off and followed Connie out the door.

It took Andy a little longer.

Pete, Ted, and Willy stood on the edge of the pond staring at a waivering pattern of bubbles. The Nashtoba Scuba Club was fanned out below along a knotted rope, traversing the length and width of the pond. In the distance, lined up along the corral where Willy had banished them, stood Greg Hempstead, Rawling, Lillian Bowles, and, after a while, Claire Simmons. When Claire arrived, Rawling left. Shortly after, so did Greg Hempstead. Scott Beaton appeared briefly and disappeared. Pete saw nothing of John Forbes or Joan Pitts. The mother and daughter stood together at the rail until Lillian went inside, and Claire remained alone, clutching the fence.

They found the stair treads first. It was almost dark when they found the malathion and the sprayer.

Connie collected her favorite pair of clippers from the basement and attacked the perennial bed, cutting back everything within an inch of its life while she did some heavy-duty thinking.

Finally she straightened up and looked around her, her eyes coming to rest on the house. It was strange how Sarah seemed to hit on the crux of the matter, she thought. Connie loved Annabel and Clara, not their house. As a matter of fact, she felt as if she were caught in a web in it, stuck in the past in it—a past that wasn't hers to begin with. She'd tried, but she'd been unable to move Annabel's iron doorstop or Clara's antimacassars. It was going to have to be someone else who did it. So what was the solution? Cramming back into the cottage with Pete and turning this house into the Bates sisters museum? Clara and Annabel would have hated that.

It grew dark, and the dry leaves and dusty earth seemed to further aggravate Connie's bronchial tubes. She began coughing. She raked up her cuttings, threw them on the compost heap, and went inside. Once inside, she remembered something else Sarah had said. Maybe it's time *Factotum* moved out. He wouldn't like it of course, but if she tossed the idea out and gave him time, the way Sarah said . . . Connie looked at the clock. Of course, if Pete were going to continue to live at the farm, the whole point was pretty damned moot.

He called at ten o'clock. "I just got back," he said. "As they say, things are afoot."

"Oh," said Connie. She may not have sounded as interested as she should have.

A silence fell that didn't belong there.

"You've eaten?" he asked.

It was ten o'clock, for chrissake. "Yes, I've eaten."

"About this morning," said Pete finally. "If I sounded like a jerk—"

Suddenly Connie had had it. Her lungs hurt, her back ached, her hands were raw, and she was tired of eating tuna out of a can while Pete dined on lobster Newburg with some little twerp. "Yes, you were a jerk," she said. "You were a royal pain in the ass. You were a class A moron. You were a—"

"All right, all right. Can we try again, please?"

"Try again? Sure. Why not? Your place or theirs?"

There was a second pained silence. "I'll walk up the beach," said Pete. "I'll be there in five minutes."

"No," said Connie, "I'll meet you." If he walked in and so much as looked sideways at one of Annabel's antimaccassars, she'd kill him. She hung up, grabbed her leather jacket, and went out.

It was black and blustery now, and the surf rumbled fifty yards away from her. She followed the sound through the path in the scrub until her eyes adjusted to the dark, and then the pale sand rose to meet her. She pushed through it fast, hunched into her jacket, head tucked in, and was almost at the edge of the marsh when she saw him, a lean black shape against the ghostly grass.

"Friend or foe?" he called, and despite the wind, she could tell by those two words that he sounded like she felt—tired, hurt, lonely.

"Friend," she answered.

They sat side by side in the sand.

"How's the cough?"

"Rotten." She coughed to demonstrate.

"I don't like the sound of that. Why don't you call Hardy Rogers?"

"It's just dust. And garbage fumes. And all the lust steaming around me."

"Uh-oh," said Pete. "Maxine and Andy?"

"Rita's going to kill me."

"So what does she expect you to do, jump between them?"

"If I did, they'd throw me down and use me for a mattress. So what happened at the farm?"

"They searched the pond. They found the missing bottle of malathion and the sprayer. And two waterlogged stair treads without a speck of dry rot in them. As far as I can tell, before they went into the pond, they would have matched the remaining treads perfectly. Forbes bought the pesticide at Beston's Store. He admits it. He denies chucking it in the pond, though."

"Did Willy arrest him?"

"Can't. All they know is that he bought pesticide at his employer's request. Forbes is scared, though. I've been watching him."

"And how's the Beaton kid taking all this?"

"Did you know he graduated from Amherst last June?"

"He did? So what's he doing at the farm?"

"There was some other job offer, but it fell through. He's sick of the farm, though. He wants to come work at Factotum."

"Good. We could use him."

Pete didn't answer. After a minute he wrapped his arm around her. Connie laid her hand on his thigh. Connie was damned if she was going to bring up moving anything. If Pete wanted to talk about it, let him bring it up.

She felt it coming as his thigh muscles tightened. "About this morning," he said. "About this moving in."

Sarah was right. They could sort through this. And Connie could contribute her half toward it. "You were right, you know. I've been thinking it over. The Bates house is still too much the Bates house. It *would* be hard for me to change it. Knowing you and me, we'll have problems enough without adding that one."

"Right," said Pete. She could feel him relax again.

"But you were right about my place, too. You felt squashed in before. It's gotten worse since."

"And I've thought about *that*. Why don't we move Factotum?"

Pete didn't speak. He didn't have to. His thigh had reknotted.

"It's not that easy," he said finally.

"Why not?"

"First we'd have to find a place for Factotum. And then we'd have to move everything. Who's got the time to do that? You're tied up at the Hermitage and I'm tied up at the farm."

"We'll be through with the Hermitage in a week. We have to be. And you should be through with the farm right now. You said it yourself before. The cops are there now, and it's not your problem."

"It's not that simple."

"Why not?"

"There's the funeral, for one thing."

Connie pulled back. "And what's that got to do with it?"

"It's got to do with the fact that I don't think this is the time to be talking about moving Factotum."

The cold and damp was beginning to get to Connie. She could feel her cough reactivating. But they could sort through this. He just needed a little time. Both Sarah and Connie knew this. Two out of three wasn't bad. "Okay," she said after a minute. "So don't move Factotum. Just move the refrigerator."

"The refrigerator?"

"The one in your closet."

"It's an ice box," said Pete. "An antique. It belongs to Jerry Beggs. I'm refinishing it."

Connie coughed again.

"Look," said Pete. "You shouldn't be sitting out

here in the sand. It's been a long day. Tomorrow will be longer. We don't have to settle this tonight."

Connie scrambled to her feet. "No, we don't. Let's just forget it."

Pete stood up, too. "Do you want to—"

"No," said Connie. "I don't."

CHAPTER
20

Pete couldn't sleep. Around three A.M. he'd decided that the reason for his unrest was Connie's unrealistic expectation that he should settle all life matters less than twenty-four hours after Anthony Simmons had been murdered. Couldn't she see he had a few other things on his mind? He knew these people. He'd been working day in and day out at that farm. He was needed over there. Despite Willy's protestations to the contrary, he needed Pete, and yes, the *widow* needed him. He was her only port in the storm. It was pretty callous of Connie to think he could settle something as big as moving Factotum right smack in the middle of everything that was going on at the farm.

Once he'd sufficiently settled the blame, he drifted off and dreamed of refrigerators again, but this time it was the one in his closet, the old ice box. Pete dreamed it smelled. In the dream he got up and opened the ice box and maggot-filled tomatoes spilled onto the closet floor.

Pete got to the farm early. The sky was still blue—as it was almost unceasingly on Nashtoba in October—and the sun still glittered on the pond as if its surface had never been disturbed. Nothing else moved.

The first sign of life Pete encountered was Scott Beaton, coming from the barn to intercept him.

He didn't say hello. He began with, "Never mind about the job."

"Never mind? You're staying here?"

"Yes," said Scott. "Thanks anyway." He walked away.

Pete went on to the house.

Joan Pitts answered his knock. "Ah," she said. "You." It wasn't the perfect maid, but it wasn't the renegade of yesterday either. Something had changed in her attitude toward Pete. For one thing, she looked at him. For another, she offered information. "Looking for someone in particular?"

"Mrs. Simmons," said Pete.

"Mrs. Simmons is in the stable."

"Is Forbes there?" asked Pete, alarmed.

"Mr. Forbes has gone. It is my understanding—" Here the maid paused and something in her eye glimmered—the reflection of a keyhole maybe. "It appears that Mr. Forbes gave his notice. Effective immediately. He arrived at the house early and spoke with Mrs. Simmons in the den. After he left, Mrs. Simmons sent for Mr. Beaton and spoke with him in the den for some time. Then Mrs. Simmons and Mr. Beaton left for the stable together."

"Thank you," said Pete. He changed direction, but before he went out the door, he stopped. "How is Mrs. Bowles?"

"Mrs. Bowles has just sent word she wishes to remain in her room. I'll be taking breakfast up."

"And Rawling?"

Something flickered briefly in the maid's face, something almost real. She said nothing but nodded toward the window that faced the pasture.

Pete looked out. Rawling and Greg were walking side by side toward the pond. As Pete watched, he could see Greg Hempstead's head bending toward hers again and again, but Rawling's ramrod straight spine never waivered.

"Oh, Pete."

Pete turned. It was Claire. She didn't look well— her face was flushed, her eyes bright, her lips trembling. She followed Pete's gaze. She made an odd sound, not quite a moan, not quite a sigh. "Will you come in, Pete? I'm afraid I'm done in. Things seem to keep happening." She turned to Joan. "Perhaps we could have coffee and pastry in the sunny room."

She led Pete down the hall, past her husband's den. She nodded at the closed door. "I can't go in there again. Somehow I felt I needed to talk to John and Scott from there. I needed my husband's strength behind me. John Forbes came to see me. He quit."

"I heard."

Claire walked into the sunny room and collapsed into the nearest wicker chair. Pete sat across from her. "It's all crumbling around me. I don't know what to do." She looked up at Pete with swimming eyes.

"You're doing fine. Just fine. So Forbes quit. So good riddance. You talked to Scott?"

She nodded. "I gave him a raise. I told him as soon as I could I would try to find someone to help him but that he would be in charge."

So that explained Scott's change of heart. Not only no more Forbes, but more money. "See?" said Pete. "Good decisions all around. Things aren't crumbling, they're rebuilding. I'll help out wherever I can."

"Will you?"

"Sure."

"There's the barn," said Claire. "I want it *done*. I can't bear to look at it."

"I'll take care of it." But Pete's reassurance didn't help her fevered look any. She leaned forward, then she slumped back in her chair and turned her face away from him.

When she spoke, her voice was so low Pete could hardly hear her. "She was there," she said. "In the barn."

"Who?"

"The day he was killed. The day I came to get you to go riding. I turned around. I turned around just before we reached the pond, and I saw her. I saw her go into the barn."

"Who?"

She shook her head. "I can't bear to tell you. I'll die before I tell them. It would be like killing him twice. She's despised me from the first, of course. I knew that. But I never dreamed she would try to hurt me. She meant it to be me, but it wasn't me." Suddenly Claire leaned forward and gripped Pete by the wrist. "Don't tell them! Promise me you won't tell them! I don't care! It's done. He's gone. I can't do it to him, I can't. He loved her so much. It's better that she stay free for him. It's all I can do for him. You won't tell them. Promise me, Pete. Promise me!"

She had him by both biceps now. He could feel her nails through his shirt. Pete pried her loose and eased her back into her chair. She huddled down inside her thick sweater. The sweater was the same green as the chair cushion, and it seemed to turn her into part of the furniture, to make her disappear. She looked so small and cold and scared. Pete could imagine her at nineteen, looking much the same. Suddenly he was

filled with rage against someone he'd never laid eyes
on—a police officer in Millburton, New Hampshire.

He stood up and walked around the room.

"You have to tell them," he said at last.

"I won't. I can't. It doesn't prove anything. It's not
a crime, going into the barn."

"It doesn't matter what it does or doesn't prove,
Claire." He could hear himself trying to sound stern.
Too stern. He sat down across from her. "You have no
choice. You have to tell the police what you saw. What
they do with the information isn't your concern."

"I'm so tired," said Claire. "This morning has been
exhausting. I can't think straight. I don't know what's
right anymore."

Pete stood, reached down, and helped her to her
feet. "Come here." He settled her on the wicker
couch, in the sun. He picked up an afghan in mixed,
muted greens and covered her. "Lie down. Go to
sleep. I'll be back this afternoon, and we'll talk to
Willy."

Claire lay down. "You'll stay with me when I talk to
him?"

"I'll stay."

She closed her eyes.

He was just shutting the door behind him when she
sat up and called wildly. "Pete!"

He popped his head back in. "Still here."

"This police chief. Anthony says . . . Anthony said
he's a friend of yours?"

"We're tight. Very tight. I think he's got the hots for
my sister."

Claire smiled.

Pete shut the door and listened for a minute.

Nothing stirred.

Pete called the station from the phone in the den,
but the chief wasn't in. He left a message. Then he

went to the end of the hall and looked out the window. He could just make out the two shapes of Greg and Rawling walking by the pond. He stole up the stairs quietly and walked past the master bedroom. There was a closed door that he took to be Lillian's. He walked into the next open door and found what he was looking for.

Rawling's room.

She and Greg were sharing a room, but they didn't look used to it. There was a clear dividing line across the top of the dresser separating their semipersonal items. On one side Pete found Mennen Speed-Stick deodorant, a man's leather shaving kit, an Ace comb. On the other side was a wire hairbrush trailing a few strands of long, auburn hair, a tube of Chapstick, a generic drugstore brand of fragrance-free, dye-free body lotion, and an assortment of hair clips and combs. The more personal items had been stashed out of sight. Pete knew because he looked, feeling like slime.

Still, he sifted through closets and drawers. And what exactly did he think he was looking for? Pete didn't know. He just knew that seeing Rawling enter the old barn just before Anthony was murdered wasn't enough to condemn her. If the early attempts and the final murder were tied together, if it had all been Rawling's not-very-subtle attempts to harass Claire or to scare her off, there should be more. But what? A book on the use of pesticides? Old shoes still wet from the pond? Rusty nails? Sawdust? Monofilament line?

He found none of the above.

When he finally did find something of significance it didn't sink in right away—Greg Hempstead's Hertz rent-a-car receipt in the inside pocket of his duffel bag. Okay, so Hemptstead rented a car to drive here.

Odd that he didn't have a car of his own, but not that odd. Pete looked at the form and only half saw it. Then something caught his eye that rang a bell, and he looked again. It was Greg Hempstead's address. Pete had heard of it before. Once before to be exact. *In some ways Nashtoba reminds me of the place I lived before Connecticut. A little town in Vermont. Swippingsdale. Have you heard of it?*

Greg Hempstead hadn't given Hertz any Keene, New Hampshire, address. He'd given them one in Swippingsdale, Vermont, the town Claire Simmons used to live in.

CHAPTER
21

Sarah Abrew liked Sundays. The paper was thick on Sunday and less grim, and Pete didn't, as a rule, work on Sunday, or at least he didn't work at anything else. She usually got a nice long visit out of Pete and like as not a few good laughs out of the paper. Pete might miss a weekday morning here and there, but he never missed Sunday at Sarah's. So when Sarah heard Connie's battered Triumph in the drive instead of Pete's truck, she knew things were more amiss than she'd thought.

Connie came in, slammed onto the couch in her usual unladylike fashion, and began to cough. Sarah, whose method of dealing with illness was to refuse to acknowledge it, raised her voice above the coughing and said, "So where is he today?"

Connie bounced up, pointing to the paper as she approached. "Right here."

Sarah's poor eyes saw nothing but two figures, one dark and tall, one pale and short.

"Want to hear what it says?" asked Connie. "'Claire Simmons, right, widow of Anthony Simmons, the director of Wequassett Trust, stands consoled by Peter Bartholomew, left, at the scene where Simmons's body was found crushed Friday night. (See story at right.) This is not the first time Bartholomew, owner of local odd-job firm, has been Johnny-on-the-spot at a murder scene. See story page two.'"

Sarah peered at the blurry print.

"Pete's spread is bigger than Simmons's," said Connie. "They start with the first body, the one in the bathtub, and chronicle his whole past, right up to this." She returned to the couch. She didn't offer to read either story. Sarah decided a change of subject was best.

"Did you talk about the house?"

"Sure we did. I passed along your suggestion about moving Factotum."

"What did he say?"

"He said he was too busy."

"Hogwash."

"Those weren't my words exactly, but the gist was the same. He countered with the fact that the funeral is tomorrow. Somehow that's supposed to explain everything." The newspaper rustled in Connie's hands. "Actually, maybe it explains a whole lot."

"Double hogwash," said Sarah. "You know Pete better than that."

"So I said okay, move the ice box out of my half of the closet. I'll start with that. And all of a sudden there was a conspicuous absence of further chat. He decided he was too tired to talk."

"And what did you say to that?"

"I didn't say a damned thing to that! I'd already done my bit. I'd crossed the line, as a matter of fact."

"What line?"

"What do you mean, what line? The line *he* put there. I crossed it and got nowhere. So now I'm crossing back."

Sarah peered at the long form sprawled out on her sofa. There were plenty of things she would have liked to say and a few choice adjectives she would have liked to put with them.

To Pete.

"Lines move back and forth," she said to Connie instead.

He was getting into his rented car when Pete caught up with him. "Leaving?"

Hempstead shook his head. "Running an errand."

"Mind if I tag along?"

"As a matter of fact—"

"I'll make this short," said Pete. "How long have you lived in Swippingsdale?"

Hempstead straightened his arms and pushed against the steering wheel. Then he looked at Pete. "Get in."

Pete got in the passenger's seat and shut the door, but Greg didn't start the engine.

"What's your problem?"

"You said you were from Keene, New Hampshire."

"So? I went to Keene State."

"When? Fifteen years ago? Several weeks ago you rented this car and gave your address as Swippingsdale, Vermont."

"Who told you this, your friend the cop? Ran us all through the computer, is that it?"

Pete decided to let this theory stand and move on. "You knew Claire before you came here?"

Greg shook his head. "I never laid eyes on her. I knew her first husband. Fritz sent me a picture when they got married a couple of years ago. I was out of town. When Rawling asked me to come with her on this trip, I had no idea that Rawling's new stepmother Claire was the same woman who'd married my friend Fritz." He continued to look straight ahead. "Fritz killed himself last Christmas. Under the circumstances, I decided it would be more tactful not to mention the Swippingsdale connection to his widow."

Pete leaned back in his seat. "I didn't know that," he said. "He . . . Jesus. First that, and then this. Poor Claire."

Greg gave him a stony look. "Excuse me if I think of it more like 'poor Fritz.'"

"Yes," said Pete quickly. "I'm sorry. Of course. It's just—" It was too much for anyone, let alone someone as physically and emotionally fragile as Claire Simmons. A rape, a suicide, a murder. "Does Rawling know?"

"Know what?"

"That you knew her first husband. That he killed himself."

Greg peered at him. "What's all this to you anyway?

Pete thought he sounded more curious than belligerent. Then he noticed the cords in Greg's neck were again sticking out.

"I just wondered. I had a talk with Rawling a while ago, and she was pretty blunt about how she felt about Claire. I wondered if this other connection—"

"This other connection, as you call it, has nothing to do with Rawling and Claire. Rawling knows nothing about my friend Fritz, and how she feels about Claire is, to a certain extent, understandable. Now if you don't mind leaving me to go about my business—"

Pete got out.

But where to next? Claire was sleeping. He walked

slowly toward the house. He would have to remember to tell Willy that Forbes had quit. And he'd have to tell him about Greg's real address.

He was surprised that it was Lillian Bowles who opened the door to him. She seemed to have regained her grip and what little she had of color.

"I would like someone to tell me what's going on in this place," she said. "Where is my daughter?"

"In the sunroom, sleeping."

"I'm told the police chief is coming to speak with her again. Why is this?"

"I asked him to come. Your daughter has some information for him."

"About whom?"

Pete hesitated.

"Never mind," said Lillian. "I don't suppose it matters. You know this police chief, I'm told."

"Yes, I do. He knows what he's doing. She'll be okay with him."

Lillian Bowles studied Pete intently. "I wonder just how much you know about my daughter."

"I . . . well, I know she's had a hard time. Harder than most."

"A hard time." Lillian Bowles closed her eyes briefly. "This isn't the first husband my daughter has lost."

"I know."

"And what else do you know?"

"I know about the rape. And the chief knows. He'll be tactful."

"Tactful," repeated Lillian. "Tactful. You have no idea—" She turned away. Then she faced Pete again. "This all started with those beach plums, didn't it?"

"I guess it did."

"Yes," said Lillian. "That's when I first noticed things going wrong. With the beach plums. Anthony

188

tried to comfort Rawling." She peered at Pete. "Rawling."

Pete said nothing.

Lillian's eyes filled. She walked away, supporting herself occasionally with a hand on the wall.

Pete took a step after her but hesitated. He doubted his help would be welcome. He watched her safely out of sight and decided to do what Claire seemed to want him to do most: he collected his paint supplies and climbed back up the ladder and put in a good long session on the barn.

Connie left Sarah's feeling at loose ends. It was Sunday, and Connie was damned if she was going to work. She needed a day off. Still, lately she'd been spending her days off with Pete, and now that Pete was spending his day off at the farm . . .

She supposed she should go home and tackle the garden. She still had all the spring bulbs to put in. Still, the garden wasn't supposed to be something she *should* do; it was supposed to be something she *wanted* to do. What had changed? She no longer had the time. She no longer had the vision. She couldn't project herself as far as spring in the Bates house, and it was hard to plant spring bulbs with an attitude like that.

Connie drove aimlessly down Shore Road, but as she passed Hall's Market, she saw Rita's Dodge Omni in the parking lot. She pulled in, curious to get Rita's reaction to the picture of Pete and Claire Simmons in the paper.

But it was Maxine. She was at the magazine rack, reading *Cosmopolitan*. Connie just had time to say hi, when the door to Hall's burst open, workboots pounded across the wood floor, and Andy appeared.

"Hey, Max. I saw your car. Where've you been?"

Maxine looked up. "Here and there."

"You want to go for a ride or something?"

"No, thanks," said Maxine, and she returned to *Cosmopolitan.*

Pete had just finished the face of the barn and was repacking his truck when Claire came up to him, calling.

"Pete! Pete!"

He turned, alarmed. "What's the matter?"

"Nothing. The barn is just lovely. I wanted to thank you. I feel so much better."

"You're supposed to be sleeping."

She smiled bitterly. "I can't. I just can't. I was so tired I thought maybe I would this time, but no. Do you know what I think would do me the most good? A ride. I'd be most grateful if you'd join me."

Pete shifted back and forth on his sneakers. The idea was less than completely appealing. Then again, he had to admit on that last mad dash back to the stable there had been a certain underlying feeling of . . . well . . . exhilaration.

"Sure," he said. It was a word he used whenever he was trying to force some enthusiasm for something, but Claire didn't know that. The one word seemed to please her beyond all reason.

Connie left Hall's Market thinking of Maxine and Andy. Since when did a magazine take precedence over a new boyfriend? But before long Connie was back to thinking about Pete and what Sarah had said about lines moving. What Connie wanted to do, of course, was to take that proverbial line and shove it down Pete's throat, but after a minute's reflection she came up with another idea. There had been a moment the day before, the moment when Connie had offered to help him out at the farm, when Pete had actually lightened up. He'd thought better of the idea in the long run, but still, for a minute he looked like he could have used her there. Connie decided to take that minute and run with it. What the hell. She could move lines with the best of them. She continued down Shore Road, hung a left onto the dirt road to the farm, and kept going until she reached it.

Connie pulled into the drive behind Pete's truck, got out, and stood without moving.

Compared to the Hermitage, Heath Farm looked like some high-class sanitarium. Maybe it was all that fresh white paint or the neat fences or the absence of the old scrub oaks and bull briars. Or maybe it was the lay of the land, the way it rose and fell so gently, or the tranquility of the pond. Whatever it was, it was hard to believe there had been a murder here. Connie walked up to the farmhouse and knocked on the door.

This had to be the maid.

"I'm Connie Bartholomew," said Connie. "I'm looking for Pete. Is he around somewhere?"

The maid studied her openly. Curiously. "Little barn," she said finally. "Painting."

Connie thanked her and backed out.

She walked toward the little barn. This was where the murder had occurred, she knew. She recognized it from the paper. The outside, the south side, was freshly painted, but Pete was nowhere visible. She walked into the dim interior.

"Hello?" she called. "Pete?"

There was no answer.

How quaint, she thought, looking around the walls at the display of refurbished farm paraphernalia. She put a foot on the bottom stair tread and hesitated.

Stair treads. Dry rot. And where *does* dry rot fall on the actuarial tables?

She bolted up the stairs, through the door at the top, and found herself in what had to be Claire's studio.

There were faces all around her, and she recognized three of them—Scott Beaton she knew from behind his parents' pizza counter, John Forbes she knew from casual encounters around the island, and Anthony Simmons she knew from the newspaper. There were two heads of Anthony, one better than the other, but still, Connie could tell that the little twerp was talented. There was a work off to the side, still draped with a cloth. Connie lifted the cloth. It was dry. So was the clay. It must not have been touched in some time. Still, the figure was unfinished. Connie could only just tell that it was meant to be Anthony.

She turned full around and gazed at the shelf over the door. This was where the block of marble had been placed. She knew that from Pete. It must have been hard to lift a heavy stone block way up there. There were other, more reachable shelves to the right of the door, but of course they wouldn't have served the murderer. Poor Anthony Simmons.

Connie turned back to the sculptures and found her eye drawn to the one inferior head of Anthony Simmons, just because it didn't seem to match up to the rest.

Poor Anthony Simmons.

Then she turned and looked at the shelf.

There were marble blocks still on shelves along the wall. They looked cumbersome and close to immovable. Connie decided to test it out. She pulled a stool nearer the shelf, climbed up on it, and reached for the block. She could move it, but it wasn't easy. She noticed as she tried to move the block that the shelf slid with it, and Connie leaned closer and examined the shelf. It was nothing more than a loose board resting on hooks. Then she looked at the shelf over the door, and it occurred to her that there was another way to do this. She slid the shelf itself, inch by inch, toward the shelf over the door, until they overlapped. Yes, this would do it. Then she slid the marble block along the shelf from the wall onto the shelf over the door.

Yes, anyone could do it.

Suddenly Connie wanted out of there. What in the hell was she doing here anyway? She left the studio, ran down the stairs and outdoors.

She looked around her and again felt that sense of order or tranquility. Two riders had just struck off from the pond and were heading toward the farm side by side, cantering. So here they come, Roy Rogers and Dale Evans. Connie looked again at the riders, one small and blond, the other tall and . . .

Pete.

They were coming closer. They were looking at each other. The blond head was tipped up, the dark one bent down. The breeze caught the sound and carried it toward Connie. They were laughing. So what came next, a chorus of *Happy Trails?* In perfect harmony? Connie decided not to stick around to hear it.

She was leaning over the tulip bulbs at Beston's when a shadow blocked her light. She looked sideways and saw the impressive bulk of the police chief, peering at the pictures on the boxes.

"I've always liked these things," said the chief. "Tulips, right?"

"Right."

"You plant them now, and they come up in the spring?"

"Right."

The chief eyed her longer than seemed absolutely necessary. He had a gentle voice for a big man, but he took it down a notch anyway. "Haven't seen you in a while. How's everything?"

Connie straightened. *"Everything* is just hunky-dory. What are you doing here? Isn't there a murder you're supposed to be investigating?"

"I am investigating. Or I will be as soon as I get some batteries. My magnifying glass is growing dim."

"Hah," said Connie.

The chief squinted at her. "Actually, I'm looking for Pete. He left me a message."

"You're looking in the wrong place. I suggest you try the farm. I was just there. He and the Widow Simmons are out horseback riding."

Connie could feel the chief's squint deepen, but she didn't care. She picked up a box of red tulip bulbs.

"I like the red ones," said Willy.

"You do? Here." Connie had lost all interest in tulips anyway. She shoved the box of bulbs into the chief's large midriff, but the midriff was rock solid, and the box made little impression.

Pete sat back and said, "Whoa" the way Claire had taught him. Buster broke stride and resumed walking. Pete guided him toward the corral, feeling cocky. Then he saw Will McOwat leaning on the corral fence, and Buster must have sensed he wasn't paying attention.

Buster started trotting.

"Whoa!" said Pete, but he'd kilted forward in the saddle, and Buster seemed to take that as a sign of encouragement. He broke into a lope and shot into the barn. Pete only managed to stay in the saddle by doing some spritely ducking under the doorjamb.

Buster trotted straight into his stall, lipped some hay out of the manger, and stood calmly munching.

When Pete finally slid to the ground and limped out of the stall, the chief was standing there, laughing.

"You're no Lone Ranger."

Pete wiped his sweaty brow. "Very funny. Did you get my message? Claire has something important to tell you. Watch it with her, will you? She's scared and she's not too sure she wants to tell you what she has to tell you. She's trying to protect Rawling. I'll be there to help her along, but——"

"No, you won't," said Willy.

"I told Claire I'd stick with her when you talked to her."

"No deal, sorry. But I'll make your apologies. What was Connie doing here?"

Pete was at the stable door, about to step through it to join Claire, who had dismounted at the corral and was fussing with Dapper's bridle. He stepped back into the shadows of the stable. "Connie?"

"I ran into her at Beston's Store. She said she was just here. She said you and the Widow Simmons were out riding."

Pete stared at him. *"Connie?* Connie was here?"

"She didn't seem too happy. What's the matter now?"

"Nothing's the matter. I . . . She was *here?"*

"Something's the matter, all right, I could tell when I talked to her. Does the Widow Simmons have anything to do with it?"

"The Widow——" Pete stared at the chief again. "Whatever's wrong, it has nothing to do with Claire Simmons."

"No? Well Connie seems to think it does."

"Connie thinks——"

"Pete?" It was Claire in the stable door, with Scott Beaton behind her, leading Dapper. She came no closer to Pete or the chief. "I'll be at the house, washing up."

"We'll be right there," said Pete.

"I'll be right there," said Willy. He started after Claire, but Pete stopped him.

"There's one other thing. Two other things." He told the chief about Forbes quitting and about Hempstead's real address.

"So someone's barking up the wrong tree," said the chief thoughtfully.

"Yeah," said Pete, heading for his truck at a trot. "Connie."

CHAPTER
22

Pete knocked on her door and reached for the knob but didn't turn it. He didn't feel right walking in, and that told him something.

When she opened it, she was surprised to see him, and that told him a lot.

"Hi," said Pete.

"Hi," said Connie.

He decided to get it said. "These problems with moving in. Or out. It has nothing to do with Claire Simmons."

"It doesn't? Well it also has nothing to do with lace doilies or moving Factotum or—"

"I know," said Pete.

"So what is it?"

"I don't know. I came over here to talk about it, and I don't even know what I want to talk *about.*"

"Okay," said Connie. "Maybe we should just let it sit."

"For now?"

"For now. While you think about it."

"You're being pretty great about this."

"Oh, I don't know. Lines move back and forth."

"What?"

"There have been times when you've been pretty great."

Pete exhaled. He hadn't realized he'd been half holding his breath.

"One other thing," said Connie. A coughing spell interrupted her. Pete could hear a definite wheeze now.

"Didn't you call Hardy? You sound terrible."

Connie shook her head. When the cough subsided, she said, "About the widow."

"I told you. It isn't about her."

"Okay. I know. I guess I know." Connie paused and looked at him. Then she disappeared, and when she returned to where Pete was still standing, just inside the door, she had a newspaper in her hand. "Here. Look at this."

Pete looked at the photo and swore under his breath.

"Okay. So maybe she doesn't have anything to do with it. But you have to admit, you've been acting pretty weird. You're over there all the time. And this picture. Look at it. And I saw you today on a *horse*. You, who have told me about a thousand times how crazy it would be to put yourself at the mercy of a . . . How was it you put it? 'A half a ton of hooves and teeth and flesh'?"

"I know," said Pete. "I don't know what happened. All of a sudden I was on this horse." Pete looked at the newspaper again and shoved it away.

"Anyway," said Connie, "that wasn't what I wanted to say about the widow." She paused for more coughing. Pete tried not to think about consumption and Camille and Edward VI.

"I went into that studio today. I think you should take a look at it. See if there isn't something funny about that shelf."

"Funny?"

"Look for yourself. I don't want to influence you. Think of it the way you would if you'd done the remodeling. And there's one sculpture that's different from the others. Look at that, too. And one other thing. I slid the shelf on the wall onto the shelf over the door and made a ramp. Then I pushed the block of marble up it. Give some thought to that."

Pete looked at her curiously. "Now?"

"Now," said Connie, but she said nothing else.

"All right. I'll go now. Am I invited back?"

"You don't have to be invited," said Connie. "I thought we settled that." She coughed again, and she seemed to have some trouble regaining her breath.

"I'll look at the studio. You call Hardy."

"Now? On Sunday?"

"Now," he said.

The chief's Scout was gone. Pete decided to go to the barn first and the house after. He saw no one on his way to the barn and went up the stairs to the studio, wondering what Connie was driving at.

It didn't take him long to see it.

One isolated shelf, high over the door, essentially out of reach.

Why?

He remembered what she'd said about making a ramp with the shelf on the wall, and he tried it. Easy enough.

But he wasn't as quick to catch her point about the sculpture. In the first place, he didn't know which one Connie wanted him to look at. He started at the beginning. Each one was like an editorial, he thought, making a point of some sort. Except for that second head of Anthony. What was the point of that? Compared to the earlier one, the one showing the conflicted man, it seemed flat. And then there was the one Claire never finished. Pete removed the cloth. The third head of Anthony had advanced no further since he'd seen it last.

Pete headed for the door, but he stopped and turned and looked again at the sculptures. He stared at them for a long time.

What? *What?*

He picked up Anthony's heads and lined them up in order—an intriguing one, a flat one, and an unfinished one.

Then he turned slowly and looked at the shelf.

Pete didn't go to the house at all. He went straight to Factotum and called Charlie Shearson.

Charlie Shearson didn't much like being interrupted on Sunday and said as much to Pete. Pete couldn't care less. "Who spoke to you about redoing the studio at Heath Farm?" he asked and waited impatiently while Shearson blustered on about having more important things to do.

"Who spoke to you about the studio?" Pete repeated. "Just the studio, not the barn or the house or the—"

"Simmons spoke to me, what do you think? He hired me to redo the house and the stable and the barn, to fit up the loft in the barn with a studio. And if he hadn't raised a holy—"

"The details," said Pete. "I don't mean who hired you, I mean who talked details with you? About the studio now. Who walked through it with you, discussing what went where. The shelves, things like that."

"She did," said Shearson. "The artist. The wife. She had it all mapped out."

Pete took a long breath. "Even the shelf over the door?"

"It wasn't my idea, I'll tell you that! Hell of a place for a shelf. Can't even reach it. But she insisted it went up just like that. She wanted to display things, she said, and she had to catch the right light. Didn't catch *any* light, not as far as I could see. I made some other suggestions, but she wouldn't hear of it."

"And when did this conversation take place?"

"We'd been working over a month, I'd say, before we got to the studio. They wanted the house and stable done first. She pushed us. Nice enough, she was, but she pushed us, couldn't stand it till it was all fixed just right."

"When this conversation took place—"

"What are you getting at anyway?" Shearson snapped. "I've got things to do, like I said."

But Pete pressed on methodically. "When you talked to her about the shelf over the door, was her husband there?"

Silence. Pete counted the seconds. There were five of them. Shearson wasn't too dumb.

"I read the paper," said Shearson finally. "You mean to tell me—"

"Where was the husband?"

"He wasn't there," said Shearson. "Christ." He paused, two seconds this time, and said it again. *"Christ."*

Connie called Hardy Rogers. He told her to come right over, just as she knew he would, but she made a side trip to Beston's Store first.

She sat on the doctor's examining table and took deep breaths each time cold metal touched her back and chest. Sometimes she coughed, and when she did, Hardy stood back and glared from under huge eyebrows, waiting for her to finish.

"Well," he said finally. "Took your sweet time about coming in, didn't you? And when do you decide to do it? Sunday, of course."

"Pete came by," said Connie. "He told me to call you. I would have waited, but—"

"Pete came by. Pete always comes by. But usually it's later, after they're dead. Speaking of which, I hear he's gone and got himself mixed up in another one."

"Yes," said Connie, which brought her nicely to her other subject of the day. "About poison," she said.

Hardy busied himself pouring little white pills into a little white box.

"Accidental kinds of poisoning," said Connie. "People eating unwashed fruit with pesticides on it, things like that. Have you seen any poisoning cases like that?"

"Last case of any kind of poisoning I can recall was two years ago. Cat ate rat poison, and the fellow couldn't reach the vet. He brought it over, and I gave it a shot of vitamin K so it wouldn't bleed to death."

"That was it? Nothing more recent? Malathion on beach plums, anything like that?"

Hardy's steel blue eyes dissected her briefly, then he shook his head. "Nothing as exciting as that. This time of year it's all sinuses. Except for today. This morning it was a grapefruit seed up a kid's nose; this afternoon, it's bronchitis." He handed Connie the little white box. "That's what you've got. Bronchitis. Take these three times a day. And keep out of that dust."

"What happens if you're poisoned with malathion?"

Hardy shot her another glance. This time he looked

like he was going to ask her something, but he left the room instead, and when he came back, he had a thick book open in his hands and a pair of wire-rimmed half-glasses jammed onto his nose. "Malathion. Let's see. Here we are. Vomiting and diarrhea. Blurred vision, headache, nosebleeds. In other words, you're sick as a dog. That's if you're not dead." He peered at Connie over the glasses. "Who are you planning to poison? Pete?"

Connie grinned. "Keep the page marked, just in case."

As she slid off the table, she said, "It's too bad about those Simmonses. Nice people."

"Wouldn't know. Never met 'em. Which doesn't surprise me. I know the type—have to have a big-city specialist for everything."

Ah-ha, thought Connie, suddenly feeling pleased with herself.

Jasper Sears was hand-scooping along the ditches, where the big machines had missed. The wooden scoop with the long tines was basically the same piece of equipment that had been used on the bogs for a hundred years. Pete circled the bog using the shore route, avoiding the crow's route, which would have taken him over the fragile vines. He hove to a few feet from where Jasper was working.

"Morning," he said.

Jasper didn't stop. "What the heck is it now?"

"Do you remember when I asked you about the chemicals you used on your bog?"

"Yes," said Jasper. "And I answered. Twice now. This makes three."

"Ah," said Pete. "It's that first time I was wondering about. Who asked about the chemicals in the first place?"

"That woman," said Jasper.

"Woman?"

"The one from the farm."

Pete wasn't going to jump ahead of the facts. "Which woman? There are several at the farm."

"Oh, are there? Well, I'm talking about the one you were hugging in the paper. That narrow it down for you any?"

Pete flushed. "Claire. Claire Simmons."

"That's right. She's the one who asked me."

Be careful, thought Pete. "When did you talk to her?"

Jasper thought. "Let's see. Late August. No, early September."

"What did she ask you, Jasper?"

"She asked me what you asked me. What I put on my bog."

"And you told her?"

"Sure I told her. She was nice and friendly."

But it made no sense. It was malathion they found on the beach plums. "Nobody else from the farm asked you anything about the chemicals you used on the bog?"

"Nope."

Pete's mind had numbed up on him. He hardly heard Jasper when he said something else. "What?" he asked.

"She asked me something you didn't."

"What?"

"She asked me what I *didn't* use," he said.

When Pete left the bog, he turned left toward the farm instead of right toward home, but he didn't go far. He pulled the truck off the verge where Claire's car had gone off the road and sat there, thinking. Finally he got out and scrambled down the hill until he reached the gravel patch where Claire's car had come to rest.

Gravel.

It was a funny little gravel patch there at the bottom of the gully. There wasn't any other gravel for miles around. Pete picked up his sneaker and looked at the sole. Then he walked up the hill to his truck, thinking of Anthony and his three heads.

Pete swung into the police station, but the chief wasn't there. He soon found out why. When he got home, the chief's Scout was in his driveway, and the chief himself was just emerging from his empty house.

They went inside together and retired to the only place fit for human habitation—the kitchen.

"Beer?" asked Pete.

The chief shook his head. That meant he was still working.

"You talked to Connie?"

"Yeah," said Pete. "It's better but not good. Thanks for that."

"So what's the matter?"

"I don't know. Me, I guess."

"But not the Widow Simmons?"

"No."

The relief on the chief's face was evident, and Pete wondered if there was more than one reason for that. "I have managed to uncover a couple of pieces of information," said Pete. He told the chief about the shelf over the door and about his conversation with Jasper.

"I see," said the chief.

"And you? You talked to . . ." Pete found his voice trailing off before saying her name.

"I talked to her," said Willy.

"And?"

"And I talked to Rawling Simmons. And I found Forbes and cautioned him about any sudden change of address. And I looked into the maid. Your instincts were right. She has a record. Theft."

"Theft?"

"Theft.

"And Hempstead hasn't lived in Keene in ten years. He's from Swippingsdale, all right. But he didn't make up this Fritz Wells. From what they're telling me in Swippingsdale, old Fritz was their most eligible bachelor. He was in politics. Headed for the big time, some say. He had money, he looked like Paul Newman, he had a discreet history with some snazzy women, but he'd avoided matrimony like the plague until the ripe old age of thirty-nine. Then he met Claire Bowles. They were married last October. Two months later, the night before Christmas, he shot himself in the head."

Pete blinked.

"The honeymoon was over, I guess."

The same old joke. But this time it didn't bother Pete so much. He was busy thinking. He'd been doing a lot of it since he'd left Jasper's, and he didn't like the way the pieces fit. Neither was the math too pleasing. Claire said she and Anthony had been married three months. That put the wedding at last July. Rawling said they'd known each other eight months before that. That meant they'd met in November. After she'd been on Nashtoba one month, she spoke to Shearson about the shelf and asked Jasper about the poison. "I take it there was no question about this suicide?"

"He left a computer-generated note. Apparently he did everything on the computer, so it didn't seem odd, and they were convinced he signed it himself. The note said something like no matter how hard he tried he was never going to make a difference. He'd just bought the gun. He'd been distracted. He was one of those sincere types that politics usually annihilates. It was Christmas. Everybody shoots themselves at Christmas. At the time they felt it fit like a glove."

"And what do they feel now?"

The chief shrugged.

"What happened to Claire after he killed himself? Did you find out anything about that?"

"She left town immediately and moved in with her mother in Briar Hills, where she presumably met Anthony Simmons." Willy paused. "There was one more thing that turned up. Or maybe I should say *didn't* turn up."

"Like what?"

"The rape."

CHAPTER

23

"There's no record of the rape?" Pete repeated. "When you talked to Claire, did you ask her about it?"

Willy looked uncomfortable. "No," he said. "She was real uneasy. I listened to what she had to say about the daughter being in the barn, and I left." The chief paused. "You said the daughter doesn't much like her?"

"I did," said Pete. "But it doesn't seem to be visa versa. It—" He stopped cold.

Willy rubbed a hand across his face. "So I talked to the daughter again. She seems pretty cut up. I didn't tell her who'd supposedly seen her, but her story is the same as the first time I talked to her. You saw their Toyota pull in, you said, and she confirmed the time on that. She said she and Hempstead went straight to their room, and she didn't leave it until she heard her father's Rover. She went downstairs not long afterward to find him. She says Joan Pitts told her her father had gone to find Claire, and Joan Pitts confirms

this, although she can't say for certain that Rawling
came down from her room or in through the door or
what. Rawling went looking for her father, first to the
stable and then to the studio."

The chief paused. "Hempstead again corroborated
all that. He said he was in the bedroom with Rawling
until her father's car pulled in and even for some few
minutes, maybe as much as fifteen, afterward. Hempstead was still in the room when Rawling came out of
the barn hollering, and he ran out along with Joan
Pitts. When he got the gist of what Rawling was
saying, he sent Joan Pitts inside to call rescue and
went to the barn with Rawling, but he took one look
and knew it was no use. He got Rawling out of there.
In the course of this conversation, I told him this was
some coincidence, his being from Swippingsdale. He
told me I'd make better use of my time if I questioned
a few other coincidences around the place. Then he
clammed up."

"Now what?"

"I think I've learned everything I can from this
vantage point. I don't see how it fits, but I don't like
coincidences. I'm off to Swippingsdale. I'll be back
late. In the meantime, stay away from the farm, will
you?" The chief stood, walked to the door, and
paused there. "When did you say Polly's coming?"

"Thanksgiving."

"The day of? The day before?"

"I'm not sure. The weekend before, maybe." Pete
studied the chief. He wasn't sure, but he thought
Willy's ears looked pink. "I'll let you know?"

"Do that," said the chief.

Connie had finally given in. She was on the couch,
under a blanket, when Pete walked in.

"Did you see Hardy?"

"I saw him. And I'm filing for worker's compensation. I've infected my bronchials from inhaling all that dust. Did you look at the shelf?"

"I looked," said Pete. "It's a dumb place for a shelf. So I talked to Shearson." He filled her in on his conversation with Shearson and then the one with Jasper and, finally, the one with Willy.

Connie nodded at various points in the story. "So," she said when he ground to a halt. "What are the odds that in two years someone would bury two husbands?"

"One husband," said Pete. "Anthony hasn't been planted yet. I want to be careful with this. I want to take this step by step."

"Okay. Step one. Two dead husbands, one underground, one up. Step two. The shelf. She insists on the construction of an oddly located shelf."

"Circumstantial at best. Say she really did want to display a row of heads up there."

Connie snorted. "Okay. Step three. No rape."

"No *record* of the rape. Maybe it happened, but cops being cops, the record was erased."

"I thought you said Anthony Simmons said there was a trial and the cop went to jail. How can you erase a record like that?"

"Okay," said Pete. "So that means what? Anthony Simmons told me this long, detailed story about Claire's rape. Did he make it up?"

They looked at each other. "True," said Connie. "Anthony told you that, didn't he? Why would he do that? What would he gain by telling you his wife had been raped when she hadn't?"

"I'll tell you what he did gain by it," said Pete. "He gained me getting in on this thing in the first place and agreeing to keep the cops out. That was the only reason I went along with any of it. Because Claire Simmons was so afraid of cops."

"So what does that mean? Are we back to my theory? That Anthony was trying to kill Claire and that you would be his character witness if he got caught?"

"But Anthony is the one who got killed."

"So maybe Claire got wind of it and somehow lured him into his own trap."

"No," said Pete. "It doesn't explain the rest of it— her talk with Jasper and the shelf."

"Okay," said Connie. "So try this one for step three. *She* made up the rape story, Anthony fell for it, he passed it on to you, and you fell for it, too."

Pete shook his head. "I can't believe she's that good."

"Oh, I don't know." Connie ran a hand into the back pocket of her jeans and pulled out the crumpled piece of newspaper.

Pete groaned. The picture again. "What are you doing with that?"

"I'm thinking of laminating it. But actually, I've been thinking and thinking about it. You have to admit you've been over there more than is strictly necessary. I think you'll have to admit that? And become"—she looked at the picture again—"closer than is likely? Would you acknowledge that?"

Pete thought. "I suppose so."

"And the horse thing, of course. All of a sudden this starts to look like powerful stuff." Connie held the picture at arm's length. "You have to admit, it's a flattering shot. The strong shoulder, the compassionate tilt to the head. And look at *her*—all pale and clinging. So you know what it reminded me of all of a sudden? An old movie poster. Clark Gable and Jean

Harlow in *Red Dust.* No, more like Gary Cooper and Merle Oberon. *The Cowboy and the Lady,* how's that? You can't believe she's that good, maybe, but *I* can. Look what she's got you doing."

Pete took the picture from Connie and forced himself to look at it, study it. So his wasn't the only mind that had been running in movie clichés of late. Pete had been doing it almost from the minute he met Claire Simmons. And now he knew why. Because every scene he'd witnessed since he'd met Claire had been an act. Every scene now rolled through Pete's mind like clips from a forties film fest.

"You have the right idea but the wrong movie," he said finally. "It was more *Casablanca,* I think. This morning she stole from the actual script. She was supposedly arguing with me about turning Rawling in to the police. 'I don't know what's right anymore,' she said. She didn't exactly ask me to do the thinking for the both of us, but she came close."

"So you see my point. Say she told her husband all about this brutal rape by an officer of the law. It would make a handy explanation for any nervousness she might exhibit when she sees a cop. Second, her husband then makes a concerted effort to keep the cops away from her. He moves her to this godforsaken island and plants her down in the middle of the woods."

"Yes," said Pete. "It fits. Rawling said this was not his usual type of location."

"And she's got this not-terribly-cold dead husband, don't forget."

"Right. I don't like the calendar on all this. She married Fritz last October. She met Simmons in November. I'm sure she visited her mother in Briar Hills from time to time, and maybe that's how they met. A month later, Fritz shoots himself. Seven months after that, she marries Simmons."

"Say she's the original black widow and she's killed him. Okay, maybe not the *original* black widow but a nice, seductive reproduction with a flair for the dramatic. She'd have plenty of reason to lie low, even to be legitimately scared of cops. But she needed to convince her husband there was some *other* reason for her fears. Voilà. The rape. She wanted to make it look like someone was out to kill her, so that when she killed *him,* everyone would think he'd accidentally stumbled into a trap meant for *her.* She'd never even be suspected! But she had to walk a fine line between convincing Anthony she was in danger and keeping him from calling the cops. So again, the rape comes in handy."

"Okay," said Pete. "She made up the rape. Then we come to the beach plums. And the stairs. And the nail stuck in her horse."

"Okay. Let's take them one at a time. First, this alleged poisoning. Did anyone see her actually get sick?"

"Anthony just told me she was vomiting and had blurred vision."

"But those aren't all the symptoms. You get nosebleeds, too. I asked Hardy about it. Anyone can stick a finger down her throat and throw up or pretend not to see straight, but nosebleeds are hard to fake. And Hardy said she'd be sick as a dog. Anyone would see a doctor after something like that. She didn't. We only have one doctor, and the only case of poisoning he's seen lately was in a cat. And I also subtly wormed out of him that he'd never met any of the Simmonses. So she didn't go to the doctor after any of it, the fall from the horse, the car wreck—"

"So she visited Jasper to make sure she'd pick a pesticide that he *didn't* use on his bog. All the time she protested it was an accident, she'd purposely orchestrated it so that with some minimal checking it would appear not to be an accident at all. First she went to Jasper to see what he *didn't* use. Then she set up Forbes. She probably knew enough about the available pesticides to know that he'd have to choose malathion if she told him there were Japanese beetles on the roses . . ." Pete's voice trailed off, remembering things in a flood now. "Claire made a point of telling me how Anthony blamed Rawling for the beach plum incident. This was to explain away an outburst from Rawling about watching what I ate around there. Later, Lillian told me Anthony took considerable pains *not* to blame Rawling. Claire even staged that."

"Of course," said Connie. "She never ate any poisoned fruit. So what came next? The stairs?"

"Of course," said Pete, thinking furiously now. "She could easily have set that up. She could have removed two good stair treads and thrown them in the pond, replacing them with two pieces of rotten wood, then faked a fall that supposedly could have killed her, with the hayrake underneath. The hayrake was a nice touch. Nobody believes two coincidences: rake falling off the wall and treads breaking. Anthony was suspicious, of course. And she probably would have figured out a way to get us to look in the pond if we didn't think of it ourselves. She threw the malathion in there, too."

"And since John Forbes bought the malathion, he was blamed."

"Yes, he was. And I suppose she stuck that nail into her own saddle blanket, then in full view of witnesses got herself bounced off the horse. She knew she wouldn't be seriously hurt. She knew the fall was coming, and she knew how to fall. She *told* me that."

"And the car accident?"

"Ah, the car accident," said Pete, and he told Connie what he realized only earlier that day. When he'd found Claire, he'd noticed gravel in the treads of her sneaker. The only gravel was at the bottom of that gully, around the car. When Pete had arrived, Claire was still strapped in the car. How then did the gravel get in the treads of her sneakers?

Connie shot up on the couch. "I'll tell you how," she said, but she was interrupted by a coughing spell. When she stopped coughing, her face was flushed.

"Do you have a fever?" Pete laid a hand on her forehead, alarmed, but Connie batted it off. "Come on now. Listen to this. Claire Simmons waited until she saw you coming up the road."

"Yes," said Pete. "That must have been it. I caught a glimpse of her car through the trees. If I saw *her,* she must have seen *me,* right? So she started down the road, going at a good clip. She knew I wouldn't be able to see anything once she was into that bad turn—"

"Right," said Connie. "Right! And she had time to slow down the car and step out before it went over the edge. Then she ran down the cliff, *through* the gravel, and strapped herself in, waiting for you to come along and rescue her. Oh, she knew you were a Sir Galahad, all right. She set you up, Pete. She's set you up every step of the way. Just the way she set up Forbes and—"

"She set Forbes up for the wreck, too. He used her car to pick up some wood. He truly does hate her, and he did it to get back at her, but she used that against him. She jammed a piece of wood under the brake. So Anthony blamed Forbes for the accident and actually tried to fire him over it, but Claire couldn't let it go that far. How could she? She needed her murder suspect on hand."

"But this car accident. When you got there, didn't it seem odd that she wasn't hurt?"

"She *was* hurt. There was blood coming out of the corner of her mouth, just the way it does in the movies whenever the guy's—" Pete stopped.

"Dead."

"She said it was a cut lip. I thought she must have cut it when her head smashed against the windshield."

"So just before you got there she bit down hard on her lip. A pretty painless way to draw a little blood."

"But she *looked* dead. Really. The windshield was smashed, and her eyes were closed, and her face was dead white, not her usual color at all."

"So she skipped the makeup that day. Or carefully applied some white stuff. And the windshield broke in the crash. Doesn't it make sense that way? Think, Pete."

Pete tried, but all he could think about was what a schmuck he'd been. There were plenty of other scenes that could just as easily have been scripted, and he was seeing them all now, seeing the helpless, fragile flower looking up and batting her eyelashes at the . . . Pete looked at the newspaper picture again. Yes. At the *schmuck.*

He crumpled up the paper and shoved it in his pocket. "I tried to tell Anthony," he said. "I wasn't completely stupid. I told him somebody was trying pretty hard *not* to kill Claire. At least I was on to that. Then somehow it all just . . . She just—"

"Yeah," said Connie. "She just. But it must have given her a bad moment when she found you on the scene. Do you think she knew Anthony had hired you to look into things?"

"Yes," said Pete. "Yes, I know she did. She asked Scott Beaton about me, and he told her about the kinds of work I did. That's probably why she went to town on me, trying to blind me to what was really up. She targeted me nicely with that accident. Of *course* she faked it. All she had to do when I got close was to hold her breath and go limp. She's good at that, going limp. Other than the bloody lip there were no other visible injuries. It was all just an impression I got, you know? The shakes, the weak knees. She faked the stiffness later. And you're right about the doctor. She wouldn't let me call the rescue *or* take her to see Hardy. Either one of them would have seen through the act. But not me. All along you thought something was funny about her not seeing a doctor after any of these accidents."

"But for the wrong reason. I thought Anthony was to blame for not trying to take her. She must have been pretty good at talking him around."

Again, they fell into a thinking silence. Pete could only hope Connie was having more fun with *her* thoughts.

"What I don't get is *why*," said Pete finally. "It wasn't for the money."

"I've been thinking about that, too," said Connie. "And about Maxine and Andy."

"Maxine and Andy?"

"Yeah. Things were getting hot. Every time I walked around a corner they were all over each other. Now all of a sudden Maxine seems to be losing interest."

"What does that have to do with Claire Simmons?"

"The thrill of the hunt," said Connie. "All the time

Andy ignored Maxine she twisted herself inside out to attract his attention. Then she got it, and you know what I think she found out? It was the chase she liked, not the prize. I'd just seen the two of them at Hall's, where it looked like Maxine would rather read *Cosmopolitan* than talk to Andy. Then I went to Claire's studio. I saw those heads of Anthony and something started to click. You could tell Claire found Anthony fascinating when she did that first sculpture. By the second one, he'd become boring."

"And she didn't even bother to finish the third."

"Right. So maybe there was something of a challenge about Anthony to start with, and—"

"There was," said Pete, thinking faster. "There was! Rawling said so. He was oblivious to women. He'd spent ten years still grieving for his first wife. No one had been able to divert him until Claire came along. And this Fritz Wells. The chief described him as the town's best catch. Thirty-nine and still unmarried, a rising star on the political front, good-looking, and I'm sure all this money only added to the prestige of the thing, whether Claire needed it or not."

"But who was it this time?" asked Connie.

"What do you mean?"

"She must have killed Anthony over somebody else. Some new challenge. Who? You?"

"*Me?* Of course not. This all started long before I arrived on the scene. Besides, what's so challenging about me?"

"I see," said Connie. "That easy, huh?"

"No. That's not what I meant. I didn't . . . It wasn't . . . At least I never thought . . ."

"Yeah," said Connie, grinning. "You never thought."

Pete stood up.

"You're leaving?"

218

"I have to. I have to go back there."

"Back where?"

"The farm. There are things we haven't touched on yet. The maid's record. When, exactly, Claire and Anthony met."

"Isn't that Willy's job?"

"He's on the road to Swippingsdale. He doesn't like this coincidence about Greg Hempstead's address."

Connie peered at him strangely. "This isn't another antimaccassar, is it?"

"No," said Pete, hurt. "No, it isn't. I just . . . have to go back there. I don't know how to explain it."

"Let me try. You're ticked off. You're feeling like a jerk. You want these people to know you're not the fool they've played you for."

"All right," said Pete. "Maybe. So what else have you figured out?"

"I'm not sure. But there's something else about that place. I felt it today when I was over there. It's neat and clean. Its existence is ordered. I can see where it would have once been a nice escape, a place of peace."

"Yes, we've established that. That's why he chose it. Or she chose it. It was supposed to be her refuge from her past and from the police."

Connie looked at Pete strangely. "Okay, have it your way," she said.

CHAPTER
24

Pete pulled into Heath Farm at five-thirty. At first he was surprised to see Scott Beaton's Jeep still there and to see lights on in the stable. Then he remembered they were down to one man. That meant Scott had twice the work.

Pete walked toward the house. It wasn't quite dusk, but it was graying, and the farmhouse lights were on, turning the windows into warm, yellow squares.

A refuge? Once, maybe, but not for long. Not tonight.

Joan Pitts opened the door.

"Good evening," said Pete. "I see you haven't left town."

For a second the maid's veneer slipped, but she recovered fast. "The funeral is tomorrow. The family will discuss their future plans after that."

"Best not to plan too far ahead around here, right?"

The maid's face darkened. "What do you want?"

"Does Mrs. Simmons know about your record with the police?"

This time she left the veneer where it had fallen. "So it's true about you and the police. Really buddy-buddies, aren't you?"

"They checked on everyone. You must have known they would."

"So what? Stealing isn't killing, even in this state. And if blackmail's what you have in mind, you're out of luck. Sure, Mrs. Simmons knows about my record. She's the one who bailed me out. She's rehabilitating me."

"Nice of her."

"Yes, that's what I thought," said Joan, but she sounded bitter in the half dark.

"How much do you know about these people?"

Joan Pitts hesitated. She looked behind her, stepped through the door onto the porch, and closed it. "So you didn't come to blackmail me."

"No."

"Why did you come?"

"To see Mrs. Simmons."

"To see Mrs. Simmons. Well, let me give you some advice. Get out of here while the going's good."

"Why don't you?"

Another pause. "Maybe in my case the going's not so hot."

"Is *she* blackmailing you? If you leave, she turns you in, is that it?"

"Why don't you get out of here?"

"I came to see Mrs. Simmons."

The perfect maid returned. She opened the door and stepped back through it. "Mrs. Simmons is upstairs resting. She had an exhausting interview this afternoon with the police." She closed the door.

She was probably right, thought Pete. Get out while the going was good. But even before he'd turned around, the door opened again, and a silver head appeared.

"Mr. Bartholomew," said Lillian Bowles, "I'd like a word, if I may."

She stepped into the growing dark. It was cold, but she had come prepared, wearing a bulky car coat. Once she was outside, she rubbed her hands against each other, then dug into her pockets and began to pull out a pair of gray leather gloves but changed her mind and thrust her hands into the pockets instead.

She sat down in a porch rocker and waved Pete to another. "You don't mind sitting out here? I'd enjoy the chance to watch the night coming. I've spent too much of my life inside, I'm afraid. Do you enjoy being outside, Mr. Bartholomew?"

"Very much."

"You weren't here when the police questioned my daughter today. I understood you to say you would be present."

"I did say I would be there," said Pete, "but that was before I talked to the chief. He said otherwise."

"I see," said Lillian. "That explains it, of course. You hadn't struck me as the type who would say one thing and do another. Is that why you came back tonight? To explain it to her yourself?"

Pete evaded. "I was told she was resting."

"Yes, I believe she is."

Silence.

Lillian Bowles sat stiffly in the rocker, hands still in her pockets, not rocking. "Has your friend the police chief come to a conclusion regarding the . . . situation?"

"I don't know."

"I thought perhaps he had. He didn't stay long."

"He had to go out of state."

She looked at Pete in surprise. "He's *gone?* In the middle of a murder case?"

"At the moment. But Ted Ball is on hand."

"The young man. I see. You'll excuse me if I sound impertinent. It's only that I'm concerned about my daughter. About how long . . . I'm sure you understand."

Pete did. And his heart went out to the older woman for what she must be feeling now and for what she was most likely going to have to face in the near future. He wasn't sure what he said next, but some instinct in him that he half abhorred and half depended on took over. He told her he was sure the whole thing would be settled soon, that they could leave here and put it all behind them. He told her it was going to be all right. He told her a whole bunch of rot. And the whole time Lillian Bowles listened as if it were the Sermon on the Mount.

When Pete finally stopped talking, Lillian Bowles stood up and pulled on her gloves. "Thank you for speaking with me," she said. "You've helped me. Good night."

"Good night," said Pete.

She went inside.

Pete stayed on the porch, trying to remember why he'd come. Darkness had closed down tighter when Greg Hempstead's car pulled into the drive.

He had Rawling with him. They walked hand in hand toward the house. When they saw Pete, they stopped walking.

"Good evening," said Pete.

"Won't they let you in?" asked Rawling.

Pete nodded to Hempstead. "I was waiting for you." Well, *now* he was.

"Go on, Rawling," said Greg. "I'll be in in a minute."

As Pete would have expected, Rawling balked at being summarily dismissed.

"Please," said Greg. "I'll be up in a minute."

Rawling went.

As soon as the door closed after her, Greg said, "What?"

Pete left the porch and walked toward the lit stable. Greg exhaled, exasperated, but he followed.

"What?" he said again.

Halfway between house and stable, Pete stopped. "You knew Claire."

"I told you, I didn't."

"Yeah, that's what you told me. Pretty strange coincidence."

The two men assessed each other. "You work for them, don't you?" said Greg finally. "You work for the police?"

"I work . . . I worked for Anthony Simmons."

"All right. Whether that's true or not no longer matters to me. I should have told them myself last week."

"That you knew Claire?"

"I *didn't* know Claire. Will you listen to me? But if I'd told them what I did know, maybe Rawling's father would be alive. I just couldn't bring myself to believe it. I still can't sometimes. It was a nagging doubt I had. And maybe a bit of guilt over losing touch with Fritz."

"Claire's first husband? The one who committed suicide?"

Greg shook his head. "He didn't. That I do know. I suspected before, and now, after this, I know. I can't prove it, though. Neither can the police." Greg looked up. For a second, hope flickered over features that were otherwise bleak. "Or can they?"

"I don't know," said Pete. "But you're telling me—"

"She killed Fritz. Claire killed him." He watched Pete, but Pete didn't blink, and something changed in Greg's voice. "Ah," he said. "You, too?"

"Tell me how you know Fritz didn't kill himself."

Greg looked out over the dark pasture and exhaled. "I knew Fritz better than anyone. At least for a long time I did. I know that sounds trite. But one thing he believed intensely was that every day brings new hope. People who believe things like that don't blow holes in their heads."

No, thought Pete. *They don't.* "So what happened?"

"I tracked his widow down. I couldn't believe Fritz could have changed that much. I knew if I talked to her about him, I'd know the truth."

"And?"

Greg laughed bitterly. "I didn't. Not for a long time. She's good, isn't she?"

"Yes," said Pete. "So you tracked her down. How? You found out she went to her mother's in Briar Hills?"

"Yes. And I found out she'd married Simmons, that they were honeymooning in Spain, and that they were moving to Nashtoba directly thereafter. But I also learned that Simmons had a daughter."

Pete had been warming up to Hempstead. Suddenly he refroze. "I see. And how'd you work that? You bamboozled your way into Rawling's affections so she'd bring you along when she visited her father? That would do it, wouldn't it? That would get you close to the new wife."

"No," said Greg. "It wasn't that easy. It was—"

"What?" said a raw voice behind them, and Rawling appeared out of the dark. "What was it? It

225

was easy enough, wasn't it? Oh, you shit. You big, dumb—"

"Rawling," said Greg.

"Oh, *God*. I should have known. What's the matter with me? You said . . . you said . . . and the *picture*. I gave you the picture."

"Rawling," said Greg again, "it's not what you think. If you'll listen—"

But Rawling turned and ran.

Greg took off after her. Suddenly she stopped, turned, and walked past him as if he were a dead stump, returning to where Pete was still standing, wishing he *were* a dead stump. Preferably a dead stump somewhere else.

"I'm almost forgetting," said Rawling, "I didn't come out here for the purpose of eavesdropping. You have a phone call. It's the chief of police."

"Thank you," said Pete.

"Rawling," said Greg, but nobody sane talks to stumps.

Rawling took off. Greg followed. Pete dawdled until they'd disappeared around the far side of the house. When he finally reached the phone in the den, it was whooping loudly. The chief had hung up. Pete rang the station, but Ted Ball said as far as he knew, the chief was still on his way to Vermont.

Pete left the den, seeing no one. He went outside and stood on the porch, thinking, until Greg Hempstead came around the corner of the house.

Pete started to walk away, but Hempstead stopped him.

"Hey. You. Wait a minute. I've got something to say to you."

"Like what?"

"Like thanks a lot. Do you always shoot your mouth off about what doesn't concern you?"

"You mean this is my fault? The fact that you used her has nothing to do with it?"

"Hey," said Greg, but then he stopped, neck muscles working furiously. "Okay," he said. "I know how it sounds. But it wasn't like that. Claire and Anthony Simmons were honeymooning in Spain when I got to Briar Hills. Rawling was just back from a graduation trip, staying alone at the house. I made up some story about how I used to live in the house, and she let me in. She showed me around. We got talking, that's all. She told me she'd just gotten a call from her father from Spain, telling her about his marriage, telling her to take what she wanted from the house because he'd sold it and was moving to Nashtoba. She was feeling kind of down, I guess. Sentimental about the house. We traded stories about it."

"Stories you made up."

Greg looked away, embarrassed. "That's what got her, I think. She even gave me a picture of the house."

"So how'd you end up here?" asked Pete. "Not that it's any of my business."

"No, it isn't." But Greg seemed to want to get the story out. At least he didn't go anywhere, and after a second he resumed talking. "I hung around Briar Hills, waiting for Claire to get back, and while I was there, I saw Rawling a lot. The problem came when Rawling decided to leave before they got back. She couldn't face them. She was angry with her father for marrying behind her back, as she put it. But I wasn't the only liar—when her father called again, I heard her feed him some line about a summer course she had to go back for. Her father pressed her to come to the farm when the course let out. I had to see this Claire face to face, and by then we'd gotten to the point where I could reasonably offer to go with Rawling. So I offered, and Rawling jumped at the offer. She didn't want to face her father or the new wife alone. She needed the moral support. So that's how it worked out."

"I see," said Pete. "I apologize. I was way off, I guess."

Hempstead's neck muscles started up again. "Look. All right. On paper that's how it reads. But the thing of it is—" He stopped abruptly.

Rawling came around the corner, saw the two men, and went inside, slamming the door.

Greg Hempstead followed.

Still Pete lingered on the porch, unwilling to leave. There were more questions to be asked and more answers to be given. Finally the lights in the stable went out, and Scott Beaton crossed the lawn. He didn't see Pete lurking on the porch in the dark. He headed straight for his Jeep and was just climbing into it when Pete heard the shot.

CHAPTER
25

Are you going to stick me with pizza again? Connie asked the refrigerator. *Or have you learned that trick with the loaves and the fishes?* She opened the refrigerator. It hadn't learned any tricks. She got in the car and drove to Beaton's Pizza Shack.

Franny Beaton was working alone, ladling red sauce onto what looked like an endless row of ivory discs, talking to herself. "Sunday night," she said. "Why doesn't anyone eat home Sunday night? What happened to the Sunday dinner, the roast, the mashed potatoes, the—"

"Hi, Franny."

Franny turned, wiping away a line of sweat on her forehead with a sleeve, and Connie was struck as she usually was by Franny's appearance. Her skin was no longer so elastic, and her hair was gray around the ears, but none of that had detracted from her overriding beauty. *No wonder Pete always offered to pick up the pizza,* Connie thought.

"Hi, Connie," said Franny. "You're going to have

229

to wait. I'm all alone. Freddy's gone to the Hook for a fuse and the Doonan gang just called in an order that would feed a herd of moose. Or is it meese?"

"Moose," said Connie. "How about if I help?"

"Lord love you. There's an extra apron and there's the sink. Cheese next. There, in the bin."

Connie washed and aproned herself and went at the cheese.

"I even put in an emergency call to Scott. Of course he wasn't there. Not that he'd come if he was. Freddy's been after him and after him. 'If you're going to spend the rest of your life shoveling manure, you might as well be shoveling sausages,' he says."

Connie winced. She's been about to order a sausage pizza, and she didn't much care for the analogy.

"I tell him to leave the kid alone," said Franny. "I tell him eventually he'll see the light. There are the olives. Two with extra olives, so lay 'em on thick."

Connie scooped olives on top of cheese, refraining at great cost from snitching any. She was suddenly starving to death. "I heard Scott had a good job that fell through," she said.

"Fell through! Nothing fell through. They even waited for him for a whole *month*. His dream job. Or so he once said. The aquaculture experiment. He was to start in September. Then he took that foolish job at Heath Farm for the month of August, and next thing we know, he's told the aquaculture people to go hang. They told him to think about it, they'd give him till October first. October first came and went and nothing's changed. He's been living out there ever since."

"Living at the farm?"

"Okay, not really. He comes home to sleep. Goes to his room and reads or watches TV, never goes out. Onions on everything. I said to him what about that lovely Jenny Sorensen you used to take to the beach?

He says he doesn't like the beach. 'Since when,' I ask? He says, 'I'm going to bed.' I hear him up there, tossing and turning all night. He could have his pick, you know, a boy like that. And that's not just his mother talking."

No, thought Connie, looking at the picture of Scott over the soda machine, it wasn't just his mother talking.

"Ever since high school the girls have been coming in here looking for him. I heard a couple of them just last week, sitting at that table right over there, going ga-ga about his *back*. Oh, Lord, I forgot the Greek salads. Here, you load the oven."

Connie took the long wooden paddle Franny handed her and slid it under the first pizza, shoving it the length of the long brick oven. "Where is the aquaculture experiment? Maybe he doesn't want to leave the island."

"Oh, pooh," said Franny. "It's only over on the Hook. I could see why he wouldn't want to work in this place, with his parents and all that, but who'd want to hang around a smelly old horse farm?"

Oh, you'd be surprised, Connie thought.

CHAPTER

26

Scott was young and athletic, but Pete wasn't a complete slouch. As soon as they heard the shot, they were running, and they were neck and neck when they rounded the corner of the open door to the back kitchen. The bare bulb overhead made it all the more grim, but even complete darkness wouldn't have helped. It was the rattling sound, even more than the dark hole in her forehead, that stopped them.

"No," said Scott.

The rattle stopped. One hand, one small, white, delicate hand, twitched. *Oh, this isn't like the movies,* Pete thought. He dropped down beside her and did things he'd done before—listened for breathing, checked for a pulse. He found neither. In no time they were all there, and Pete tried to remember where they came from and in what order, but it didn't much matter. It could have been any of them. Anyone but Scott.

So he sent Scott. "Call the rescue," he said. "Once

they've been launched, find Ted. Tell him to get Willy back here. Tell him Claire Simmons has been shot."

There was a sound at the back door. Pete turned around and saw him.

So did Rawling. "Forbes!" she yelled. "John Forbes!"

Scott still stared at the small body on the floor.

"Go," said Pete softly.

Scott went.

CHAPTER
27

———

All the pizzas were in, including a small green pepper and mushroom, no sausage, for Connie, and the Greek salads were well under way when Evan Spender blew in.

He looked surprised to see Connie. "What are you doing back there?"

"She's aiding the afflicted," said Franny. "Eat home tonight, will you, Evan? Or go bum something off Rita."

"Where's Pete?"

"At the farm," said Connie. She picked up the paddle to check the oven. The smell of the pizza was driving her nuts.

"That's the way I heard it, too," said Evan. "Just checking."

"Heard what?"

"That he was there for it. Again."

"There for what?"

Evan looked at her curiously. "There for the shooting."

"What shooting?"

"Somebody shot Claire Simmons. Chief's off island. Pete's holding the fort at the farm till the chief gets back."

Pete's holding the fort. Of course. And she knew, she just knew, something was going to happen to him. Of course. Connie put down the pizza paddle. "I have to go," she told Franny.

"Scott," said Franny. "Is Scott out there? Oh, Lord, I told him after the first one to get himself out of there. If this isn't the craziest . . ."

Connie looked at Franny. Beautiful Franny. Suddenly everything fell into place. "Scott," she said. "Of course."

CHAPTER
28

The ambulance had come and gone for the second time in a week, leaving a Heath Farm corpse where it lay, now under the purview of the police. Ted Ball, obviously uncomfortable in charge, requested the household to remain in his sight in the living room while they waited for the chief.

They had arranged themselves as could have been expected. Lillian Bowles sat in her usual seat by the fire, which Pete had once again lit for her. On the whole, she seemed in better shape over the death of her daughter than she had over the death of her son-in-law, but Pete suspected it was only because she'd summoned all her reserves to deal with it. Joan Pitts sat alone on the step that framed the sitting area, as if to separate herself from the rest. It left her head slightly lower than Rawling's, who sat across from her in a chair. Greg Hempstead stood at Rawling's back. He leaned down and spoke low to Rawling, but Rawling either didn't hear or was still giving him the stump treatment. Scott Beaton had taken the chair on the other side of the fire, and he and Lillian stared into it like two halves of one trance.

"I saw John Forbes," said Rawling. "He ran by that door not a second after Claire was shot."

"I saw him, too," said Pete. He watched Ted struggle with his dilemma. He'd radioed the chief and turned him around. He'd also radioed for help from the mainland. But right now Ted Ball was the sole representative of the Nashtoba police force. He had a roomful of potential suspects and/or witnesses and a possible murderer somewhere out in the woods. Pete watched him make a decision, an unfortunate one for Pete.

"Pete, I'd like you to watch that back door."

Right. Watch the back door. Which happened to have the dead body of Claire Simmons in front of it.

To his relief Scott came out of his trance. "I'll guard the door."

"No," said Ted. "You're a . . . You have to stay here."

"He didn't do it," said Pete. "He was right in front of me when the shot went off."

Ted looked from Scott to Pete. "Okay. You go, Scott. Don't touch anything."

Ted Ball stepped outside to radio for more men to look for John Forbes. When Ted came back, Pete decided to join to Scott. It didn't seem right to leave the kid alone back there with Claire's body.

Scott stood in the back kitchen doorway, staring down at Claire.

"All right?"

Scott nodded.

Pete looked around. Claire had fallen half curled in the fetal position, as if she were asleep. The gun lay where it had been dropped, four feet away. Pete looked over the rest of the room, and something about the rag box caught his eye. Not all the rags in the rag box were white. He walked over to it and looked closer.

"What are you doing?" asked Scott.

Pete forced his voice to sound the way it had sounded a minute before. "Nothing. I guess I'll go back. You're sure you're okay?"

"I'm okay."

Pete returned to the living room. Lillian had apparently roused from her trance. She was speaking, and her eyes were glued on Joan Pitts. The paleness of her face was accentuated by two bright spots of color on her cheeks. "I believe, Joan, that is incorrect. I was there first. You spoke from behind me. You said something strange. You said, 'That's it then.' Wasn't that what you said?"

"That's it then," said Joan Pitts, a little trancelike herself. "Yes, that's what I said."

"What about that gun?" asked Hempstead. "Whoever it was, he left his gun."

"That was my father's gun," said Rawling. "He kept it in his desk."

Greg seemed displeased that Rawling had spoken. "Others knew about the gun," he said. "They must have."

"I knew of it," said Lillian. "My daughter told me soon after we arrived. Anthony had told her about it in the hopes . . ." She bowed her head and closed her eyes. When she resumed, her voice shook. "He told her in the hopes it would make her feel safe." Her first tears squeezed from below the closed lids. She fumbled at her hip as if she expected to find a pocket with a handkerchief, but the dress she wore had no pockets.

Pete went down the hall and found a green and

ivory bathroom. He picked up a box of tissues in a matching green and ivory boutique box. He brought them back to Lillian.

"Thank you," she said.

Greg Hempstead opened his mouth to say something, looked at Rawling, and closed it instead.

CHAPTER
29

Connie was roughly halfway along the road to Heath Farm when someone wobbled sideways into the beam of her right headlight. She slammed on her brakes, jumped out of the car, and ran toward him.

It was John Forbes.

Drunk.

He lunged at Connie and grabbed her by both shoulders to keep himself up. "Rocky," he said. "Damned road is too damned rocky."

Connie added a hand under an elbow to help steady him. "What are doing out here, John?"

"Came to get my stuff."

"At night? In the dark?"

"Didn't want to see 'em. Had it with the whole lot. Would a made it, too, only she came out. Had it with her tricks."

"Yes," said Connie. "I'll tell you what. Why don't you get in, and I'll drive you back."

"Back? Back? I'm not going back." John Forbes reared away from her and almost took Connie over with him. She clutched him in her arms, and her feet scrambled on the rocks. His breath stank. By the time she'd righted them, it occurred to her that if he were carrying a gun there weren't too many places she hadn't already accidentally frisked.

"I'll give you a ride home," said Connie.

"Oh," said John Forbes. "Yeah. Okay. Home."

She led him to her tiny car and half shoved, half lifted him in.

"Hope she's dead," he said when Connie had climbed into the driver's seat. "Never know, though. Saw it in the war. Shoot 'em dead center and they get up and walk."

CHAPTER
30

"Wait a minute," said Rawling. "I *saw* John Forbes run past the door. I came downstairs when I heard the shot—"

"I was with her," said Greg. "We were in our room, we heard the shot, and we came downstairs together."

Rawling twisted around and looked up at Greg. Then she turned her attention to Ted. "Are you getting this? I saw Forbes run off. He's been snooping around this house for months. He could know all about that gun. Why aren't you out there tracking him down?"

Pete looked at his watch. Two minutes since Ted's radio call. It seemed like two hours instead.

Ted Ball stared at his notepad. "I'd like to get the order straight, here. You were there first, Mrs. Bowles. Then you, Ms. Pitts. Then who?"

"Greg and Rawling were right behind me," said Joan. "I was standing at the foot of the stairs when they came down."

"Together?"

"Together."

"You hear the shot?" Pete asked her.

"Yes. I ran out of my room the second I heard it and was at the foot of the stairs when Greg and Rawling came down. We stopped there a second or two, looking at each other."

"Yes," said Rawling. "It was like none of us believed it was a shot until we saw each other's faces. Then the three of us ran. Joan, you were a foot ahead of us, but that was it. We got there together."

"So that clears all of us," said Greg. "The three of us came running. Joan came from the direction of her room, not the back kitchen. She couldn't have gotten from the back kitchen all the way around and out to the foot of the stairs by the time we came down. And that's the houseful. That settles it. Forbes then."

Yes, thought Pete, thinking about the look on Forbes's face as he ran, *that settles it.* He looked around the room. He felt cold. He walked to the fire and sat down in the chair Scott had vacated across from Lillian.

CHAPTER
31

"**W**hoa, there!" Forbes lurched sideways and grabbed Connie's wheel. The Triumph nosed into the brush and stalled.

"Jesus Christ, John, what are you trying to do, kill us?"

"Home," said Forbes. "You said you were taking me back home. You're going back to the farm."

"I'm taking you home, John. Will you look at this road? It's ten feet wide here. How am I going to turn around? I'm going this way until I can find a spot to turn."

Forbes peered out the side of the Triumph. Since he'd yanked the wheel toward him, Connie was pretty sure all he'd see from his side was the brush he'd plowed them into.

"Can't turn here," he said.

"No," said Connie. "Now for chrissake, sit there and shut up." She took a couple of deep breaths and turned the key in the ignition, but nothing happened.

"Dumb kid," said Forbes.

For a minute Connie thought he meant her, and she bristled.

"Dumb, blind kid," he repeated. He sat up straighter. The near accident seemed to have sobered him. "Couldn't see his hand in front of his face. Tried to point a few things out to him, but oh, no. He wouldn't listen. Kept telling me I was wrong, it was nothing, she was married." Forbes snorted and belched. "As if that meant anything to the likes of her. Being married."

Connie stopped trying to start the car. Here it was then. Her very own theory. "You mean Scott, don't you?" she asked. "Scott and Claire Simmons?"

"He was no match for her. Saw it from the first. She started slow, all innocent, just a little pressure here and there, a look, a word, until she'd hooked him. God knows what she told him. But he had scruples. We used to talk some, and I know. He wasn't one of those kids just out to get what he could. So I tried to talk to him about her. Got nowhere. Swore it was nothing. She was married, and that meant nothing doing. I knew better, of course. Just a matter of time. But even I didn't figure she'd go so far as to kill Simmons to get him. So then I tried to keep him busy. She was too smart for me, though." Suddenly Forbes looked at Connie and narrowed his eyes. "What's the matter? Why aren't we moving?"

"Oh." Connie tried again, and the car started. She moved off down the road. Slowly.

"'Course what she saw in that fool kid beats me," said Forbes.

But that was because Forbes was a man. Connie could look at Scott's classic features and recognize that in addition to that there was enough youth and innocence there to drive someone like Claire crazy. And Connie now felt like she knew Claire Simmons better than Forbes did. She knew she was looking for the "thrill of the hunt," and Scott Beaton would have given it to her, all right. At least he seemed to have had enough scruples to keep her at bay while she was married.

But what did Scott see in Claire? The same thing all the other men did, whatever that was. And whatever it was, it was enough to keep a promising young man from a promising career.

Connie inched the car slowly toward the farm. She had no intention of taking John Forbes home. She wanted him back where she knew the only remaining cop on the island was waiting. She wasn't stupid, was she? Here Claire Simmons had just been shot, and here John Forbes was, running down the road away from the farm. He must have liked Scott a lot to have killed Claire Simmons just to keep Scott out of her clutches. But then again, he was raving drunk. Who knew what he'd been thinking?

Suddenly there were headlights behind her. Connie looked in her rearview mirror and saw the gleam of the blue dome and enough cars following behind to set her heart thumping.

"What the—" began John Forbes. Then he grabbed the wheel for a second time and yanked.

This time the little sports car careened through the thin wall of beach plums and went plunging.

CHAPTER
32

Ted Ball checked his watch. Lillian Bowles shivered. Pete stoked the fire for her, but she didn't seem to notice it.

The other players moved around restlessly. Greg kneeled in front of Rawling's chair, forcing her to look at him, and when she did, he whispered something softly.

"No," Rawling spat back.

Joan Pitts stood and stretched. There was nothing of the maid, perfect or not, remaining.

There was a loud sound from outside. A tearing, crashing sound. Rawling jumped up and went to the window. "What was that?"

Greg Hempstead joined her. "Sounds like a car."

"Yes, I see headlights. No, I don't. That's not the road anyway. What's going on out there?"

Lillian looked up from the fire, alarmed.

Pete leaned toward her. "Are you all right?"

"She's dead," she said.

"I know," said Pete.

"It's not her fault. It can't be her fault, what's going on out there."

"No," said Pete. "Would you like to go upstairs?"

Lillian lifted her chin and shook her head.

"Okay," Pete stood up. "I'll check on Scott."

He walked down the hall to the back kitchen.

Scott Beaton was gone.

And so was the body of Claire Simmons.

CHAPTER
33

It wasn't all that much of a plunge. The little car bumped and skidded down a gentle bank and stopped in a thicket of beach plum bushes. John Forbes scrambled out and started running. Connie was out and on her feet when the first of the half-dozen men reached her—one she identified by his bulk as their very own police chief. The others, judging by their level of fitness, were straight from the state police barracks.

Willy gripped her by both arms and looked her up and down thoroughly. "Are you all right?"

She shoved him away. "Will you go get him? It's John Forbes, and he killed Claire Simmons."

The troopers tore off through the brush like a pack of hounds. Connie had a fleeting moment of sympathy for the fox.

"Are you all right?" Willy asked her again.

"Of course," she said. "We just took out a few beach plum bushes." *The* beach plum bushes. All of a sudden one of her knees, the one that always gave her trouble in times of stress, started to quiver.

Willy grabbed her again, more firmly this time. "Come on."

"He might still have the gun," said Connie. "I don't think so, but he might."

The chief pulled out his radio and spoke into it. It crackled something back. "They've got him. Come on. One of the troopers will run you home."

"I want to go to the farm."

"No. There's nothing there for you."

"Oh, yes there is," said Connie. "And ten to one, he's smack-dab in the middle of it."

CHAPTER
34

Pete darted through the outer door of the back kitchen and took a quick look around, but he saw nothing. He was about return to the house and report the missing body to Ted Ball, when he was distracted by the sounds drifting his way from the stable. Even to Pete's untrained ear the amount of stamping and snuffling seemed unusual. He turned warily toward the stable.

The sliding stable door had been left open a foot or two. Pete wedged through it without opening it further and found himself face to face with his old friend, Buster.

Pete backed out fast through the opening, thinking hard. Buster, loose in the stable. Pete didn't know what it meant, but he knew it meant something. He poked his head through the door again and was met by one huge, gleaming eyeball.

"Easy old boy," said Pete.

Buster snorted and pranced sideways.

Pete withdrew his head and slid the door shut,

thinking frantically. He could hear the horses through the closed door, stamping their feet, whinnying. Something was in there. Something besides horses. Something they didn't like. A dead body maybe? Pete wiped a sweaty palm along his thigh, gripped the handle of the door, and slid it open wide enough so he could squeeze in, but not wide enough so Buster could squeeze out.

Once inside he backed himself against the door, watching and listening.

The horses were going crazy. He heard more stamping and whinnying from the stalls and the sound of an occasional hoof against solid (he hoped) planking. In front of him Buster danced back and forth, rolling his eyes till the whites showed.

"Hey, buddy," said Pete.

Buster reared, came down hard, pivoted, and clattered down the corridor only to stop short at the midway point. At the far end of the stable, Pete saw the door to Buster's stall had been left open, but Buster would go no closer.

"Scott?" Pete called. "Are you in here?"

Buster whirled again, charged in Pete's direction, stopped, reared, snorted, and stood trembling.

"You and me both, buddy," said Pete. "You and me both."

Only the horses answered him. Someone neighed, another kicked something. Pete tried to pretend he hadn't heard wood splintering. He looked at the open stall door, and he looked at Buster, filling the corridor between them. He wiped his hands on his jeans a second time and took a step forward, jabbering.

"Okay, Buster. Okay, old pal. What's the matter, buddy? Something's got you spooked? Not me. Not me, old buddy."

Buster watched him, not moving.

"Okay," said Pete, taking another step. "See? It's just me. You remember me, don't you? The guy you almost decapitated on this beam here. You remember that, don't you?" He stretched a hand toward the long nose, and Buster tossed his head without taking his eye off him. Pete refrained from jumping backward through the door, but just barely. He stretched out his hand again, and Buster stayed still. Pete stroked the white stripe between his eyes, keeping his hand steady. "There you go. There you go. It's just me. See? We're friends, aren't we?"

Buster snorted.

Pete slid has hand down his neck and over his flank. Buster didn't move. Pete moved between Buster and the wall, keeping his hand on the horse all the time, wanting Buster to know where he was. He could feel the sweat on Buster's side. He could feel the sweat on *his* sides, running down from his armpits. He found a halter hanging on the wall and managed to work it over Buster's ears, buckling it with slimy fingers. He clipped the halter to the ring in the wall.

He was free. He patted Buster on the rump. They were both much calmer now. He walked to the open stall door and peered in.

Scott Beaton was in the stall, kneeling over the fresh bed of straw that cradled Claire's body.

Pete went in. "Scott? What are you doing?"

"I couldn't leave her there on the floor. It didn't seem right. You saw her lying there. It wasn't right, was it?"

"No," said Pete. "I guess it wasn't. But I don't think we can leave her in here either. For one thing, Buster doesn't seem to like it. What do you say we—"

What do you say we *what?* Dump her on the floor again?

Pete stood up and gripped Scott by the elbow.

"Come on. Let's go back inside. She'll be fine where she is."

He was guiding Scott across the lawn when the cavalry arrived—the police chief, Connie, and two state troopers.

The troopers took Scott off in the cruiser. The police chief went into the stable.

Pete and Connie stood on the lawn.

"What are you doing here?"

"I heard what happened," said Connie. "I was worried. I figured you'd do something crazy."

Pete put his arm around her. "Not to worry. I can swim, remember? I can even tame wild horses."

From the stable a hoof clattered into a wall and Pete jumped. Connie snorted.

The chief rejoined them. "Forbes is in custody," he said.

"For what?" asked Pete.

"For shooting Claire Simmons," said Connie. "I found him running down the road away from the house. She was after Scott. Forbes hated her. He says she deserved it. He told me all about it."

"He told you he did it?"

"No," said Connie. "Not that. But—"

"Hold on," said Pete. He went into the house.

They were still all there, Greg and Rawling together at the window, Joan Pitts on the step, Lillian in her chair by the fire. Pete walked over to the fire and gave it another poke. Then he swiveled on his heels until he was facing Claire's mother. "Lillian? I was just speaking with the chief. He's arrested Forbes for killing your daughter."

The silver head tipped up, but at first what Pete had told her didn't seem to register. Then her eyes cleared and swung toward the door where Will McOwat now stood. She attempted to get up, but she seemed to have stiffened from sitting so long. Pete helped her up, and he helped her walk all the way across the living room until she stopped in front of the police chief.

"Let him go," she said.

The chief squinted, first at her, then at Pete.

"Let the poor man go," Lillian repeated. "*I* killed my daughter."

CHAPTER
35

Pete watched a rainbow of opposing emotions wash over the chief's face—puzzlement, disbelief, pain, and yes, finally, relief. They had killed each other. It would be left among them, among these strangers. But when he addressed Lillian, his face was again blank. He gave her the proper caution and advised her that she would be taken to the station, where she would be asked to give a formal statement.

"A moment, please," said Lillian. She returned unaided to her chair by the fire and sat down heavily. "I would ask you to allow me one moment to collect myself. Please."

The chief shot Pete a look. Pete returned to the fire and sat by Lillian. The chief jerked his head at Ted Ball, and Ted began to clear the room quietly.

"It's so odd," said Lillian finally. "I've never completely believed in guns. I don't mean that in the sense that I disapprove of them, I mean it in the sense that I've never believed they work. They're so small, guns. So insignificant. And yet they change everything."

She looked into the fire and blinked. "But I'd do it again," she said softly. *"She'd* do it again. Fritz. And my poor, poor Anthony. If only I'd acted before. If only I'd been able to save Anthony." She looked up at Pete. "You see, I thought it might be different this time. You came. You told me you were hired by Anthony. I'd heard about you, and I thought maybe this time Anthony was on his guard, that you'd be able to save him. I tried to tell you. I tried to tell Anthony. But finally I could see it was no use. Men. She can make them do anything."

"Why didn't you tell the police?" asked Pete.

Lillian looked up at him, confused. "What good would that do? They're men, too. She would have gotten around every one of them. Hadn't she already? This evening, in speaking with you, Pete, you made me see that it was going to be just the same all over again. You told me the chief had abandoned the case and had left the island. He was without a clue. You assured me we'd be able to leave here and go on as before. Didn't you, Pete?"

Pete felt the chief's eyes drilling into him. "Not exactly. The chief was working on the case from the other end. He knew about Claire already. But I didn't want to worry you."

Lillian seemed to think that over for a second or two. "Oh, well," she said finally. "It doesn't matter. Even if she'd been arrested, she would never have gone to jail. She would have found a way. She would have found some man to do her bidding." Lillian looked up at Pete again. "She always did, didn't she?"

"Yes," said Pete. "She did."

It was two A.M. They were in Connie's living room. For some reason they had elected to sit apart, across from each other, in Clara's and Annabel's doily-covered chairs, and for some time now neither of them had spoken.

"We had the 'who,'" Connie said finally. "I mean the first 'who,' didn't we? Claire did kill Anthony."

Pete nodded. "Lillian confirmed it. Claire killed Anthony Simmons and Fritz Wells, and Lillian knew it. I have a feeling Joan Pitts knew it, too, but one was kept silent by fear of being sent to jail, and the other was kept silent by—" Pete hesitated, at a loss how to phrase it.

"Mother love," said Connie. "But somehow, somewhere, it got worn down. But why now? Why after it was all over?"

"Because it wasn't all over. There was Scott. And now that Claire was free and clear, she would probably eventually have succeeded in snagging him. He must have had some pretty strong feelings for her, considering that scene with the body."

"And to have given up his dream career so he could stay around the farm."

"Lillian knew it was just a matter of time before someone else caught Claire's eye, and then it would be Scott's turn to go."

"But what I don't get is how you arrived at the second 'who.' How did you figure out it was Lillian who killed Claire? There was John Forbes. You saw him at the scene. You saw him run away."

"That's just it, I saw him. I saw his face when he saw Claire lying on the floor. He was as surprised and shocked as anyone. He must have been in the stable, collecting his things, just the way he told you, and he heard the shot, too. He ran up to the back door, looked in, and there she was. He'd already been implicated by Claire over the poison and the car accident, as we said before. He hated Claire and let it show, and she got even. He knew he was a main suspect because he'd made little if any effort to conceal his distaste for her. He probably figured he'd get blamed for this, too. So he ran."

"That still leaves a lot of other people."

"It did at first. But I knew it wasn't Scott because he was in my line of vision when the shot came. And the story that Rawling and Greg and Joan Pitts told about meeting up at the foot of the stairs seemed true. The timing was such that it would have been impossible for one of those three to have done it and then met up with the others. Besides, Lillian practically told us she did it. She said she knew about the gun. And when Joan tried to say she was first in the room, Lillian corrected her. She said she was there first. So where did she come from? From the back kitchen. She never moved."

"But still," said Connie, "she's Claire's *mother*. You can't tell me just because she was first on the scene you automatically decided she was the one who killed Claire."

"There were other things, too. My mind has been racing all night. She said this evening that she tried to tell me, and I see now that she did. She told me things weren't what they seemed, but I thought she was referring to me, my job as handyman. And she hinted at trouble in Claire's past, but I thought she was referring to the rape. She even warned me that Anthony wasn't the first dead husband. I think she wanted me to figure it out, but she just couldn't bring herself to tell me. And she thought *Claire* had hired me. Maybe she thought Scott was out now, and Claire was after me." Pete paused.

"She wasn't, though. She never was, was she? You *were* too easy, weren't you?"

"Maybe I was. I remember when we talked about divorce. I tried to explain my situation with you, but I made a mess of it. It could easily have sounded like I was footloose and fancy-free when actually I was the opposite."

The opposite? And what exactly was the opposite of footloose and fancy-free, wondered Connie. Hog-tied and brainwashed?

"Actually," Pete went on, "I think with me the whole challenge was the horses. She smelled out my fear. She wouldn't let go of it." Pete shuddered, and Connie surmised that he'd suffered something in that stable that he wasn't admitting.

"Back to Lillian," said Connie. "You said she thought Claire hired you?"

"Yeah. And she was so relieved when I told her no, Anthony had hired me. I think she then thought Anthony had wised up to Claire and had hired me to thwart her. But even that thought could give Lillian no peace. If I caught on to Claire, what would happen to her? Lillian hadn't reconciled herself to her daughter's destruction at that point. And Claire's fall off Dapper scared her to death. I thought she was afraid for her daughter, but in hindsight I've realized it was *Anthony* she told to be careful that night. The nail in the horse brought her face to face with reality. She saw what Claire was doing, and she couldn't deny it to herself any longer. The horse was one accident too many."

"So that's it. On the basis of her relief that Anthony had hired you, on the basis of her fear for Anthony's safety, you decided Lillian put a hole in her daughter's head."

Pete grinned sheepishly. "It was the gloves actually. Tonight we sat on the porch and talked for some time. She had a pair of gray leather gloves, and when she first came out, she put them in her pocket. Then, when she was going inside, she put them on. It struck me as odd at the time, putting on gloves to go inside, but I thought she was just rattled. Until I saw them again in the rag box in the back kitchen."

"Her gloves?"

"She must have made her decision to kill her daughter while we were on the porch, talking. She said as much later. I'd managed to convince her the cops weren't going to stop her daughter. So she put on the gloves when she went in so she wouldn't leave fingerprints on Anthony's gun. Everyone knew about the gun, so as long her prints weren't on it, it wouldn't incriminate her."

"But she left her gloves. In the rag box. Why?"

"She took off her coat in Anthony's study. I don't know why. Reflex maybe. Or most likely she was perspiring with anxiety. She would have been better off to leave it on. But after she shot Claire and she heard people coming, she realized she shouldn't be seen with the gloves on. Her dress had no pockets. I noticed that later. So she shoved the gloves into the rag box, figuring no one would notice them in all the confusion."

"But how was it she happened to trap Claire in the back kitchen? It was a funny place for either of them to be."

"Not for Claire. She always snuck in that way when she came from accosting Scott in the stable. At least that's what Lillian said later. She saw Claire sneak out that way, so she got the gun, went out to the back kitchen, and lay in wait for her. She knew she wouldn't have long to wait. Claire always insisted they sit down to dinner on the dot of seven."

Yes, she did, and Connie had started to find the habit annoying. Or at least she had started to find

Pete's harping on it annoying. "But why the fuss about fingerprints if she was going to confess anyway?"

"She wasn't planning to confess. She's a tough lady. She likes her fresh air and she had no intention of getting locked up for this unless she had to. But she couldn't let John Forbes take the fall in her place. I know, I watched her face. You should have seen her. The minute I told her the chief had arrested Forbes—" Pete stopped.

"You told her."

"I had to. I knew when she found out she'd do the right thing, but it would only be harder for her later. So I figured I'd help her."

Yes, thought Connie, *that's what Pete would figure.*

For a long time neither of them spoke.

Finally Connie saw Pete look down at the arm of the chair, where his hand rested on the circle of lace. He stood up. "It's late. I'll hit the road."

Connie wasn't surprised. He wasn't one to stay under false pretenses. Still, he crossed to her chair and leaned over her. His lips touched her and he drew back, but not very far. They touched again and kept going. Thoughtfully. Hungrily. Still, it didn't seem to tell him what he wanted to know.

CHAPTER 36

Greg Hempstead was sitting on the trunk of his car in front of the funeral home, smoking a cigarette.

"There's no funeral," he said as soon as Pete got in range. "Rawling canceled it. It was all Claire's sham, she said. She's in there with him. She's decided to take him back to Briar Hills and bury him."

"So you're out here, fending people off?"

"What people? I wanted to go in, but she won't let me." Hempstead looked down at his cigarette in disgust. "I quit these things two years ago." He crushed it out on the sole of his shoe and tossed the dead butt in the bushes.

"Okay," said Pete. "I guess I'll shove off. Tell her I came, will you?"

"Sure."

Pete started to walk away, but Hempstead stopped him.

"Hey. Wait a minute." He slid off the car and caught up with Pete. "About what I was saying to you last night. About finding Rawling and—"

"Forget about it," said Pete. "You were right. It doesn't concern me."

"True," said Hempstead. "But just so you know. I'm not leaving it like this with Rawling. I'm giving this thing a shot. I just wanted you to know that."

"Well, good. Good luck to you."

Hempstead grinned. "Yeah. I'll need it. What I did in Briar Hills was bad, but it's what I did once we got here that was so tough for her to swallow. Despite what I suspected about Claire, I wouldn't take Rawling's side against her. I was just trying to keep a lid on Rawling. I didn't want her to cause a scene and leave here before I found out what I wanted. So I defended Claire, and it made Rawling feel like the evil stepdaughter."

Which explained why Rawling was crying in the woods that day. Yet another example of Hempstead using her. Yeah, he'd need some luck, all right.

"I don't mind telling you, I've got my work cut out for me," said Hempstead.

"Yeah," said Pete. "Scary."

Hempstead seemed to think about that. "Yeah, it is," he said finally. "But you know what's strange? It's not losing Rawling that scares me. It's if I *don't* lose her. What do I do then? I don't know the rules for that part. It's all new territory."

Pete thought about it all the way home. All new territory. A territory with new rules. And more to lose if you broke them. Yes, it was scary.

He went into his bedroom to change out of his funeral tie and jacket and stopped, dismayed, at the door. He'd scrambled to get ready on only a few hours' sleep that morning, and his bedroom was littered with the signs of the battle. Yesterday's dirty clothes were tossed in a heap. Drawers hung open. All the single socks he'd sorted through to get a pair that matched were jumbled together on the bed. The remains of his entire tie collection, all two of them, festooned the chairbacks, and a wet towel lay on the rug.

Pete moved around the room, straightening up. He went to the closet to hang up a clean shirt he had tried on and rejected, but he couldn't find the empty hanger it had come from. He tried to slide the full hangers along but the old ice box jammed them. He stood still and looked at the ice box. So why didn't he move it? She wasn't asking for much.

Sure enough, within seconds of thinking the thought, his pulse started to race and his skin clammed up.

Yeah. Scary.

He threw the clean shirt on the floor and went into the kitchen to make lunch, but he was too keyed up to sit. He took his ham and cheese sandwich in one hand and a Coke in the other and left the house via the porch. He intended to walk the beach, eating as he went, but when he reached the edge of the marsh, he turned around and sat down instead.

There it was, his house, a typical Cape, with the steeply pitched roof, designed in a previous century for the same purpose it served to this day, to battle the winter winds and keep the household snug. There was history to the house. Some of it was his.

And some of it was his and Connie's.

Pete stood up and turned around, gazing out over the golden marsh, thinking of all the hours he had looked at it with Connie.

He went inside through the porch to the kitchen. He disposed of his lunch paraphernalia and walked out into the hall to the old living room that was now Factotum.

Rita was at the window, looking out.

"What are you doing?"

Rita didn't budge. "Will you get a *load* of them? They've been in that truck for twenty minutes. *Arguing.*"

Pete remembered what Connie had said about the thrill of the hunt. He went to the window and looked out. He could see Maxine's hands flailing the air, fingers spread wide, the nails painted purple now. When Andy made a point, he did it one-handed, with the fingers together, cutting the air with a karate-type chop. Both mouths moved, not necessarily in turns.

"So now what? They're going to spend half of every day fighting in the truck? We'll never get a full day's work out of Andy again. That's if he doesn't plain quit. *Ooooh,* I could—" Rita stopped mid-could and shook herself from head to toe, fists clenched.

"There's always Scott," said Pete.

Rita turned from the window and glared at him.

"Why not? Don't you like Scott?"

Rita pointed one long, peach-colored nail out the window. "*Look* at that. You see it right before your eyes, and you still don't get it. Look what she did over dumpy little Andy. Can't you see what evils she'll resort to if she gets a crack at an Adonis like Scott Beaton?"

"Andy's not dumpy," said Pete. But then he realized something that might have saved him some time had he picked up on it a sooner.

"Scott *is* pretty good-looking, isn't he?"

Rita turned around and gazed at Pete disgustedly. Then she looked out at the truck again, thoughtfully.

"Oh, go ahead," she said finally. "How much worse can it get? Go ahead. Hire Scott Beaton."

CHAPTER
37

Pete pulled his truck into the drive at Heath Farm, but he hesitated before getting out. He'd looked for Scott at the pizza place, first, but somehow he hadn't been too surprised when Franny said the farm was still the best place to look.

But Pete sat in the truck and looked in front of him. Nothing had changed—the gleaming house and stable, the neat fences, trim fields, still pond, green woods. Claire Simmons may have hidden here, but Pete suspected that this farm had been *his* hiding place, too—a place in which he could immerse himself in other people's woes rather than face his own insecurities. Who else had hidden here? Lillian? Joan? Maybe even Scott Beaton?

The door to the house opened, and Joan Pitts came out. She shielded her eyes against the sun and came toward him. Pete got out of the truck.

"Come to say good-bye?" she asked.

"Yeah. I guess."

His eyes strayed to the old barn, and Joan's went with him. "What's going to happen to the place?"

"Rawling's selling out."

"And you?"

Her eyes twinkled, making her look young for once. "Why? Looking for a maid?"

Pete grinned, thinking of his room. But then he remembered something. "You aren't really a maid, are you?"

"Nope. I worked in a department store in Swippingsdale. They caught me with my hand in the till, so to speak. Claire happened to be there, and she bailed me out. Then she hired me."

"Out of the goodness of her heart."

"You were pretty much right the first time," said Joan. "She needed an accomplice of sorts. When Fritz was killed, I vouched for her presence elsewhere."

"But if she went, you went, was that it?"

"That was it."

"But she didn't use you as an alibi for Anthony."

"Why should she?" said Joan. "She had you. All I had to do was shut up about everything else."

"That next morning, when I tried to get you to go up to her room. Why didn't you?"

Joan Pitts looked away. "There are some things even I can't stomach. I didn't know Fritz much, but I kind of liked old Anthony."

"Yeah," said Pete. "Me, too."

But it brought them back to the previous question. "Really," said Pete. "If you're looking for a job—"

Joan Pitts laughed. She was getting younger by the minute. "Out here? In the middle of nowhere? No thanks. I'll be moving along. Now what are you doing here?"

Pete gave up. "Looking for Scott."

"Thataway." She pointed to the stable.

Pete held out his hand, and Joan Pitts shook it.

In contrast to Joan Pitts, Scott looked like he'd aged a decade or two. Pete found him head down over a horse's hoof. Buster's. Pete tried to remember the exact minute when he had taken leave of his senses and actually climbed up on the brute. Still, he and Buster had been through a war or two together. Maybe it was time to start treating him as a comrade. Pete stretched out a hand and rubbed Buster's white stripe. Buster blinked. Pete gazed into the big brown eye, looking for some sort of insight, but all he saw was his own fish-eyed reflection.

Pete turned to the other comrade-in-arms. "Still on the payroll, Scott?"

Scott looked up. "I told Rawling I'd stick around until she moves them out."

"Oh," said Pete. "Well, if you still want a job when they leave, there's one at Factotum."

"Thanks," said Scott. "I think I'd like that." He bent down to the hoof.

"Okay, then," said Pete. "Let me know when you're through here. Or maybe you'd like to take a little time off in between. Seems like you've been through enough."

"Yeah," said Scott. Then he straightened up and looked at Pete. "Tell me something, will you? Was it just me, or was she—"

"Oh, she was," said Pete.

CHAPTER

38

Sarah Abrew heard the familiar tires and closed her eyes, gathering her strength.

"Well, hello," she said when he came in. Then she looked at the odd-shaped box in his hands. "Is that it? Is that my—"

"Bat house," said Pete. He laid it across her lap and showed her the narrow end where the bats came in and described, the way he always did when he knew she couldn't see something, the rungs in the dark interior where the bats would cling upside down by their feet.

"I thought you'd forgotten. Either that or you were avoiding me."

"I didn't forget," said Pete.

And see how neatly he avoided that, Sarah thought.

Pete went to the window and looked out. "I see a good tree for it. The pine just to the right of that patch of myrtle. I'll go hang it up."

"No," said Sarah. "Sit."

Somewhat to her surprise, Pete sat.

"So what's the matter?" she asked finally. "Cold feet?"

"No," said Pete. "Not exactly. At least not much. It's just that now I know what it's going to take."

"And you figure it's not worth it?"

"No," said Pete. "It's not that. It's just . . . I'm wondering if I have it in me. I'm not sure I can pull it off, you know? I mean, it's scary."

"So tell her that."

"Tell her what? That I'm scared?"

"Why not?" said Sarah. "It's the first time in a long time that you've made a lick of sense if you ask me."

CHAPTER

39

Connie was alone in the Hermitage. Neither Andy nor Maxine had showed up, but Connie didn't care. She was getting close to the end. The trash was discarded, the walls and floors and ceilings scrubbed down, the furniture salvaged and repaired where possible, tossed where not, and now she was attempting to deal with the curtains.

She was sitting on the hermit's bed upstairs, buried in folds of material fresh from the dry cleaner's, wondering who the idiot was who invented curtain hooks, when she heard tires in the drive. She pretended she didn't know whose. She heard the door open. She didn't move.

"Hello?"

She got up.

She was on the top step when he reached the bottom. She kept walking. He did, too. They met on the landing halfway up. Or halfway down, of course, depending on your point of view.

He grinned at her and then looked away and then

grinned again and then reached out and rubbed her upper arm nervously. "So how are you?"

"Okay. And you?"

"Okay. Better. I—" He stopped. He looked around him, then waved a hand at the nearest step in an attempt at Cary Grant-style gallantry. "Care to sit down?"

Connie sat down.

Pete joined her.

"I've been thinking," said Connie.

"Yeah," said Pete. "Me, too."

"And this is what I don't get. Why did Claire have to *kill* these guys? Why didn't she just divorce them? You described Anthony as a reasonable sort. He wouldn't have bucked her if she wanted out, would he?"

"No, I don't think so. But I talked to her about divorce. I don't think divorce was neat enough for her." Again, Pete looked around. "You were there. You saw the place. Did you get the sense of it?"

"A little. How perfect everything was."

"How everything fit?"

"Yes," said Connie. She looked around her and sighed. "And how clean it was. And nothing was unfinished. Or almost nothing. There was the barn, of course."

"Yes," said Pete. "And that barn drove her crazy. In the middle of all the turmoil, all she cared about was the fact that the barn wasn't painted. And did you notice the little things? How everything matched? Even Claire. She matched her room and her car and her horse."

"And she was neat."

"She was more than just neat. She changed table-cloths between courses. And when we talked about divorce, she mentioned that very thing—how un-neat it all was. There were too many loose ends for her. I can see where in her mind death would tie things off much more nicely."

Connie had to admit she had a point. "Nifty theory," she said. "Have you got any others?"

"About Claire, no. About me, I think so." Pete rubbed his palms on the thighs of his jeans.

Connie wanted to rub her palms on hers, but she didn't.

"I guess it comes down to this. I was sitting out at the farm, in my truck, and it struck me what you said about the place being an escape. A place of peace. You meant for Claire." Suddenly Pete looked sideways at her. "Actually, maybe you didn't. Maybe I'm slow to this. But anyway, here it is." He rubbed his palms on his jeans again. "I admit I'm a little scared, okay? About moving in together. I mean, let's face it, we're bound to have a few problems. There were problems before, and since then we've each lived alone a long time. We've probably formed some pretty good ruts."

"So what's the big solution? Separate but equal—"

"Wait," said Pete. "Please. I want to explain this thing. It just struck me, sort of out of the blue, when you suggested that I move in, that, my God, this is it. We're dropping the big one. And it scared the hell out of me. Actually, I didn't realize that was how it struck me until today. At the time, I just knew I didn't want to talk about it. I didn't want to think about it. I pretended to myself it was because I didn't want to move into this house or that there wasn't room in my house or because you drank beer with spaghetti and used the wrong tomatoes—"

"The wrong what?"

Pete waved a hand. "Nothing. It didn't have anything to do with it. And I knew it. I knew if we really sat down and talked about it, none of those things would turn out to be insurmountable. So I guess subconsciously I decided we just wouldn't sit down and talk about it. And I guess that's where the farm came in."

"The escape."

Pete nodded. "I mean, think about it. I'm not this stupid as a rule, but all of a sudden I'm falling for every dumb trick in the book. You said it before, and it hit me today when I was standing next to that horse. Me. On a horse. I must have been pretty desperate if in order to avoid one little conversation I'm out riding around on a *horse.*"

"So," said Connie, "here's that one little conversation. Or maybe not so little."

"Not little, maybe, but at least short and to the point. So, okay. So it's not going to be any day at the beach. And so I'm scared. I admit that. But so what? Either we move in together or we don't. And if we don't, that's it. We've bluffed each other out." Pete twisted sideways. "So what do you say? You still want to go for it?"

Connie looked down at the step under her sneakers. "There's still the little matter of where this famous experiment gets carried out."

"Ah," said Pete. "It's just possible I've even figured that out." He cleared his throat. "I'm assuming you meant what you said about the Bates house? You wouldn't die if you had to leave it or anything like that?"

"Actually," said Connie, "I've been thinking that I might come to life a little if I left it. But what would I do with it? I'm not sure I'm ready to sell it."

Pete grinned. "No burning the bridges, huh? But you could rent it out, couldn't you? At least while we try this out? And you could still keep up the garden if you want to—you'd be right down the beach."

"I would, huh? I'd be just down the beach? Under the ice box?"

"I was thinking more like on top."

Connie peered at him.

"We can leave Factotum where it is and go up."

"Up?"

"Add on a couple of big dormers and we'll have a whole second story. We'll leave the bottom for Factotum, but the whole top floor will be just for us."

Connie felt that one telltale knee of hers start to quiver. She pressed down on the kneecap with the flat of her hand. "And if it doesn't work out? Us, I mean?"

"So I'll have lost my one true love, but I'll have gained some floor space. Even trade, don't you think?"

Connie laughed. "I don't mind telling you I'm a little scared myself."

"Good," said Pete. "That means this time we start out on the same foot."

CHAPTER
40

It was the last day of October. There was a sun but it gave off little heat, and the old men sat on the steps of Beston's Store with their collars turned up.

"So," said Ed Healey. "Seems odd, don't it? Came and left with hardly a trace."

"Good riddance to bad rubbish," said Bert.

"What in the blue blazes are you two talking about?" said Evan.

Both men turned to him in surprise. That was strong language for Evan.

"What do you mean, left without a trace? First off, who left? Both of them dead as two doormice. And if you think they left no trace, you just pop into Beaton's Pizza or over to Forbes's place or Factotum or—" But Evan's voice trailed off, and he stared into space.

Ed and Bert exchanged glances. Finally Ed cleared his throat. "Speaking of Factotum, it's a shame about that old hermit's place."

"Should've burned it to the ground, that's what I say," said Bert.

"I wouldn't blame Pete if he wanted to burn that distant cousin at the stake," said Ed.

"What do mean, you wouldn't blame Pete? Connie's the one who did all the work," said Evan. "Then the cousin calls up and says he's changed his mind, and he doesn't want the place. Fought with them over the bill, too. Said it couldn't possibly have taken two whole weeks just to clean up one house."

"I suppose you know those two fools are moving in together," said Bert.

"Yep," said Evan. "And guess who's gonna rent the Bates place?"

"Who? Don't tell me they've got more foreigners coming in here trashing up the place."

"Not really," said Evan. "Just the chief of police. And guess what he's doing as we speak?"

"Counting his bullets?" asked Bert.

"Planting tulip bulbs. Forty-eight of 'em. Red."

Bert hooted.

"So now the Hermitage is on the market," said Evan. "Heath Farm, too. And Pete's taking off his roof and adding on to his house."

"A lot of changes going on around here," said Ed. He shifted his weight and settled more securely into the spot on the bench he'd occupied pretty much nonstop for the past twenty years.

Evan Spender walked over to the rusty machine that still sold Cokes in long green bottles for a quarter. He put in his quarter, pulled out his Coke, and looked up at the sky. "Gonna rain before night," he said.

Ed Healey looked up with Evan. "Yep," he said. "Wouldn't be surprised if it did at that."

Bert Barker snorted. "If it rains, I'll eat my hat. And what I'd like to know is this: while Pete's ripping up his cottage, who am I supposed to get to clean my gutters?"

"Yep," said Ed. "Sure are a lot of changes around this place."